Subscribe now and save
cover price!

MW01224148

($11.80 savings
on regular cover price of $51.80)

$70 Two Years
($33.60 savings
on regular cover price of $103.60)

GRAND STREET

Name

Address

City   **State**   **Zip**

Payment enclosed ☐   **Bill me** ☐

☐ Please enter my new subscription *and* the following gift subscription

☐ Please enter only the following gift subscription

Please charge my

AmEx ☐   **Mastercard** ☐   **Visa** ☐

Gift Subscription to:

Recipient's Name

Address

Account Number

City   **State**   **Zip**

Exp. Date

Last minute? For immediate service,

Signature (A gift card will be sent in your name)

All foreign (including Canadian) orders $55 per year. Institutional orders $50 per year. Payable in U.S. funds.

call 1-800-807-6548
2357A

Subscribe now and save 23% off the
cover price!

$40 One Year
($11.80 savings
on regular cover price of $51.80)

$70 Two Years
($33.60 savings
on regular cover price of $103.60)

Name

GRAND STREET

Address

City   **State**   **Zip**

☐ Please enter my new subscription *and* the following gift subscription

☐ Please enter only the following gift subscription

Payment enclosed ☐   **Bill me** ☐

Please charge my

AmEx ☐   **Mastercard** ☐   **Visa** ☐

Gift Subscription to:

Recipient's Name

Address

Account Number

City   **State**   **Zip**

Exp. Date

Last minute? For immediate service,

Signature (A gift card will be sent in your name)

All foreign (including Canadian) orders $55 per year. Institutional orders $50 per year. Payable in U.S. funds.

call 1-800-807-6548
2357B

no postage necessary
if mailed in
the United States

BUSINESS REPLY MAIL
First Class Mail   Permit No. 301   Denville, NJ

Postage will be paid by Addressee

GRAND STREET
Subscription Services
P.O. Box 3000
Denville, NJ 07834-9878

no postage necessary
if mailed in
the United States

BUSINESS REPLY MAIL
First Class Mail   Permit No. 301   Denville, NJ

Postage will be paid by Addressee

GRAND STREET
Subscription Services
P.O. Box 3000
Denville, NJ 07834-9878

FINE ARTS WORK CENTER IN PROVINCETOWN

SUMMER WORKSHOPS & RESIDENCIES 1996

one-week workshops • June 23–August 31

Fiction

Dean Albarelli
Anne Bernays
Michael Cunningham
Peter Ho Davies
Maria Flook

Pam Houston
Tama Janowitz
Fred Leebron
Carole Maso
Richard McCann

Rick Moody
Ann Patchett
Susan Power
Heidi Jon Schmidt
A.J. Verdelle

Poetry

Mark Doty
Marie Howe
Yusef Komunyakaa

Cleopatra Mathis
Gail Mazur
Susan Mitchell
Robert Pinsky

Liz Rosenberg
Tom Sleigh
Charlie Smith

Memoir & Biography

Hope Edelman
Lucy Grealy

Justin Kaplan
Susanna Kaysen

Michael Ryan

Screenwriting & Genre

Pat Cooper

Nelson Gidding
Jackie Manthorne

Bill Phillips

for catalog or more information, contact:

Peter Ho Davies, Summer Program Coordinator
Fine Arts Work Center, 24 Pearl Street, Provincetown, MA 02657.
Tel: 508-487-9960 • Fax: 508-487-8873

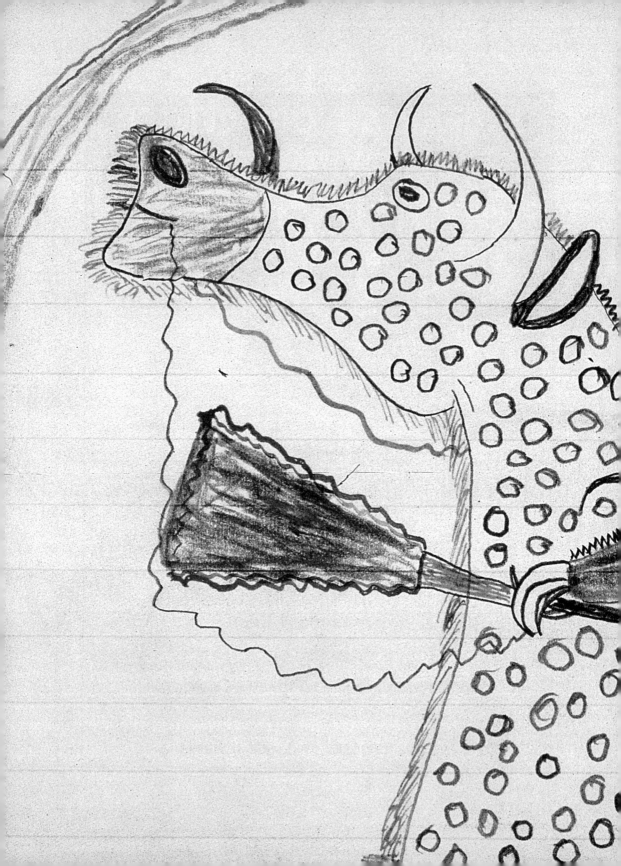

GRAND STREET

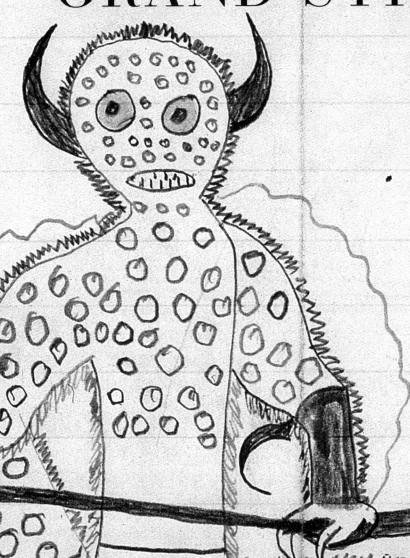

Dreams

Front cover: ADOBE LA, *La Mona (The Doll)*, 1995.
Back cover: Jim Shaw, *Dream* (detail), 1995.

"Gags" by Luis Buñuel is translated and excerpted from the French volume *Le Christ à Cran d'Arret* (Paris: Plon, 1995). Copyright © 1995 by Plon.

"Religion, Eroticism, Death" by Luis Buñuel and Max Aub © 1984 Max Aub, and Heirs of Max Aub.

"The Rifles" from *The Atlas* by William T. Vollmann. Copyright © William T. Vollmann, 1996. Reprinted by arrangement with Viking Penguin, a division of Penguin Books USA, Inc. To order the book, please call (800) 253-6476.

Grand Street (ISSN 0734-5496; ISBN 1-885490-07-0) is published quarterly by Grand Street Press (a project of the New York Foundation for the Arts, Inc., a not-for-profit corporation), 131 Varick Street, Room 906, New York, NY 10013. Contributions and gifts to Grand Street Press are tax-deductible to the extent allowed by law. This publication is made possible, in part, by a grant from the National Endowment for the Arts.

Volume Fourteen, Number Four (*Grand Street 56*—Spring 1996). Copyright © 1996 by the New York Foundation for the Arts, Inc., Grand Street Press. All rights reserved. Reproduction, whether in whole or in part, without permission is strictly prohibited.

Second-class postage paid at New York, NY and additional mailing offices. Postmaster: Please send address changes to Grand Street Subscription Service, Dept. GRS, P.O. Box 3000, Denville, NJ 07834. Subscriptions are $40 a year (four issues). Foreign subscriptions (including Canada) are $55 a year, payable in U.S. funds. Single-copy price is $12.95 ($18 in Canada). For subscription inquiries, please call (800) 807-6548.

Grand Street is printed by Hull Printing in Meriden, CT. It is distributed to the trade by D.A.P./Distributed Art Publishers, 636 Broadway, 12th floor, New York, NY 10012, Tel: (212) 473-5119, Fax: (212) 673-2887, and to newsstands only by B. DeBoer, Inc., 113 E. Centre Street, Nutley, NJ 07110 and Fine Print Distributors, 500 Pampa Drive, Austin, TX 78752. *Grand Street* is distributed in Australia and New Zealand by Peribo Pty, Ltd., 58 Beaumont Road, Mount Kuring-Gai, NSW 2080, Tel: (2) 457-0011.

GRAND STREET

Editor

Jean Stein

Managing Editor

Deborah Treisman

Art Editor

Walter Hopps

Poetry Editor

William Corbett

Designer

Jim Hinchee

Editorial Assistant

Julie A. Tate

Assistant Editor

Jackie McAllister

Interns

Steven Lee

Caroline Linder

Christina Persico

Administrative Assistant

Lisa Brodus

Contributing Editors

Hilton Als, Dominique Bourgois, Colin de Land,
Anne Doran, Morgan Entrekin, Raymond Foye,
Jonathan Galassi, Stephen Graham, Barbara Heizer,
Dennis Hopper, Hudson, David Kornacker, Jane Kramer,
Erik Rieselbach, Edward W. Said, Jeremy Treglown,
Katrina vanden Heuvel, Gillian Walker, Drenka Willen

Founding contributing editor

Andrew Kopkind (1935–1994)

Publishers

Jean Stein & Torsten Wiesel

CONTENTS

Religion, Eroticism, Death

—Mexico, circa 1968

LUIS BUÑUEL (*Reading from a sheet of paper he has taken from his pocket*) The twenty dreams are all here. They're very schematic. I wrote them down for myself, to remember. I can flesh them out for you, but that isn't the point. They are dreams I've dreamed dozens of times, all of them; the least frequent are five to ten times.

MAX AUB Over how long a period?

LUIS BUÑUEL Over the last fifteen or twenty years.

First, there's the famous train. I've had this dream at least twenty times: something with a train, a station. The train is leaving, I'm carrying my suitcases, and whoosh! it leaves me behind. Another train: I get on, put down my suitcases, get off the train, and say, "Well, I think I'll take a little stroll around the platform." I get sidetracked and the train leaves without me. Good-bye suitcases. *My suuuuitcases* . . . I've dreamed variations on that one many times. I miss the train; I lose my suitcases; I get to the baggage claim and it's very complicated, lots of red tape I have to deal with . . . . And the train always leaves without me.

8

Edward Ruscha, from *Hollywood Boulevard*.

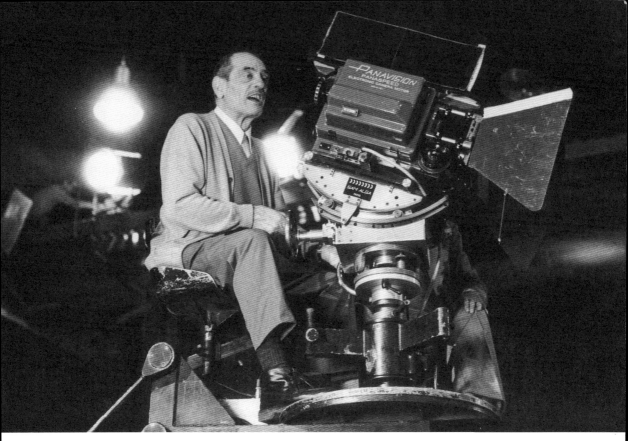

Luis Buñuel, circa 1960.

Another dream: heights. Sometimes it's on a mountain, or a hill-top, or in a very tall building. I'm frozen in a place that has only a small ledge. It's a very common dream. Sometimes I manage to get down, or I wake up. Fifteen or twenty years ago, I used to jump off and nothing happened to me. I'd say, "I'm dreaming," and jump. But now I don't dare.

Another: My father and my mother are alive—even though I know they're dead. I feel this enormous sorrow and at the same time a deep compassion for them, especially my father. I'm sad that he is dead, but must mask those feelings in front of him. He's very serious at the table, and I'm making conversation. Suddenly I say, "I know you're dead." What a thing to say. . . .

Here's another: I'm supposed to be in a play and I don't know my lines. Anguish. This is a very long dream. I see an enormous room with rows of seats, a stage. Everyone is ready to go on and I have to play a certain role and I don't know which one.

MAX AUB   Is there an audience?

LUIS BUÑUEL   Usually not. Sometimes there is, but other times the audience hasn't arrived yet. I don't know the part; I'm just studying it. It's impossible for me to learn something that I'll have to perform immediately. Then the play begins. I sneak away, and I feel awful. Who will they get to take my place?

Almost all my dreams are painful.

Another: fornication. I've been dreaming this one forever, for forty years. There is almost always some problem. My neighbors are watching through the window, or they come in the room at the wrong time, or I can't find my penis, or my penis is blocked. I mean I have a great plan of action, I'm filled with lust, but . . .

MAX AUB   That window is very important.

LUIS BUÑUEL   Right. The neighbors are watching me through the window. I am with a girl I liked a lot forty years ago in San Sebastián. All her brothers are on the balcony, and I say, "All right, the woman's here with me." I pull the drapes, but I can't do anything.

Another: I have no work and no hope of getting any. Anguish. Despair. . . This one is very long, because things happen in the dream. I'm looking for work. It's impossible, and no one gives me anything. Extreme despair.

1 0

Luis Buñuel with Zachary Scott on the set of *The Young One*, 1960.

MAX AUB   Did that one start after you came to Mexico?

LUIS   Oh, maybe fifteen or twenty years ago. All these dreams are repeated
BUÑUEL   . . . I can't tell you exactly when they began; they're all from my later
                 life, the last twenty, twenty-five years. It's especially in the last fifteen
                 that they've been so repetitive. Some of them I've dreamed for
                 twenty or thirty years.
                      Another: I don't have any money and I don't dare ask my
                 mother because she's already given me so much. I don't know what

I'm going to do. I'm not thinking about my family. It's the anguish of not having money. Terrible.

Another: I'm in my childhood home. There are ghosts. I used to be very afraid, but not now. Now I arrive at my house; I go up-stairs, which is dark, and I say, "I am going to prove that I can distinguish the ghost from whoever's there." It's dark. I go in and close the door of the anteroom. I'm afraid. Suddenly the ghost makes a sign: a noise, a chair moves, I don't know. Then I say, "Bastards! Sons of bitches! Come out, show yourselves once and for all," things like that. I insult the ghosts, but with a healthy dose of fear, you know? Then a corpse appears. Terrible anguish, but I stand up to it rather well.

Another: From a psychoanalytical perspective, this one is very clear. Also dreadful. I've dreamed it seven or eight times, all since I filmed *Evil Eden* [1956] in Catemaco.* The dream is about warm, slightly oily water, still and glaucous, at the edge of a jungle. It is only the edge of the jungle, but the trees are very tall and cast their shadows across the water. I'm in the water and swimming peacefully, almost floating, because the water is rather viscous, like oil—as I said—glaucous, that is, greenish, like green eyes. That must mean the mother, right? No doubt about it. I've dreamed the lake, the trees, the earth, the amniotic fluid. I'm swimming peacefully enough, but I'm afraid. I'm afraid of the jungle, but I feel a certain voluptuousness at the same time. Total silence. Nothing moving. The mother.

Another, very frequent: spiders, in a thousand variations. I'm somewhere, and there are spiders everywhere. Or I go to bed and see spider legs coming from every direction. There are a thousand variations. Unbearable.

---

* A town in the state of Veracruz, Mexico.

Here's one a lot of people have: animals. This one's very well known. I'm running away from a bull or a tiger. I'm going to a bull-fight. The bull gets loose, I'm running down corridors, the bull is chasing me, I close a door but the bull is very powerful . . . and I wake up.

Another important one: I have been an accomplice to murder. I killed someone, with a number of friends, maybe eight or ten years ago. We buried him together and so on. Now ten years have gone by, and suddenly I learn that one of my partners in crime—I don't know who he is—has been arrested by the police. They've found one of the dead man's arms. Great panic that the police will discover me.

Another: the only ineffable or religious dream I've had. In the midst of very moving, extraordinary music, marvelous music, the Virgin appears to me, the Mother Without Stain, stereotypical in her blue robe, her white . . .

MAX AUB   The Virgin of your films.

LUIS   I sink into a feeling of supreme peace. I believe that I understand—
BUÑUEL   through feelings, not reason—certain of the mysteries of religion. The emotion from this dream lasts a long time. It is the only positive dream I have.

Another: a narrated dream I included in its entirety in *The Discreet Charm of the Bourgeoisie*. I used this dream in which I'm walking down a street and meet a friend. "What are *you* doing here? I saw you with Pepito." "What? What do you mean with Pepito? Pepito died fifteen years ago." "You're right, he died. But I saw him here." A young girl wearing a white tunic walks up. She looks at us with the greatest tenderness, and it turns out that we are all dead. I put that into *The Discreet Charm of the Bourgeoisie* exactly as I dreamed it.

Another: This one, along with the one about the Virgin, is the most emotional dream I've had. I see myself with my dog Tipi, a dog

I used to have at home, a mongrel I loved a lot, and he's barking at me as if asking for something. He's next to Jeanne*, where she's knitting, and the dog sees me and comes toward me, barking, asking me for something. When I wake up I feel a terrible anguish, an overwhelming sense of pity for Tipi. Emotion, and a premonition of my death. It creates a deep anguish in me that sometimes lasts for days. And I say, "It's true, it is my death, because the dog's dead."

Another: defecating or being naked in public. You must have had this one, too. I find myself on La Reforma or on Campos Elíseos, and there I am, sitting there defecating. And people are passing by and I'm pretending . . . I don't know what to do and then finally I get up. . . . Very unpleasant.

Another dream: storm, rain, lightning. I'm looking for shelter. This one's a long dream, too. Woods, a pretty country house with large windows. It's beginning to rain. Panic, lightning. I want to get out of the storm. I go inside, into a room with lots of mirrors, and things happen. The storm continues, the lightning, the panic, and the anguish.

Another good one, one I don't dream anymore though I dreamed it about thirty times: I make objects, sometimes people, levitate by placing my hands on them. In some dreams I fail. "How about that chair? I made it rise off the floor yesterday." Nothing. I fail. Sometimes I succeed. Suddenly I see that the chair is rising ten feet off the ground. "That's wonderful!" everyone is saying.

Another: I'm deceiving my parents. I'm still in school. I'm in my last year of the *bachillerato*†, and I can't finish, though it's time. Then I say, "What about my mother? Well, what the shit, I'm making a living, I have a career, so let her get upset." But the exams are going

---

* Buñuel's wife.

† An advanced high-school diploma, similar to the French *baccalauréat*.

to be the next day and I haven't been to class—history, geography—for several months; it's a very bad time. Then I say, "Well, I'm going to tell my mother to take a flying leap. I have a career, after all. I have a way to make a living."

And the last dream is one of autofellatio, in which I can suck my own member. My cock must be very small in the dream, because it fits perfectly in my mouth. But I get no pleasure from it. It's stupid, I don't like any part of it. "What luck," I say, "to be able to blow myself, right?" But no, nothing.

MAX AUB   That one, is it an old one?

LUIS
BUÑUEL   The autofellatio dream is an old one. I must have dreamed it some six or eight times. And those are the twenty I remember. . . . Yes, that's everything: religion, eroticism, death.

Translated from the Spanish by Margaret Sayers Peden

LUIS BUÑUEL

Gags

—From Luis Buñuel's film notes, Hollywood, 1944

1. In the solitude of the night, someone is trying to break in through one of the castle's exterior windows. That someone ends up breaking the lock and enters cautiously. The entrance hall is immersed in total darkness. The intruder pulls out his flashlight and begins to shine it around him, but just at that moment, someone turns on the light. Stretched out on the ground, in armchairs, on the staircase, more than two hundred soldiers are sleeping. Some of them wake up and complain. *Turn out the light. Let us sleep. What a stupid joke.* Completely bewildered, the intruder smiles sheepishly and climbs back out the window. No one stops him, because no one can imagine that a thief would make it into a house with two hundred guards.

2. The hosts and their guests, about six or seven people in all, are climbing the main stairs to go to bed. On the second floor, they open the doors to several different rooms, bid each other goodnight, and retire. Shortly afterward, one of the guests steps cautiously out of his room and sets off on a mysterious expedition. When he reaches the stairs, he hears the voices of people coming up. They are exactly the

16

same people as a moment before. Once again they bid each other goodnight and go into their separate rooms.

3. In the middle of the night, a thief is trying to break open the safe. Suddenly, he sees a light and hears footsteps. He sees one of the female guests coming toward him with a lighted candle. He doesn't have time to hide, but the young woman walks right past him, indifferent to his presence. She is asleep. The thief breathes again. The young woman disappears behind the curtain that covers the door to the next room. No sooner is she out of the thief's sight than she puts her candle down on a chair and begins to spy on the thief through the folds of the curtain.

4. Through the silence of the night, a strange noise comes from the garden—as if someone were kicking a drum. A guest looks out the window of his room. He sees a man trampling on a violin. Furiously, the man crushes the instrument under his feet.

5. A loud knock on the door of the castle. The activity in the castle is at its peak. Someone goes to open the door. In the doorway, a Napoleon appears, in his characteristic pose. Taking advantage of the surprise his appearance causes, he enters, climbs the stairs, and disappears out of sight of the bewildered guests.

6. A well-known gag: a man arrives at the castle and asks to be seen immediately by the lord. The butler offers him a seat in the vestibule and asks him to sit and wait. A moment later, the butler returns and asks the man to follow him. The visitor remains seated and doesn't answer. The butler asks again, without receiving a response. He touches the visitor's shoulder and the visitor falls to the ground like a stone. He is dead. This version of the gag is identical except that, as he falls, the visitor wakes up and angrily slaps the butler. He had simply fallen asleep.

1 7

7. In the middle of a battle, or in a moment of danger, someone fires a revolver. As if in a dream, the bullet moves very slowly out of the barrel and falls at the feet of the person who fired it. He is terrified and wants to run but cannot. He seems to be nailed to the floor.

8. We see, from a distance, and without being able to hear what they are saying, the male and female leads playing cards. The young woman appears bored, only marginally interested in the game. Switch to a close-up: we hear their conversation. It is an exchange of the most passionate vows of love imaginable. "My love, what unbearable anguish it is always to have to hide." "Only death will unite us forever." "I adore you." "Not to be able to hold you in my arms, to kiss your eyes a thousand times, and your lips . . ." She gathers the cards to deal, and the male lead puts his hand on hers. "I could die of pleasure just touching your hand." We see them again from a distance. He seems to be telling her sharply that it's his turn to deal. This scene is witnessed by several people, hence the characters' dissimulation.

9. On the mantelpiece or on a wall hangs a magnificent portrait of a bride, with a white veil and orange blossoms. Someone asks who the woman is. It is the daughter of the host who died fifteen years ago in tragic circumstances on her wedding day. Later, in the middle of the night, as rain whips the trees in the garden, one can imagine the bride, alive, her dress soaked through, gazing sadly at the castle. Hands cover her mouth and pull her out of sight.

10. Someone, the detective for example, is inspecting the castle. Suddenly, his attention is drawn to the noises that are coming from one of the rooms. He approaches. The door is closed. He hears what sounds distinctly like a party: music, loud voices, bursts of laughter. Someone, between laughs, announces that he is leaving. The detective barely has time to hide before the door opens and a coffin glides out.

11. Strange noises in the night, as if someone is randomly beating a sledgehammer against the floor. Sometimes these noises are followed by the sound of furniture falling or dishes breaking. Hearing the noises come closer, a man opens the door to his room. Terrified, he sees a huge rhinoceros calmly walking down the hall.

12. It is rumored that a thief is going to break into the castle despite all the precautions taken. Suddenly a servant announces that two men have just carried a large trunk into the vestibule below. Everyone goes downstairs. Someone whispers: "So there it is. The technique is not exactly ingenious." He pulls out his revolver and calmly orders that the trunk be opened. When the lid is raised, more than a hundred birds fly out, cheeping and chirping. After having flown twice around the room, the flock disappears up the stairs.

13. A young girl is reading alone in the hall. There is a large carpet on the floor, thanks to which she doesn't hear the rhinoceros approaching. When its muzzle is almost touching her arm, it grunts. The girl turns her head, and instead of reacting in fear as we would expect her to, she seems angry and scolds the animal: "Not again! Go on, go away!" Kicking at it, she chases it out of the room.

14. As the girl is sleeping, a secret door to her room opens and we see a shadow approach her bed. The shadow pulls what looks like a dagger out of its bag. When it reaches the bed, after carefully kissing the girl, it cuts a lock of hair from her head with its scissors—which is what the dagger turns out to be.

15. In a room, centered between four tall candles, is a coffin in which a beautiful woman—possibly the bride—is lying. As the hero approaches her, the cadaver opens her eyes and says: "Can't you just leave me alone?"

16. In the passageway of the castle, one of the suits of armor is bleeding from its chest. The helmet is open and there is clearly no one inside it. In fact, the blood is flowing from a crack in the ceiling. The observer climbs the stairs to the room above the crack. In the middle of the room lies the body of the old lord, bleeding. Hundreds of birds are pecking at his corpse and flying around the room.

17. A storm. An owl in dead leaves. Rain against a windowpane. Storm music. A woman is preparing to leave the castle. She puts on her raincoat, but once outside she discovers a completely calm night. The elements of the storm were fictional: The music came from a record player, and the rain against the window was dripping from the flowerpots on the floor above. The owl is stuffed, posed in the window of a natural-history display case.

18. Introduced to each other, A and B shake hands. Suddenly, B screams and drops A's hand. All the fingers on A's right hand have been amputated.

19. The detective finds a pretext for leaving the castle and comes back disguised as an old peasant, in order to be able to act more freely. Despite the perfection of his disguise and his fake beard, everyone recognizes him right away. "But this is ridiculous, why are you wearing a disguise?" says one. "What a beautiful disguise, I almost didn't recognize you," says another. This gag should not be comical.

20. At some point in the plot, a small box falls into the hands of a young woman who has spoken about it with fear in earlier scenes. When she opens it, her face registers the most intense terror. She faints. The male lead arrives and, after having helped the girl, he also looks into the box. His expression changes, his eyes dilate. Horrified, he closes the box. At that moment, something happens, a fire for

example, which annihilates both people and the box, so we will never know what it contained.

21. A terrible punishment: a person is chained in the dungeon of the castle. His arms are bound tightly to the wall. A slight incision is made in the palm of his hand and fly and beetle larvae are planted there. Some time later, a hundred worms swarm in his hand.

22. An argument. A picks up a knife and tries to stab B. B jumps back and draws a sword out of a display of weapons. A grabs a revolver. B flees. When he reaches the cannon, he fires at A.

23. A woman with a magnificent head of hair is fleeing her suitor. Her hair gets caught in the door, which her suitor slams shut.

Translated from the French by Deborah Treisman

SAÚL YURKIEVICH

Revolution

—for Emilio Pernas

Chairs will sit on us
floors will sweep us up
coat hooks will hang us
we'll be pushed by doors
kicked by balls
dealt by cards
wrinkled by papers
dampened by handkerchiefs
struck by matches
dissolved by sugars
stirred by spoons
drunk by waters
and it will serve us right.

Translated from the Spanish by Cola Franzen

ADOBE LA

Architects, Artists and Designers Opening the Border Edge of Los Angeles

Huellas Fronterizas:

Retranslating the Urban Text in Los Angeles and Tijuana

Learning from Tijuana

F ive stories tall and butt-naked, *La Mona (The Doll)* (shown on the cover of this issue) struts her stuff in the dusty Tijuana suburb of Colonia Aeropuerto. Distressingly—to the gringo eye at least—she looks like the Statue of Liberty stripped and teased for a *Playboy* centerfold. In reality, she is the home of Armando Muñoz Garcia and his family.

Muñoz is an urban imaginer somewhere on a delirious spectrum between Marcel Duchamp and Las Vegas casino entrepreneur Steve Wynn. "Give me enough rebar and an oxyacetylene torch," he boasts, "and I'll line the border with giant nude Amazons." In the meantime, he eats in *La Mona*'s belly and curls up to sleep inside her enormous breasts. When ADOBE LA's Gustavo Leclerc asked Muñoz why he built a house with pubic hair and dimples, he growled back, "Why not?"

Porque no?, Leclerc agrees, is an appropriate slogan for the West Coast's most astounding metropolis. Like Swift's floating sky-city of Laputa in *Gulliver's Travels*, Tijuana seems to defy the ordinary laws of gravity. With an estimated 1.4 million inhabitants, it is now larger than San Diego, San Francisco, Portland, and Seattle. Yet its formal economy and public budget are barely sufficient for a city one-third its current size. Grass roots audacity makes up the difference. "The Tijuanenses," according to Leclerc, "are world champions at the art of flying by the seat of their pants. Nothing fazes them. Just look at the exuberance of *La Mona* with her fist raised triumphantly in the air."

In these photographs, ADOBE LA—"Architects, Artists and Designers Opening the Border Edge of Los Angeles"—a Los Ange-les–based group formed in 1992, after the Rodney King riots, has tried to capture the ironic optimism that undergirds the apparent chaos and callousness of the largest border city. Unhappy with the invisibility of Latino immigrants in the media and politics, the three Mexicans and one Salvadoran who make up ADOBE LA have celebrated their quiet heroism in a series of provocative installations, performances, and documentaries.

The quartet's individual portfolios reveal a shared fascination with the unmapped spaces of immigrant life. Mexico City–born painter Alessandra Moctezuma, for example, has explored the tropical com-plexity of images in the dreamscapes of Latin American women. Leda

Ramos, who grew up in a Salvadorean neighborhood near down-town L.A., has portrayed the daily dislocations between the intimacy of Latino family life and the alienations of sweatshop labor. Ulises Diaz runs a workshop for young graffiti artists from the mixed black and Latino neighborhoods of South Central L.A. And Leclerc, who describes himself as "a voluntarily defrocked corporate architect," has experimented with new forms of "intercultural public space."

Although ADOBE LA's previous work, including their much admired contribution to the Museum of Contemporary Art's *Urban Revisions* show, has focused on Latino street culture in Los Angeles, it was inevitable that the group would turn its attention back toward the border. This led to the current ongoing research project, *Huellas Fronterizas: Retranslating the Urban Text in Los Angeles and Tijuana.* "Tijuana," Moctezuma explains, "anchors a continuous fabric of Mexican life that stretches all the way to Santa Barbara and beyond. Functionally, it is as much a part of Southern California as Laguna Beach or San Bernardino. And, in terms of vernacular architecture and popular culture, it has the most salsa. If Orange County is Wonder Bread, Tijuana is chile verde."

The populist flavor of Tijuana, of course, is scarcely savored by the day tourist from the Midwest. The radical shortage of water, and thus of formal landscaping, gives the city an arid, almost Saharan visage that reads immediately as *Danger: Third World.* Moreover, Tijuana remains stigmatized by its past life as a *zona roja* for the U.S. Pacific fleet. Yankees still fear contamination by their own moral sewage.

Yet for young Tijuanenses, who work in modern offices or Japanese branch plants, the handful of seedy bars left on Avenida Revolution, just like the zebra-painted donkeys, are nostalgic flot-sam from a largely vanished world. In the context of today's indus-trialized border economy, "sin-tourism" is an insignificant factor. Moreover, Tijuana's income from North American tourism is now dwarfed by Mexican shoppers' purchases *en el otro lado*. Last year, patriotic Tijuanenses—angered by the Clinton administration's creeping militarization of the border (e.g. the INS's "Operation Gatekeeper")—attempted to flex their new market power in a boy-cott ("Operacion Dignidad") against San Diego County businesses. NAFTA, they reminded Yankees, is a two-way street.

One traditional Tijuana stereotype, however, retains its validity.

Since the beginning of the population boom in the early 1950s, the city has suffered from chronic shortages of water and urban infrastructure. In large part, this environmental crisis is the result of deliberate disinvestment by a federal government that for decades has used Tijuana as a cash cow to finance modernization in more central regions. The ambitious, if belated, program of public works since 1980 has focused on the largely foreign-owned *maquiladora* belt (*Nueva Ciudad Industrial*) near the airport, rather than on the city's two hundred struggling neighborhoods (*colonias*).

Faced with official neglect, the rank-and-file Tijuanenses have built the city as they have built their homes and lives: from the ground up, in small, hopeful increments. In the absence of public investment, neighborhoods improvise their own infrastructures. Thousands of old tires, for instance, shore up dangerously eroding hillsides. Communal associations, including trade unions, build nurseries, schools, and soccer fields in districts ignored by the government. And, over time, cardboard squatters' camps slowly metamorphose into reasonably middle-class streets, replete with carports and satellite dishes.

Indeed, the true grit of Tijuana is most authentically revealed in the histories of its homes. A friend of mine once took me to his parents' house in Colonia Libertad, two blocks from *la línea*, the sinister steel wall that now defines the border. The spacious two-story home, he explained, had begun life in the 1950s as a small one-room concrete hut that housed nine people. As a child he had shined shoes and sold Chiclets to condescending tourists. Now, twelve structural additions later, the growth of the house recapitulates his family's rising fortunes. Now a Ph.D. psychologist living in Northern California, he was bringing his parents an electric dishwasher for their new kitchen.

Tijuana's bootstrap brand of urbanism—ADOBE LA points out—is antipodal to the monolithic utopias advocated by Le Corbusier and other modernists, where the city is the outcome of a single magisterial vision. In the Do-It-Yourself City, bricolage supplants master planning, and urban design becomes a kind of *art brut*, generated by populist building practices. If only by default, the masses become the city's true auteurs, and architecture is not so much transcended as retranslated through its dynamic vernacular context.

A Tijuana icon almost as surprising as *La Mona*, for example, is the dramatic spherical theater at the municipal Cultural Center (completed in 1982). It is, of course, a realized version of Etienne-Louis Boullée's *Project for a Cenotaph for Sir Isaac Newton (1784)*—one of the great unbuilt utopian designs in the history of architecture. In Cambridge or Paris, it would be a striking enough sight; but on the banks of the bone-dry Tijuana River, it becomes magic realism. The city that defies gravity exalts its discoverer.

The city's other public monuments, however, are mostly sterile eulogies to the PRI's* discredited franchise on Mexican history. Everything touched by the bureaucratic hand of Mexico City seems to wither and die in the relentless Tijuana sunshine. Villa and Zapata look as dispirited upon their official pedestals as the statues of Marx and Lenin that once frowned over Eastern Europe. When presidential nominee Colosio was assassinated in a Tijuana *colonia* in 1993, popular grief built a pyramid of flowers and letters at the site where he fell. Now there is a memorial plaza which Moctezuma calls "the most desolate patch of official concrete in all of Mexico."

La línea, by contrast, has unexpected energies. A steel knife slicing through daily life on both sides of the border, it is also, in Leclerc's words, "a superb stage for subversive practices of all kinds." "While the Migra† is playing hide-and-seek with the *mojados*†† in the hills, kids from an adjacent *colonia* organize a soccer game on the U.S. side. Street vendors sell tamales. Artists build illegal installations. And Tijuana simply yawns in the face of its paranoid neighbor across the wall."

The members of ADOBE LA, meanwhile, have burnt their cultural green cards in public. "In a sense, we are Pete Wilson's worst nightmare," says Leda Ramos. "We are *coyotes* with sketchbooks and video cameras. We are trying to build an underground railroad of ideas between artists and activists in Mexico and Southern California. We openly celebrate the Latin American genius for urban improvisation and, at the risk of vast misunderstanding, we advocate the 'Tijuanization of L.A.'"

Y porque no?

---

* Partido Revolucionario Institucional.

† The Immigration and Naturalization Service.

†† Undocumented border-crossers.

Cross A Parted Sea

in the Green
pastures   God is a Negro
his cigars cost a dime

Heaven is a fish fry every day
where angels (wings pinned to
their white robes) are singing

and even in heaven the catfish
bite & drinking peach wine
is the only sin my father knows

my mother is dusting the Lord's
wings sweeping heaven's floor
the little ones

eat too much watermelon
and they sing (all heaven
does) the spirituals before

there was a bondage
and the children
of Israel crossed a parted sea

Elegy for My Father 1945

A Soldier Home   a southern boy
in the army   whiskey   never left
my side and when I played
my guitar   the south   spoke
my mind   now   with my duffel bag upon
my back uniform   still   on campaign ribbons
                         on my chest
Captain bars
bright across my   shoulders
I came home   south   (o where
the land   so beautiful
is a sorrowful one)
of shantytowns
Nigger Towns
Coal Towns
windows   stuffed
with   cardboard
& me   a southern
poor Negro   (church of God
in me prophecies of the nigger)

mad as The once angry Mississippi I thought
of (you) my father   working for five dollars
a day southern poor (long day poor
father)
now home I bring (to you and the south)
the   war
and cast
down my bucket
father
where you are

THE SPRU

Under construction since 1942, Howard Hughes's giant 200-ton flying boat—popularly dubbed the "Spruce Goose" (a name Hughes loathed)—was completed in 1947 at a cost of $25 million (roughly $166 million in 1996 dollars). Faced with wartime aluminum shortages, Hughes and his partner, shipbuilder/car magnate Henry Kaiser, had used wood, mainly birch and some spruce (from which the aircraft gained its nickname), to develop the largest plane the world had ever seen. With its eight tremendous, 3,000-horsepower engines and

FLIGHT OF

HOWARD HUGHES AT THE CONTROLS OF THE SPRUCE GOOSE PRIOR TO ITS FIRST FLIGHT.

THE 200-TON FLYING BOAT LEAVES THE WATER ON AN UNSCHEDULED ONE-MILE FLIGHT.

CE GOOSE

four-bladed propellers dwarfed by an immense hull and a prodigious wingspan of 320 feet, the Spruce Goose was originally designed as a partly government-funded prototype for tank and troop transport. It had the world's largest and most advanced hydraulic system, as well as the first fuel-dumping system for emergencies and the first airborne spiral staircase.

Soon after the seaplane's completion, Hughes appeared before a congressional committee investigating several of his wartime contracts and was called to task for spending $18 million of Federal funds ($120 million in 1996 dollars) on a plane that had never flown. On November 1, 1947, the craft was taken for float testing for the first time. Positioned on

THE SPRUCE GOOSE CROSSES THE SURFACE OF LOS ANGELES HARBOR AT 90 MILES PER HOUR.

THE HUGHES FLYING BOAT IS TUGGED ACROSS LONG BEACH HARBOR TO A PUBLIC DISPLAY AREA NEXT TO THE QUEEN MARY.

a small platform atop the craft's broad back, Hughes was barely visible as he personally directed operations through a walkie-talkie. Then, on November 2, the plywood flying boat skimmed across the surface of Los Angeles Harbor at ninety miles per hour. On the same day, to prove a point to his congressional investigators, Hughes lifted the mammoth ship into the air on an unscheduled flight. The flight lasted just over a minute: the Spruce Goose flew for one mile, reaching a height of seventy feet.

But the behemoth never made it into the air again. Awaiting future flight opportunities, the Spruce Goose was moved to a three-acre, climate-controlled hangar in the port of Long Beach, California, where a team of some twenty-five assistants was instructed to turn the engine over several times a week. In 1975, the Spruce Goose was offered as a donation to the Smithsonian Institution in Washington, DC. However, when the Smithsonian leaked its plan to keep the cockpit and break down the rest of the flying plane into several sections to be distributed to other museums across the country, Hughes retracted the offer and sold the

plane instead to the Aero Club of Southern California for $1. In 1980, four years after Hughes's death, it was tugged along a three-mile route to a permanent display area across the harbor. But the Spruce Goose floundered as a tourist attraction, and the Walt Disney Company, which temporarily operated the seaplane as an exhibit, eventually gave up its lease. The Spruce Goose was finally sold in 1992 to Evergreen International Aviation, and was moved to McMinnville, Oregon, where it will soon become the centerpiece of Evergreen's aviation museum.

[BACKGROUND] THE GIANT SEAPLANE LIES AT ANCHOR READY FOR ITS FIRST TAXI RUNS. HUGHES AND ASSISTANTS CAN BE SEEN STANDING ON SMALL PLATFORMS ON TOP OF THE SHIP.

[INSETS] TOURISTS VIEW THE SPRUCE GOOSE INSIDE THE EXHIBIT DOME AT THE PORT OF LONG BEACH. THE SPRUCE GOOSE'S OFFICIAL OPENING TO THE PUBLIC WAS CELEBRATED WITH AEROBATICS AND A RIBBON-CUTTING BY ACTOR AND ONE-STAR GENERAL JIMMY STEWART.

Text by Jackie McAllister

VICTOR PELEVIN

From *Omon Ra*

I t was May, the peat bogs around Moscow were on fire, and a pale sultry sun hung in the smoke-veiled sky. The Political Instructor of the Special Cosmonauts' Detachment, Urchagin, gave me a book to read by a Japanese author who had been a kamikaze pilot during the Second World War, and I was astounded by the similarity between my state and the feelings he described. Just like him, I didn't think about what lay ahead of me, but lived for the present day— engrossing myself in books and leaving the world completely behind as I gazed at the fiery explosions on the cinema screen (on Saturday evenings they showed us war films), even worrying seriously about my grades, which weren't too good. The word "death" existed in my life like a note reminding me of something I had to do that had been hanging on my wall for ages—I knew it was still there, but I never paused to look at it. My friend Mitiok and I never discussed the subject, but when we were finally told it was time for us to begin practicing on the actual space equipment, we glanced at each other and seemed to feel the first breath of an icy wind.

From the outside, the moonwalker looked like a large laundry tank set on eight heavy tram wheels. Numerous different items protruded from its fuselage—various-shaped antennae, mechanical arms, and so forth. None of these worked, and they were really only there for television, but they were very impressive all the same. The lid of the moonwalker was covered with small oblique incisions: this was not deliberate, it was simply that the metal sheeting it was made from was the same as they used on the floor in the metro, but then again, it made the machine appear more mysterious.

The human psyche works in peculiar ways: it needs details first of all. I remember when I was small I often used to draw tanks and airplanes and show them to my friends, and they always liked the drawings with lots of lines that didn't really mean anything, so I actually began adding them on purpose. In just the same way, the moonwalker managed to look like a very complicated and ingenious piece of equipment.

The lid hinged up to one side—it was hermetically sealed with rubber padding and had several layers of thermal insulation. Inside, in a space about the same size as the turret of a tank, there was a slightly modified sports-bike frame, with the pedals and just two gear-wheels, one of which was neatly welded to the axle of the rear pair of wheels. The handlebars were ordinary semi-racers—they could just turn the front wheels slightly via a special transmission system, but I was told the necessity shouldn't arise. Shelves, empty for the time being, protruded from the walls; attached to the center of the handlebars was a compass, and attached to the floor was the green tin box of a radio transmitter with a telephone receiver. Set in the wall in front of the handlebars were the black spots of two tiny round lenses, like the spy-holes in apartment doors; through them I could see the edges of the front wheels and a decorative mechanical arm. On the opposite wall hung the radio speaker, a perfectly ordinary square block of red plastic with a black volume control: the Flight Leader explained that in order to counter the sense of psychological isolation from the native land, all Soviet space vehicles received programs broadcast from Moscow's Beacon radio station. The large, convex external lenses were covered by blinkers above and at the sides, so that the moonwalker had something like a face, a crude and likeable face, like the faces they draw on melons and robots in children's magazines.

When I first climbed inside and the lid clicked shut over my head, I thought I would never be able to stand being cooped up and cramped like that. I had to hang over the bicycle frame, distributing my weight between my hands on the handlebars, my legs braced against the pedals and the saddle, which didn't really support part of my weight so much as determine the position my body had to adopt. A cyclist bends over like that when he's trying to get moving really fast—but at least he can straighten up if he wants to, whereas I couldn't, because my back and my head were practically jammed against the lid. But then, after about two weeks of practice, when I began to get used to it, it turned out that there was quite enough space in there to forget about feeling cramped for hours at a time.

The round spy-hole lenses were immediately in front of my face, but the lenses distorted everything so badly there was no way I could tell what was there outside the thin steel wall of the hull. A small spot of the ground just in front of the wheels and a ribbed antenna were powerfully magnified in clear focus, but everything else dissolved into zigzags and blobs, as though I were gazing down a long dark corridor through tears on the glass lenses of a gas mask.

The machine was fairly heavy, and it was hard to get it moving—I even began to doubt whether I would be able to power it across seventy kilometers of lunar desert. Just one turn round the yard was enough to make me really tired; my back ached and my shoulders hurt.

Every other day now, taking turns with Mitiok, I went out into the yard, stripped down to my undershirt and underwear, climbed into the moonwalker and strengthened the muscles on my legs by riding round and round the yard, scattering the chickens and occasionally running over one of them—not deliberately, of course, it was just that through the lenses there was no way to tell a huddled chicken from a newspaper, for instance, or a leg-wrapping the wind had blown off the clothesline, and I couldn't brake fast enough, anyway. At first Urchagin drove in front of me in his wheelchair to show me the way— through the lenses he was a blurred gray-green blob—but gradually I got the hang of it, so I could drive round the entire yard with my eyes closed. All I had to do was set the handlebars at a certain angle, and the machine went round in a smooth circle, coming back to its starting point. Sometimes I even stopped looking through the spy-holes and just let my muscles work away, putting my head down and thinking my own thoughts. Sometimes I remembered my childhood; sometimes I used to imagine what the rapid approach of the final moment before eternity would feel like. And sometimes I tried to finish off really old thoughts that resurfaced into consciousness. For instance, I thought about the question "Who am I?"

It was a question I often used to ask myself as a child, when I woke early in the morning and stared up at the ceiling. Later on, when I was a bit older, I began to ask it in school, but the only answer I got was that consciousness is a property of highly organized matter, according to Lenin's theory of reflection. I didn't understand what these words meant, and I remained as astonished as ever. How was it that I could see? Who was this "I" who saw? And what did it mean, to see? Did I see anything outside me, or was I simply looking at myself? And what did that mean—outside myself and inside myself? I often felt like I was on the very threshold of the answer, but when I tried to take the final step, I suddenly lost sight of the "I" that was about to cross the threshold.

When my aunt went out to work, she often asked an old neighbor to look after me, and I used to ask her the same questions, taking real pleasure in seeing how hard it was for her to answer them.

"Inside you, Ommy, you've got a soul," she said, "and it looks out through your eyes, but it lives in your body like your hamster lives in that saucepan. And this soul is a part of God, who created all of us. And you are that soul."

"But then why did God stick me in this saucepan?" I asked.

"I don't know," said the old woman.

"And where is he?"

"Everywhere," said the old woman, gesturing with her arms.

"Then that means I'm God, too?" I asked.

"No," she said. "Man isn't God. But he's made in God's image."

"And is Soviet man made in God's image, too?" I asked, stumbling over the unfamiliar phrase.

"Of course," said the old woman.

"Are there many gods?" I asked.

"No. There is only one."

"Then why does it say in the handbook that there are lots of them?" I asked, nodding towards the atheist's handbook standing on my aunt's bookshelf.

"I don't know."

"Which god is best?"

The old woman gave the same answer again: "I don't know."

Then I asked: "Can I choose for myself, then?"

"You choose, Ommy," the old woman laughed, and I began rifling through the handbook, which had heaps of different gods in it. I especially liked Ra, the god the ancient Egyptians believed in thousands of years ago. Probably I liked him because he had a falcon's head, and pilots and cosmonauts and all sorts of heroes were often called falcons. I decided that if I really was made in a god's image, then it should be this one. I remember taking a large exercise book and copying the following excerpt into it:

In the morning Ra, illuminating the Earth, sails along the heavenly Nile on the bark Manjet, in the evening he transfers to the bark Mesektet and descends into the underworld, where he does battle with the forces of darkness as he sails along the nether Nile, and in the morning he reappears on the horizon.

In ancient times, people could not know that the Earth really circles the Sun, said the handbook, and so they invented this poetic myth.

Under the article in the handbook was an old Egyptian picture showing Ra transferring from one bark to the other: two identical boats were drawn up side by side, and a girl in one was handing a girl in the other a hoop with a falcon sitting in it—that was Ra. What I liked most of all was that in among all the weird and wonderful items in the boats there were four grim five-story houses which looked just like the ones built in the Moscow suburbs in Khrushchev's time.

From then on, although I responded to the name "Omon," I always thought of myself as "Ra": that was the name of the hero of the imaginary adventures I had before I fell asleep, when I closed my eyes and turned to face the wall—until the time when my dreams were affected by the usual developmental changes.

I wonder if anyone who sees a photograph of the moonwalker in the newspapers will imagine that inside this steel saucepan, which exists for the sole purpose of crawling seventy kilometers across the moon and then halting for eternity, there is a human being, gazing out through two glass lenses? But what does it matter? Even if someone guesses the truth, he'll never know that this human being was me, Omon Ra, the faithful falcon of the Motherland, as the Flight Leader once called me, putting his arm round my shoulder and pointing through the window at a brightly glowing cloud.

It felt like I was riding on a pedal boat through thick reeds with huge telegraph poles sticking up out of them. The pedal boat was strange somehow, unusual, the pedals not in front of the seat, but improvised from an ordinary bicycle: set between the two thick, long floats was a bicycle frame with the word "Sport" on it. I hadn't any idea where all these reeds and the pedal boat had come from, or what I was doing there. But I wasn't really bothered about it. Everything around me was so beautiful I just wanted to ride on and on and keep looking, and probably I'd have been quite happy to go on like that for ages. The sky was particularly lovely—long, narrow, lilac-colored clouds hung above the horizon, looking like a string of strategic bombers. It was warm; I could just hear the propeller splashing in the water, and there was an echo of distant thunder from the west.

Then I realized it wasn't thunder. At regular intervals everything in me—or everything around me—was shaken, and my head began to buzz. With every successive blow all my surroundings—the river, the reeds, the sky over my head seemed to fade a little more. The world was becoming as familiar in its finest details as the door of the toilet at home seen from the inside, and it was all happening very quickly, until I noticed that the bicycle was no longer on water or surrounded by reeds, but inside a transparent sphere that separated me off from everything around me. Every blow made the wall of the sphere thicker and more solid; it let through less and less light, until finally there was total darkness. Then the sky over my head was replaced by a ceiling, a feeble glow of electric light appeared, and the walls began to change their shape, closing in on me and bending out to form shelves stacked with glasses, cans, and other stuff. And then the rhythmical shuddering of the world became what it had been from the very start—a telephone ringing.

I was sitting on the saddle inside the moonwalker, clutching the handlebars and leaning right down over the frame; I was dressed in a padded jacket, a fur cap with earflaps and fur boots; an oxygen mask hung round my neck like a scarf. The ringing came from the green box of the radio screwed to the floor. I picked up the receiver.

"Why, you fucking useless shithead!" a monstrous bass voice boomed in my ear in a tone of anguished suffering. "What're you

doing in there, wanking?"

"Who's that?"

"Head of Central Flight Control Colonel Khalmuradov. Are you awake?"

"What?"

"Fuck you, that's what. Make ready, one minute to launch!"

"Ready in one minute, sir!" I muttered in reply, biting my lip in horror and grasping for the wheel with my free hand.

"You asshole," the receiver hissed indistinctly and began croaking—the man yelling at me was obviously holding the receiver away from his face while he talked to someone else. Then there was a ping in the phone, and I heard a different voice, mechanical and impersonal, but with a strong Ukrainian accent:

"Fifty-nine . . . Fifty-ate . . ."

I was in that state of shame and shock that makes a man groan out loud or scream obscenities; the thought that I'd almost made an irrevocable mistake obscured everything else. As I followed the numbers exploding in my ears, I tried to remember what had happened and realized I probably hadn't really done anything all that terrible. All I could remember was lowering a glass of boiled fruit from my mouth and getting up from the table after I suddenly lost my appetite. The next thing I knew, the phone was ringing and I had to answer it.

"Tirty-tree . . ."

I noticed the moonwalker was fully equipped. The shelves that had always been empty before were densely stacked—on the bottom shelf there were cans of "Great Wall" Chinese corned beef, covered in gleaming vaseline, on the upper shelf there was a map case, a mug, a can opener, and a pistol in a holster, everything secured by wire. Resting against my left hip was an oxygen cylinder with the word "Inflammable" on it, and against my right hip an aluminum milk can that reflected the light of the small electric lamp glowing on the wall. Under the lamp hung a map of the moon marked with two black

circles: under the lower circle were written the words "Landing Site."
Hanging beside the map on a piece of string was a red marker pen.

"Sax-teen . . ."

Beyond the two spy-holes there was total darkness—which was what
I should have expected, I realized, since the moonwalker was covered
by the rocket's nose cone.

"Nine . . . Ate . . ."

I recalled Comrade Urchagin's words: "Those final seconds of the
countdown, what are they but the voice of history speaking through
millions of television screens?"

"Tree . . . Two . . . Win . . . Blast-off."

Somewhere far below me I heard a rumbling and roaring that grew
louder with every second until soon it was beyond all imagining, as
though hundreds of sledgehammers were pounding on the rocket's
iron fuselage. Then the shuddering began, and I banged my head
against the wall in front of me a few times—if not for the fur cap, I'd
probably have beaten my brains out. A few cans of corned beef fell to
the floor, then everything suddenly keeled over so sharply I thought
for a second we were going to crash—and the next moment there
was a distant voice in the telephone receiver that I was still pressing to
my ear:

"Omon! You're flying!"

"We're off," I remembered my instructions and yelled, just like
Gagarin did when he was first catapulted out into space.

The roaring became a steady, powerful rumbling, while the shud-
dering became the kind of vibration you feel in a train when it's already
picked up speed. I put the receiver back on the hook, and the phone
immediately rang again.

"Omon, are you all right?"

It was Sema Anikin's voice, speaking over a monotonous recitation
of information about the first section of the flight.

"I'm fine," I said. "But why are we . . . Ah, I see . . ."

"We thought they'd have to postpone the launch, you were so sound asleep. The moment's calculated to the split second. The entire trajectory depends on it. They even sent a soldier up the gantry and he kicked the nose cone to wake you up. They were trying to call you on the radio for ages."

"Aha."

We said nothing for a few seconds.

"Listen," Sema began again, "I've only got four minutes left, not even that. Then I have to detach the first stage. We've all said good-bye to each other, except for you. . . . This is our last chance to talk."

I couldn't think of the right words to say, and all I felt was embarrassment and weariness.

"Omon!" Sema called me again.

"Yes, Sema," I said, "I hear you. We're flying, d'you understand?"

"Yes," he said.

"How are you feeling?" I asked, realizing just how senseless and insulting the question was.

"I'm okay. How about you?"

"Me, too. What can you see?"

"Nothing. There's no way to see out. The noise is terrible. And the shaking."

"Up here, too," I said, then stopped.

"Okay," said Sema, "my time's up. You know what? Think about me when you land on the moon, okay?"

"Of course," I said.

"Just remember there was a guy called Sema. The first stage. Promise?"

"I promise."

"You've got to get there and finish the job, you hear me?"

"Yes."

"Time's up. Good-bye."

"Good-bye, Sema."

There were several hollow knocks in the receiver, and then through the crackle of interference I heard Sema's voice loud and clear as he sang his favorite song.

"O-oh, in Africa there's a river as long as this . . . O-oh, in Africa there's a mountain as high as this . . . O-oh, crocodiles and hippos . . . O-oh, monkeys and rhinos . . . O-oh . . . Ah-ah-ahah . . ."

On the word "rhinos" there was a crackling like a piece of tarpaulin ripping, and a moment later there were just short beeps, but just a second before that—if it wasn't my imagination—Sema's song turned into a scream. I was jolted again, my back hit the ceiling, and I dropped the receiver. From the change in the roaring of the engines, I guessed the second stage had begun firing. Probably the most terrible thing for Sema was switching on the engine. I imagined what it was like— breaking the safety glass and pressing the red button, knowing all the while that a second later the huge gaping openings of the rocket tubes would spring into violent life. Then I remembered Ivan, and I grabbed the receiver again, but it was still beeping. I hit the hook a few times and yelled:

"Ivan! Ivan! Can you hear me?"

"What is it?" I finally heard him say.

"Sema, he's . . ."

"Yes," he said, "I heard it all."

"Are you going soon?"

"In seven minutes," he said. "D'you know what I'm thinking about now?"

"What?"

"I suddenly remembered how I used to catch pigeons as a kid. You know, we took this big wooden crate and sprinkled bread crumbs under it and stood it on edge, and we propped up the opposite edge with a stick with about ten meters of string tied to it. Then we hid in the bushes or behind a bench, and when a pigeon wandered under the crate, we pulled the string. Then the crate fell on it."

"That's right," I said. "We did the same."

"And you remember, when the crate comes down, the pigeon starts trying to fly off and beats its wings against the sides, so the crate even jumps about?"

"I remember," I said.

Ivan didn't say anything else.

In the meantime it had turned quite cold. And it was harder to breathe, too—after every movement I wanted to catch my breath, as if I'd just run up a long flight of stairs. I began lifting the oxygen mask to my face to take a breath.

"And I remember how we used to make bombs with cartridge cases and the sulphur from matches. You stuff it in real tight, and there has to be a little hole in the side, and you put several matches in a row beside it . . ."

"Cosmonaut Grechka," the bass voice in the receiver was the one that had woken me with abuse before the start of the flight. "Make ready."

"Yes, sir," Ivan answered without enthusiasm. "And then you tie them on with thread—insulating tape's better, because sometimes the thread comes loose. If you want to throw it out of the window, say from the seventh floor, so it explodes in mid-air, then you need four matches. And . . ."

Stop that talking," said the bass voice. "Put on your oxygen mask."

"Yes, sir. You don't strike the last one with the box, though, the best thing is to light it with a dog-end. Or else you might shift them away from the hole."

I heard nothing after that except the usual crackle of interference. Then I was bounced against the wall again, and the short beeps sounded in the receiver. The third stage had fired. The fact that my friend Ivan had just departed this life at an altitude of forty-five kilometers—as simply and unpretentiously as he did everything—

strangely failed to make any impression on me. I didn't feel any grief; quite the opposite, I felt a strange exhilaration and euphoria.

I suddenly realized that I was losing consciousness. That is, I didn't notice when I lost consciousness, I noticed when I regained it. A moment ago I was holding the receiver to my ear, and now it was lying on the floor; there was a ringing in my ears, and I gazed down at it in stupefaction from my saddle up under the ceiling. A moment ago the oxygen mask was hanging round my neck like a scarf—and now as I shook my head in an effort to rouse myself, it was lying on the floor beside the telephone receiver. I realized I needed oxygen, so I reached for the mask and put it to my mouth—I felt better instantly, and I could feel I was very cold. Fastening all the buttons of my padded jacket, I put the collar up and lowered the earflaps of my fur cap. The rocket was shaking slightly. I wanted to sleep, and even though I knew it wasn't a good idea, I couldn't fight it—I folded my hands on the handlebars and closed my eyes.

I dreamed of the moon—the way Mitiok used to draw it in our childhood: a black sky, pale yellow craters, and a distant mountain range. Walking slowly and smoothly toward the blazing orb of the sun hanging above the horizon was a bear, with its front paws held out in front of its muzzle: it had the golden star of a Hero of the Soviet Union on its chest and a trickle of dried blood ran from the corner of its mouth, which was set in a pitiful grin. Suddenly it stopped and turned its face toward me. I felt it watching me, and I raised my head to glance into its motionless blue eyes.

"I, and this entire world, are nothing but a thought someone is thinking," the bear said in a quiet voice.

I woke up. Everything was very quiet. Clearly some part of my consciousness had maintained contact with the outside world, and the sudden silence had affected me like an alarm clock going off. I leaned down to the spy-holes in the wall. The nose cone had already separated from the rocket, and there in front of my eyes was the Earth.

I tried to work out how long I'd been asleep, but I couldn't put any definite figure on it. It must have been a few hours at least: I felt hungry already, and I began rummaging through the things on the upper shelf—I thought I'd seen a can opener there, but it wasn't there now. I decided it must have been shaken off onto the floor, and started looking around for it, but just at that moment the phone rang.

"Hello!"

"Stand by, Ra. Omon, can you hear me?"

"Yes, Comrade Flight Leader."

"So far everything seems to be going okay. There was just one difficult moment, when the telemetry malfunctioned. Not that it actually malfunctioned, you understand, they simply activated another system in parallel and the telemetry failed to operate. They even lost control for a few minutes. That was when you were short of air, remember?"

He was speaking in a strange way, quick and excited. I decided he must be feeling very nervous, though just for a moment I suspected he was drunk.

"You gave everyone a good scare, Omon. Sleeping like that. We almost had to postpone the launch."

"I'm sorry, Comrade Flight Leader."

"Never mind, never mind. It's not your fault. They just drugged you too heavily before the trip to Baikonur. So far everything's going just fine."

"Where am I now?"

"On the working trajectory already. You're flying toward the moon. You mean you slept through the escape from Earth orbit, too?"

"I must have. You mean Otto's already . . ."

"Yes, Otto's gone already. Surely you can see the nose cone's already separated? But you had to do two extra orbits. Otto panicked at first. He just wouldn't switch on the rockets. We thought he'd chickened out, but then the lad pulled himself together. . . . Anyway, he

sent you his regards."

"And Dima?"

"What about Dima? Dima's okay. The automatic landing system isn't used during the inertial section of the flight. Though he still has the corrections to make . . . Matiushevich, can you hear us?"

"Yes, sir," said Dima's voice in the receiver.

"Okay, you rest for now," said the Flight Leader. "Stand by tomorrow at 15:00 hours, then correction of trajectory. Over and out."

I put down the receiver and pressed my eyes against the spy-holes to gaze at the blue semicircle of the Earth. I'd often read how all the cosmonauts were astounded by the sight of our planet from space. They wrote about some fabulously beautiful misty effect, and how the cities with their shining electric lights on the dark side reminded them of huge bonfires, and how they could even see the rivers on the daylight side well: none of it's true. The thing the Earth seen from space resembles most is a large school globe. I was soon sick of the sight; I rested my head as comfortably as I could on my arms and went to sleep again.

When I woke up, the Earth was no longer visible. All I could make out through the spy-holes were the white spots of the distant and unattainable stars, blurred by the lenses. I imagined the existence of a huge, immensely hot sphere hanging entirely unsupported in the icy void, billions of kilometers from the closest stars, those tiny gleaming dots, of which all we know is that they exist, and even that's not certain, because a star can die, while its light will carry on traveling out in all directions, so really we don't know anything about stars, except that their life is terrible and senseless, since all their movements through space are predetermined and subject to the laws of mechanics, which leave no hope at all for any chance encounters. But then, I thought, even though we human beings always seem to be meeting each other, and laughing, and slapping each other on the shoulder, and saying good-bye, there's still a certain special dimension into which our consciousness sometimes takes a frightened peep, a dimension in which we also hang quite motionless in a void where there's no up or down, no yesterday or tomorrow, no hope of drawing closer to each other or even exercising our will and changing our fate; we judge what happens to others from the deceptive twinkling light that reaches us, and we spend all our lives journeying toward what we call the light, although its source may have ceased to exist long ago. And me, I thought, all my life I've been journeying toward the moment when I would soar up over the crowds of what the slogans called the workers and the peasants, the soldiers and the intelligentsia, and now here I am hanging in brilliant blackness on the invisible threads of fate and trajectory—and now I see that becoming a heavenly body is not much different from serving a life sentence in a prison carriage that travels round and round a circular railway line without ever stopping.

We traveled through space at a speed of two and a half kilometers a second, and the inertial sector of the flight lasted about three days, but I had the feeling I'd been flying for at least a week. Probably because the sun passed in front of the spy-holes several times a day, and every time I was able to watch a quite incredibly beautiful sunrise and sunset.

All that was left now of the immense rocket was the lunar module, made up of the correction and braking stage, where Dima Matiushevich was sitting, and the descent vehicle, that is, the moonwalker on its platform. In order to save fuel, the nose cone had separated before escape from Earth orbit, and now there was open space beyond the fuselage of the moonwalker. The lunar module was flying backward, so to speak, with its main rocket pointing toward the moon, and gradually the way I felt about it changed: at first the lunar module rose higher and higher above the Earth, until at some point it gradually became clear that it was falling toward the moon. I hurtled out of Earth orbit with my head pointing downward and it was only later, after a day or so of the flight, that I found myself with my head upward, falling with ever increasing speed down a black well, clutching the handlebars of my bicycle and waiting for its nonexistent wheels to collide silently with the moon.

I had time for all these thoughts because for the time being I had nothing to do. I often felt like talking to Dima but he was always busy with all his complicated corrections to the trajectory. Sometimes I picked up the receiver and heard his incomprehensible exchanges with the engineers at Central Flight Control:

"Forty-three degrees . . . Fifty-seven . . . Yaw . . ."

I listened to all this for a little while, then gave up on it. As far as I could understand, Dima's main task was to catch the sun in one optical device, the moon in another, measure something and transmit the result to Earth, where they had to check the actual trajectory with the projected one and calculate the length of the corrective impulse required from the engines. Judging from the fact that I was jerked about quite roughly on my saddle several times, Dima seemed to be coping with his task.

When the shocks stopped, I waited about half an hour, picked up the receiver and called him:

"Hello! Dima!"

"Yes, I hear you," he said in his usual dry manner.

"Have you corrected the trajectory, then?"

"Seems like it."

"Was it difficult?"

"It was fine," he answered.

"Listen," I said, "where did you pick up all that stuff? All those degrees and things? We didn't have any of that in class."

"I served two years in a strategic rocket detachment," he said. "The directional system's much the same, only you use the stars. And without any radio communications—you work it all out yourself on a calculator. Make a mistake and you're fucked."

"And if you don't make a mistake?"

Dima didn't answer that one.

"What were your duties?"

"Operational Officer. Then Strategic Officer."

"What does that mean?"

"Nothing complicated. If you're sitting in a tactical operations rocket, you're an Operational Officer. If you're in a strategic rocket, then you're a Strategic Officer."

"Is it tough?"

"It's okay. Like working as a watchman back in the everyday world. Twenty-four hours' duty in the rocket and three days off."

"So that's what turned your hair gray . . . I suppose all of you are gray."

Dima didn't answer that one either.

"No. More likely the training flights."

"What training flights? Ah—that's when they write in fine print on the back page of *Izvestiya* that it's forbidden to sail into such and such a sector of the Pacific Ocean, is that it?"

"That's it."

"And do they have training flights often?"

"It depends, but you pull a straw every month. Twelve times a year, the entire squadron. All twenty-four of you. That's what turns the guys' hair gray."

"And what if you don't want to pull a straw?"

"Pulling a straw is just an expression of speech. What actually happens before the training flight is the Assistant Political Instructor goes round and gives everyone an envelope. Your straw's already in it."

"And if you get a short straw, can you refuse?"

"In the first place, it's a long straw, not a short one. And in the second place, no. All you can do is write an application for a cosmonauts' detachment. But you have to be really lucky."

"Are many people lucky?"

"I've never counted them. I was lucky."

Dima answered my questions reluctantly, with lots of rather impolite pauses. I couldn't think of anything else to ask, so I put down the receiver.

I made my next attempt to talk to him when there were only a few minutes left to braking. I'm ashamed to admit it, but I was overcome by a callous curiosity—would Dima change before . . . ? I wanted to check whether he would be as taciturn as he was during our last conversation, or whether the approaching end of his flight would make him a bit more talkative. I picked up the receiver and called him:

"Dima! This is Omon. Pick up the phone."

The answer I got was:

"Listen, ring me back in two minutes! If your radio's working, switch it on now!"

Dima hung up. His voice sounded excited, and I thought they must be talking about us on the radio. But Radio Beacon was broadcasting music—when I switched on I just caught the fading tinkle of a synthesizer; the program was just ending, and after a few seconds there was a silent pause. Then came the time signal, and I learned that in a place called Moscow it was two in the afternoon. I waited a bit and then picked up the receiver.

"Did you hear it?" Dima asked excitedly.

"Yes," I said, "but only the very end."

"But did you recognize it?"

"No," I said.

"It was Pink Floyd. 'One of These Days.'"

"How come the workers requested that?" I asked in astonishment.

"They didn't, of course," said Dima. "It's the theme tune for the program *Life of Science*. From the album *Meddle*. Pure underground."

"You mean you like Pink Floyd?"

"Me? I'm a fan. I had all their albums. What d'you think of them?"

It was the first time I had heard Dima speak with such enthusiasm.

"Not bad in general," I said. "But not all their stuff. They have this album with a cow on the cover."

"*Atom Heart Mother*," said Dima.

"I like that one. And there's another one I remember—a double album with them sitting in a yard, and on the wall is a picture of the same yard with them sitting in it . . ."

"*Ummagumma.*"

"Maybe. I don't think that's music at all."

"That's right! It's not music, it's shit!" a bass voice roared in the receiver, and we said nothing for a few seconds.

"You're wrong," said Dima when he finally spoke. "At the end there's a new version of 'Saucerful of Secrets.' A different timbre from on *Nice Pair*. Different singer, too."

I'd forgotten that.

"What do you like on *Atom Heart Mother*?" asked Dima.

"There are a couple of songs on side two. One's quiet, just a guitar, and the other has an orchestra. The ending's beautiful—tam ta-ta ta-ta ta-ta ta-ta tam-taram tra-ta-ta . . ."

"I know it," said Dima. "'Summer '68.' And the quiet song's 'If.'"

"Maybe," I said. "So what's your favorite record?"

"I don't have a favorite record," Dima said haughtily. "It's not records I like, it's music. On *Meddle*, for instance, I like the first song. About the echo. It makes me cry every time I listen to it. I translated it with a dictionary. 'Overhead the Albatross pa-ra-ram, pa-ram . . . And help me understand the best I can . . .'"

Dima swallowed and fell silent.

"Your English is very good," I said.

"Yes, that's what they told me in the rocket division. The Assistant Political Instructor said so. But that's not the point. There was one record I didn't manage to find. During my last leave I went to Moscow specially, took four hundred rubles with me. I asked around everywhere, no one had even heard of it."

"What record was that?"

"You wouldn't know it. Music from a film. It's called *Zabriskie Point.*"

"Ah," I said, "I did have that one. Not the record, I had it on tape. Nothing special really . . . Dima, why have you gone all quiet? Hey, Dima!"

The receiver crackled for a long time before Dima asked:

"What's it like?"

"How can I put it?" I said. "Have you heard *More*?"

"Sure."

"It's kind of like that. Only they don't sing. An ordinary kind of soundtrack. If you've heard *More*, you can reckon you've heard it. Typical Pinky—saxophone, synthesizer. The second side . . ."

There was a beep in the phone, and my skull cavity was filled with Khalmuradov's loud roar:

"Ra, come in! What are you fucking chattering about up there? Haven't you got anything to do? Prepare the automatic system for soft landing!"

"The automatic system's ready!" Dima replied, reluctantly.

"Then commence orientation of the braking motor axis to the lunar vertical!"

"All right."

I glanced out into space through the moonwalker's spy-holes and saw the moon right up close. The picture that met my eyes would have been just like the Ukrainian flag, if its top half were blue instead of black. The phone rang. I picked it up, but it was Khalmuradov again.

"Attention! At the count of three activate the braking motor on the command of the radio altimeter!"

"Read you," replied Dima.

"One . . . Two . . ."

I hung up quickly.

The motor fired. It worked intermittently, and about twenty minutes later my shoulder was suddenly thrown against the wall, then my back was bounced against the ceiling, and then an intolerably loud crash shook everything; I realized that Dima had passed on to immortality without saying good-bye. But I wasn't offended—apart from our final conversation he'd always been taciturn and unsociable, and I had a feeling that sitting for days at a time in the gondola of his intercontinental ballistic missile, he'd understood something which meant he never needed to say hello or good-bye again.

I didn't notice the landing. The shuddering and rumbling suddenly stopped, and looking out through the spy-holes, I saw the same pitch blackness I had seen before the start of the flight. At first I thought something had gone wrong, then I remembered that according to plan I was supposed to land during the lunar night.

I waited for a while, not knowing what I was waiting for. Suddenly the phone rang.

"Khalmuradov here," said the voice. "Is everything in order?"

"Yes, sir, Comrade Colonel."

"The telemetry will be activated in a moment, and the guide-rails will be lowered," he said. "You will proceed down onto the surface and report. But use the brakes, you understand?"

Then in a quieter voice, holding the receiver away from his face, he added: "Hun-der-ground. What a bastard."

The moonwalker swayed and I heard a dull thud from outside.

"Proceed," said Khalmuradov.

This was probably the most difficult part of my assignment—I had to drive down out of the descent module along two narrow guide-rails lowered on to the lunar surface. The guide-rails had special slots to accommodate the flanges on the moonwalker's wheels, so it was impossible to slide off them, but there was still the danger that one of the guide-rails might land on a boulder, and then the moonwalker might tilt and overturn on its way down to the ground. I turned the pedals a few times and felt the massive machine lean forward and begin to move under its own momentum. I pressed the brake, but the force of inertia was too strong, and the moonwalker was dragged downward; suddenly there was a clanging sound, the brake went slack, and my feet turned the pedals backward several times with terrifying speed. The moonwalker rolled forward irresistibly, swayed, and came to a halt, standing evenly on all eight wheels.

I was on the moon. But I had no feelings about the fact at all; I was wondering how to put back the chain that had slipped off the cogwheel. Just when I finally managed it, the phone rang. It was the Flight Leader. His voice sounded solemn and official.

"Comrade Krivomazov! On behalf of the entire aviation officers' corps present here at Central Flight Control, I congratulate you on the soft landing of the Soviet automated space station 'Luna-17B' on the moon!"

I heard popping sounds, and I realized they were opening champagne. There was music, too—some kind of march; I could hardly hear it, it was almost drowned out by the crackling in the receiver.

My youthful dreams of the future were born from the gentle sadness of those evenings, far removed from the rest of life, when you lie in the grass beside the remains of someone else's campfire, with your bicycle beside you, watching the purple stripes left in the western sky by the sun that has just set, and you can see the first stars in the east.

I hadn't seen or experienced very much, but I liked lots of things, and I thought that a flight to the moon would take in and make up for all the things I had passed by, in hopes of catching up with them later; how could I know that you only ever see the best things in life out of the corner of your eye? As a kid I often imagined the landscapes of other worlds—rocky plains flooded with dead light and pitted with craters; distant, sharp-pointed mountains, a black sky with the huge brand of a sun blazing on it among the glittering stars; I imagined meter-thick

layers of cosmic dust; I imagined boulders lying motionless on the surface of the moon for billions of years—for some reason I was really excited by the idea that a boulder could lie in the same place without moving for so long until one day I bent down and picked it up between the thick fingers of my spacesuit glove. I thought about how I would raise my head to see the blue sphere of the Earth, and this supreme moment of my life would link me with all the moments when I felt I was standing on the threshold of something wonderful beyond comprehension.

In fact the moon proved to be a narrow, black, stuffy space where the faint electric light only came on rarely; it turned out to be constant darkness seen through the useless lenses of the spy-holes, and restless, uncomfortable sleep in a cramped position with my head resting on my arms, which lay on the handlebars.

I traveled slowly across the surface, about five kilometers a day, and I hadn't the slightest idea what the world around me looked like. But then, of course, this kingdom of eternal darkness probably didn't look like anything—apart from me, there wasn't anybody for whom it could look like anything, and I didn't switch on the headlight, in order to save the battery. The surface of the ground beneath me was obviously even and the machine moved smoothly over it. I couldn't turn the handlebars at all—they must have jammed on landing—so all I had to do was keep turning the pedals. But my journey into space had been so long, that I refused to allow gloomy thoughts to get me down, and I even managed to feel happy.

Hours and days went by. When I halted, it was only to lower my head onto the handlebars and sleep. It was so horribly uncomfortable to use the toilet that I preferred to wait till the final moment, like I used to during quiet hour in kindergarten. The corned beef was gradually running out, there was less and less water in the milk can; every evening I extended the red line on the map in front of me by another centimeter, and it crept closer and closer to the small black circle where it was supposed to come to a stop. The circle was like the symbol for a metro station; it irritated me that it had no name, and I wrote one beside it—*Zabriskie Point.*

With my right hand squeezing the nickel-plated knob in the pocket of my padded jacket, I had been staring for an hour at the label of one of the cans, with its words "Great Wall." I was having visions of warm winds over the fields of distant China, and I wasn't really interested in the tedious ringing of the phone on the floor, but I picked it up after a while.

"Ra, come in! Why don't you answer? Why aren't we moving? I can see everything here with the telemetry."

"I'm having a rest, Comrade Flight Leader."

"Report the reading on the gauge!"

I glanced at the figures in the opening in the small steel cylinder.

"Thirty-two kilometers, seven hundred meters."

"Now put out the light and listen. Looking at the map here, we can see you're very close."

I felt my heart sink, although I knew there was still a long way to go to that small black circle that gazed at me from the map like the barrel of a gun.

"To what?"

"The landing module of 'Luna-17B.'"

"But I'm 'Luna-17B,'" I said.

"Never mind, so were they."

It seemed he was drunk again. But I understood what he was talking about. It was the expedition to obtain samples of the lunar soil; that time two cosmonauts had landed on the moon, Pasiuk Drach and Zurab Pratsvania. They had a small rocket with them which they used to send five hundred grams of soil back to Earth; after that they lived on the lunar surface for one and a half minutes, and then shot themselves.

"Careful, Omon!" said the Flight Leader. "Be cautious now. Reduce speed and switch on the headlights."

I flicked a switch and pressed my eyes to the black lenses of the spy-holes. The optical distortion drew the blackness around the moonwalker into an arch that stretched out ahead of me in an endless tunnel. All I could make out clearly was a small section of the rough, uneven rocky surface—it was evidently ancient basalt; every one and a half meters or so there were long low outcrops perpendicular to my line of movement; they reminded me of sand hills in the desert. The strange thing was I didn't feel them at all as I moved along.

"Well?" asked the voice in the receiver.

"I don't see anything," I said.

"Turn off the headlights and proceed. Don't hurry."

I went on for another forty minutes. Then the moonwalker collided with something. I picked up the phone.

"Earth, come in. There's something here."

"Switch on the headlights."

Right in the center of my field of vision lay two hands in black leather gloves. The extended fingers of the right hand lay over the handle of a small shovel which still held a little sand mixed with small stones, and the left hand gripped a Makarov pistol that gleamed dully. There was something dark between the hands. Looking closer, I could make out the raised collar of an officer's padded jacket with the top of a fur cap protruding above it; the man's shoulder and part of his head were concealed by the wheel of the moonwalker.

"What is it, Omon?" the receiver breathed in my ear.

I described briefly what I could see.

"What about the epaulets, can you see them?"

"No, I can't."

"Move back half a meter."

"The moonwalker doesn't travel backward," I said. "It has pedal braking."

"Damn . . . I told the chief designer," mumbled the Flight Leader. "I wonder who it is, Zura or Pasha. Zura was a captain, and Pasha was a major. Okay, switch off the headlights, you'll flatten the batteries."

"Yes, sir," I said, but before I carried out the order, I took another look at the motionless hand and the fabric top of the fur cap. I couldn't get moving for a while, but then I gritted my teeth and put all my weight on the pedal. The moonwalker jerked upward and then, a second later, back down again.

"Proceed," said Khalmuradov, who had replaced the Flight Leader on the phone. "You're falling behind schedule."

I saved energy by spending almost all the time in total darkness, frenziedly turning the pedals and only switching on the light for a few seconds at a time in order to check the compass, although this was quite pointless, since the handlebars were useless anyway. But they ordered me to do it. It's hard to describe the sensation: darkness, a hot, cramped space, sweat dripping from your brow, a gentle swaying—perhaps an embryo experiences something of the sort in its mother's womb.

I was aware that I was on the moon, but the immense distance separating me from the Earth was a pure abstraction for me. I felt as though the people I spoke with on the phone were somewhere close by—not because I could hear their voices clearly in the receiver, but because I couldn't imagine how the entirely immaterial official relationships and personal feelings that linked us together could be stretched so far. But the strangest thing was that the memories connecting me with childhood could extend over such an incomprehensible distance, too.

When I went to school, I used to spend the summers in a village outside Moscow. It stood on the edge of a main highway, and I spent most of my time in the saddle of my bike, sometimes riding up to thirty or forty kilometers a day. The bicycle wasn't very well adjusted—the handlebars were too low, and I really had to bend down to them—like in the moonwalker. And now, probably because my body had been set in that pose for such a long time, I began having light hallucinations. I seemed to drift off into a waking sleep—in the darkness it was particularly easy—and I dreamed I could see my shadow on the asphalt rushing past below me, and the white dotted line in the middle of the highway, and I was breathing air smelling of diesel fumes. I began to think I could hear the roar of trucks rushing past and the hissing of tires on asphalt, and only the next radio contact brought me back to my senses. But afterward I dropped out of lunar reality and again was transported back to the Moscow highway, and I realized how much the hours I'd spent there had meant to me.

On one occasion Comrade Kondratiev came on the radio to talk to me and began declaiming poetry about the moon. I was wondering how to ask him to stop without being offensive, when he began reading a poem that I recognized from the very first lines as a photographic image of my soul:

> *Life's vital bonds we took for lasting truth,*
> *But as I turn my head to glance at you,*
> *How strangely changed you are, my early youth,*
> *Your colors are not mine, and not one line is true.*
> *And in my mind, moon glow is what I see*
> *Between us two, the drowning man and shallow place;*
> *Your semi-racer bears you off from me*
> *Along the miles toward the moon's bright face,*
> *How long now since . . .*

I gave a quiet sob, and Comrade Kondratiev immediately stopped. "What comes next?" I asked.

"I've forgotten," said Comrade Kondratiev. "It's gone clean out of my head."

I didn't believe him, but I knew it was pointless to argue or plead.

"What are you thinking about now?" he asked.

"Nothing really," I said.

"Nobody thinks of nothing," he said. "There's always some thought or other running round your head. Tell me, I'd like to know."

"Well, I often remember my childhood," I said reluctantly. "How I used to go riding on my bike. It was a lot like this. And to this day I don't understand it—there I was, riding along on my bike, with the handlebars way down low, and it was really bright up ahead, and the wind was so fresh . . ."

I stopped speaking.

"Well? What is it you don't understand?"

"I thought I was riding toward the canal . . . So how can it be that I . . . ?"

Comrade Kondratiev said nothing for a minute or two and then quietly put down the receiver.

I switched on Radio Beacon—I didn't believe it was really Beacon, even though every two minutes they assured me it was.

"Maria Ivanovna Plakhuta from the village of Nukino has given the Motherland seven sons," said a woman's voice, soaring out over the factory lunchtime in distant Russia. "Two of them, Ivan Plakhuta and Vassily Plakhuta, are now serving in the army, in the tank forces of the KGB. They have asked us to broadcast the comic song *The Samovar* for their mother. We're doing just as you asked, lads. Maria Ivanovna, here singing for you is People's Jester of the U.S.S.R., Artem Plakhuta, who was just as delighted to accept our invitation as he was to be demobilized from the army with the rank of senior sergeant eight years before his brothers."

Then the balalaikas began to jangle, the cymbals clashed a couple of times, and a voice filled with feeling, leaning hard on the letter "r" as if it were the person crushed next to him in a crowded bus, began to sing:

"*O-oh, the wa-terrr's on the boil!*"

I switched it off. The words sent a shiver through me. I remembered Dima's gray head, and the cow on the cover of *Atom Heart Mother*, and a cold shudder ran slowly down my spine. I waited a minute or two until I was sure the song must have finished, and turned the black knob. For a second there was silence, and then the baritone leapt out of hiding straight into my face with:

"*We gave the skunks our tea to drink,*
Fed them water fiery hot!"

This time I waited longer, and when I finally switched the radio on, the announcer was speaking: "Let us remember our cosmonauts, and all those whose earthly labors make possible their shiftwork in the heavens. For them today . . ."

I withdrew into my own thoughts, or rather, I suddenly found myself immersed in one of them, as though I had fallen through thin ice, and I only began to hear anything again a few minutes later, as a ponderous choir of distant basses was laying the final bricks in the monumental edifice of a new song. But even though I was completely unaware of the real world, I carried on mechanically pressing the pedals, with my right knee turned out as far as possible—that way I felt less pain from the blister my boot had given me. I was struck by a sudden idea. If now, when I closed my eyes, I was—as far as a person can actually be anywhere—on a phantom highway outside Moscow, and the nonexistent asphalt, trees, and sunshine became as real to me as if I actually were dashing down a slope in my favorite second gear; if—forgetting about *Zabriskie Point*, which was not very far off now—I was sometimes happy for a few seconds, didn't that mean that already back then in my childhood, when I was simply a part of a world submerged in summer happiness, when I really was dashing along the asphalt strip on my bicycle, riding against the wind into the sun, without the slightest interest in what the future had in store for me—didn't that mean that even then I was really already trundling across the black, lifeless surface of the moon, seeing nothing but what penetrated into consciousness through the crooked spy-holes as the moonwalker slowly solidified around me?

We're spaceward bound tomorrow
But there's no grief or sorrow
Alone in the sky.
The moon's riding high.
You ripe ears of barley, good-bye.

Translated from the Russian by Andrew Bromfield

Keeping an Appointment

Like you I nearly died once.
While I drove myself from the doctor
who explained the operation's urgency, my hands
began to spasm and I drew
into a Sinclair and called
the woman who was going to marry me.
To heighten the drama
by sharing it. Called her,
who stopped speaking to me one day
years later, with reason, like a faucet
turned off. I sobbed
the first exciting prospect of my death,
my exquisite loneliness.
And as she gasped blind sympathy,
I heard behind me in the pitiful afternoon
the far-off howling of dogs from a horizon
I of course did not believe in
any more than in my love for her.

Something

More than ten years later, she was reading in the bathroom one of the books he had given her and reached to set the book on the window ledge to make use of her hands otherwise when the book tipped and she tried to catch it to keep from losing her place but it slipped and fell anyway and a note-card slid out with some writing on it and she caught herself thinking This, maybe this is the note he left.

The Bricoleur
of
Broken Hearts

MMind of an engineer, soul of a poet: a real crisis," George
Herms says.* He was first-semester Engineering, Univer-
sity of California, Berkeley, fixated on the football season.
It was 1953. He was eighteen. By New Year's Eve, he was in jail in
Southern California.

By 1955, George was orating in a thicket of limbs and pot smoke
in Wallace Berman's Crater Lane pad in Beverly Glen on the rim of
Los Angeles. It would be months before Allen Ginsberg delivered
Howl in San Francisco. George met his Merlins at Crater Lane:
Berman, an assemblagist who built "temples"; Robert "Baza" Alexan-
der, a printer who wrote poems; Marjorie Cameron, an occultist who
drew her nightmares in notebooks. They prayed to Charlie Parker,
played "Wine Spoe-de-o-dee," mailed postcards that looked like art.
Each swam in that American midnight river in nothing but his skin.
George considered where he came from and how to swim with it.

"I had stage fright," he remembers. He was reading from a roll
of shelving paper he had covered single-spaced on a trek to Mexico
with his typewriter and a copy of Philip Lamantia's surrealist poems.
Baza may have breathed in his ear, *Suck me baby with your eyeball
mind.* Berman's *Panel* stood beside him, a totem (photograph of
wife Shirley, the word *Veritas*, a stone crossed with leather in a box).
George thought, "Maybe I can cut off a section of the roll, put it in
a box with an old tin can. That can be my contribution."

He went back to engineering. Between the fall of 1956 and the
summer of 1957, he worked at Servomechanisms, Inc., operating
computers. He lived in Hermosa Beach. After work and on week-
ends, George combed the sand under the condemned Pier, the
vacant lot with empty foundations, the alleys between garages.
He filled his rooms with castoffs. "I was trying to make poems out of
objects."

George found Bobby down one of those alleys. He knew him
from childhood: Bobby Driscoll had been in seventeen movies, one
of them *Treasure Island.* When George was twelve, Bobby was ten;
Bobby was George projected. When George met Bobby in Hermosa
Beach, the studios wouldn't cast him: He was twenty, searching. They
became friends. *(cont'd on p.89)*

---

*All quotations are taken from conversations between George Herms and
Merril Greene, 1976 and 1995.

Immediate Occupancy, 1985/86.

Fuji Vision, 1986.

Blind Trust in the Muse, 1987.

Song for Hope, 1987.

Beauty's Lid, 1990.

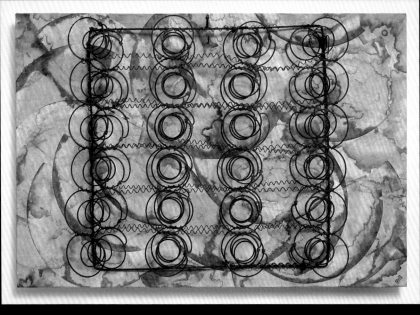

Seat of Coffee Filter Consciousness, 1991.

Pandora's Box, 1992.

Aleph Me, 1992.

(cont'd from p.80) Bobby was "the classic example of the perfect actor": He could "*become* what he *pretended*." George tried to imagine how it would feel to "give everything" to become someone else. Some days Bobby woke up and didn't know who he was. Bobby was an addict and gave George some heroin once. "It's anesthesia," George said. "You don't move."

George *had* to move. "I'm a doer; I make things. When I have a dream, I like to get it into a form where I can pass it on." He *knew* who *he* was. "You carry a landscape within you. It's sort of a permanent thing." He was a small-town boy from Woodland, California, born 1935. He was "middle everything": "middle-class, middle of the Central Valley," which was "flat as the middle of a frying pan." The emptiness got to him sometimes; he wanted to fill it up. He felt the planned grid of streets, of furrows, ditches, farm roads. He pictured the Joads' truck. (Everyone read Steinbeck.) His father was a farm agent who believed in the New Deal.

George worked among his castoffs, "stoned by the light of common day." He could not reclaim Bobby. He *could* reclaim himself. He could accomplish this reclamation project by degrees. Work was a virtue: patience, a virtue; so was self-discipline. He would use his engineer's control, his poet's abandon, to rescue the world's refuse, and thereby rescue himself. He would create a "Department of Dreams," one of "Visionary Prophecy." This was *his* New Deal: a little model of the world, for poets.

Later that summer, George led Wallace Berman to the vacant lot where the bungalows had been knocked down. George had carried everything he'd made from his house on Hermosa Avenue to the open plot.

It was everywhere, wedged in the sand, leaning against the foundations. George called it his "Secret" exhibition; he would put it first on his vitae. He moved away from Hermosa in August. He left his work in the field.

—Merril Greene

Zinacantán Dreams

We only come to sleep, we only come to dream.
It is not true, not true that we come to live on the earth.
—Tochihuitzin Coyolchiuhqui, Aztec shaman

Zinacantán is a small Mayan community in the highlands of Chiapas, the southernmost state in Mexico. Its inhabitants, who have seen their population double to 25,000 since 1980, have discovered that the rugged mountains do not shelter them entirely from the media, the world economy, or the Zapatistas' pan-Mayan peasant rebellion. Nevertheless, they maintain a traditional way of life. They work their fields by hand, celebrate the old gods, and affirm the truth of myths and dreams while defending themselves against ancient demonic forces and modern social pressures.

Throughout the Classic Maya period (200–900 A.D.), the Chiapas highlands remained outside the political and cultural dominion of the major Mayan centers. When the cities fell, Zinacantán became a thriving market, gaining impressive local control over the trade in precious feathers, salt, and amber. Despite perpetual warfare with the lowland Chiapanecs, Zinacantec merchants maintained a network of trade relations that stretched from Guatemala to Tabasco in central Mexico, and north to the Aztec Empire. In 1524, however, Zinacantán capitulated without a hint of resistance to a handful of Spanish invaders, doubtless believing that the town would profit from the defeat of its enemies, the

Zinacantán Center.

9 1

Chiapanecs and the Chamulans. Four years later, the Spaniards established the town of San Cristóbal de las Casas as the political and commercial center of Ladino* supremacy in the highlands. Zinacantán continued to be the Indian "capital" of the region and Zinacantecs served the Spanish forces as warriors and porters in expeditions in the highlands and in the Lacandón jungle.

For three centuries Zinacantán has endured a fate as bitter as that of any Indian segment of Mexico. "History" has been for the Zinacantecs what they defined in a sixteenth-century dictionary as "the book of suffering, the book of hardship"—punctuated by famines and epidemics, tributes and taxes, servitude and destitution. As late as 1910, the plight of the Chiapas Indians was "probably the worst of all in the nation."[†] From the fall of Porfirio Diaz to the defeat of the reactionary forces of General Pineda in 1924, Zinacantán was invaded by waves of contending armies, and the land-reform policy promised by the Revolution did not reach Zinacantán until the early 1940s.

D reams have long played an important role in the Zinacantec system of beliefs. Shortly before the arrival of Cortés in 1519, the capital of the Aztec Empire, Tenochtitlan, was shaken by a series of ill omens.

> Anyone dreaming anything about the end of the Empire was ordered to the palace to tell of it. Night and day, emissaries combed the city, and Tenochtitlan paid tribute in dreams. . . . But finding no good in the thousands offered, Moctezuma killed all the offenders. It was the massacre of the dreamers. . . . From that day there were no more forecasts, no more dreams, terror weighed upon the spirit world.[††]

Once the conquistadors had subdued the native people, the friars set about converting the multitudes to Christianity, asking, "Have you practiced witchcraft? Do you believe in the devil? Do you believe in dreams?"

While Western culture takes great pains to distinguish between dreams and "reality," the Zinacantecs would call our wisdom sheer

---

* The Chiapas and Central American term for *mestizo*, or a Mexican who is not considered to be Indian. The term can be extended to include foreigners.

† Daniel Cosio Villegas (ed.), *Historia moderna de México* (Mexico City: 1956).

††Laurette Séjourné, *Burning Water: Thought and Religion in Ancient Mexico* (London: Thames and Hudson, 1957).

blindness. We concern ourselves only with what transpires "on the earth's surface," as the Zinacantecs describe the material world. In Zinacantán, however, it is the inner reality that motivates, explains, and clarifies the irrational, hazardous events of life. There must be a reason for poverty, sickness, and death. And that reason is not to be found "on the earth's surface" but in the "soul." Dreams are the means by which we "see with our souls."

When still a fetus, every Zinacantec is bestowed with a soul by the ancestral gods, who reside in the surrounding mountains and jealously guard and sustain the souls of their descendants, so long as they live in humility and righteousness. The soul, say some, is lodged in the back of the head; others locate it in the heart. The soul is believed to be composed of thirteen parts. It is immortal, but it, or parts of it, may be dislodged from the body by fright, by the excitement of sexual intercourse, by a divine beating, or by witchcraft.

It is a Zinacantec truth that people are resentful and envious of the good fortunes of others. If their anger and hatred of a particular person becomes sufficiently strong, they may seek the aid of a shaman who is known to wield his power with malevolent effects. One of the principal practices employed by a shaman who indulges in witchcraft is to "sell the soul" of his enemy to the Earth Lord. Everyone must be on guard lest his soul be devoured by the soul of one of these witches, which emerge every night to hunt their victims. To further confuse and frighten his enemies, it is said, a witch's soul rolls three times before a cross, and transforms itself into an animal—a black dog, a cat, a long-haired goat, a cow, or a horse. Dreams, then, are not mere portents, they are fields of battle.

Furthermore, there is a matrix of ominous associations with the earth. Since the Earth Lords are thought to be Ladinos, to meet with a Ladino in one's dream is to confront death. Snakes are the Earth Lords' daughters, so encounters with serpents and women alike may have horrifying connotations. Earth Lords, like Ladinos, are fabulously wealthy; to discover treasure, to receive money is to receive an infernal gift. Water, too, being within the Earth Lords' domain, is icy to the touch. Food and drink that are happily consumed in one's dreams are products of the netherworld, transferring their subterranean chill to the dreamer's body.

Sickness and death are prophesied with overwhelming regularity. The calamitous tone of Zinacantec dreams would seem to render each new dawn unbearable were it not for a series of qualifications, equivocations, and uncertainties that clothe the dreamer in protective armor. Dream interpretation finally depends on the individual circumstances of the dreamer and his state of mind. Whatever may be interpreted as divine advice and consent lightens the dreamer's burden. While many nightmares may seem to the dreamer to be a severe trial, they can constitute a powerful ego-building force, reinforcing his or her relationship with the gods and with the self. The dream is a measure of the man.

In 1959, when I arrived in Zinacantán as a member of the Harvard Chiapas Project, I dedicated myself to learning their Tzotzil Mayan language and collecting their folktales and myths. But the Zinacantecs' eagerness to tell me their dreams and to ask for my interpretation seemed to open another door into their lives. So, in the privacy of my house, they revealed to my tape recorder years and years of dreams.

Though I was merely a familiar figure to the majority of this company of dreamers, they described with undisguised enthusiasm the wanderings of their souls. The dreams of Zinacantán reveal an uncompromising world of fear and affirmation, where coincidence and clairvoyance are commonplace and the demonic and divine are immanent. Though their souls wander on perilous paths, Zinacantecs bear their fate with astonishing grace and humor.*

Romin Teratol

Romin was conceived in 1933, reputedly in the woods, the son of a Zinacantec salt merchant and a Chamulan woman. He was raised by his grandmother, mother, and maiden aunt. At twelve, Romin watched his corn crop fail. He volunteered for the coffee plantations on the coast and worked on thirteen plantations in two months. Later he became a puppeteer and an agent of the National Indian Institute, the Mexican counterpart of the Bureau of Indian Affairs. At the age of twenty-six, after one rejection and a lengthy courtship, he married a woman of high social standing within the community.

Romin's "friends" and "enemies" change roles with lightning speed, yet in a pinch he is a loyal friend. Romin is deeply religious and conservative. He is an affectionate father, scrupulously filling his shoulder bag with fruit for his children whenever he goes to market. Yet, when he hears his son crying in the house, he knocks on the door and shouts, "I will sell you to the Ladinos in San Cristóbal,

---

* This introduction and several of the following dreams are adapted from versions published in Carol Karasik (ed.) and Robert M. Laughlin's *The People of the Bat: Mayan Tales and Dreams from Zinacantán* (Washington: Smithsonian Press, 1988).

Robert Laughlin (left) and Zinacantán resident, Zinacantán, circa 1959.

I am the baby-eater." In his dreams, Romin is constantly defending himself against the attacks of wild beasts, murderous men, and lecherous women. His wife is often the victim of his scoldings and near-mortal assaults.

An Owl Screeches, I Kill a Black Cat

I, Romin Teratol, dreamt at dawn on Thursday, February 28th. It seemed as if I was sleeping at my mother's house. It was dark. Then a screech owl* arrived and called by the side of the house. I was very scared because it is said that if a screech owl comes and calls next to the house we will die, because that bird is a messenger of death. So I went out to find it and kill it.

A man was standing behind the house with his pine torch flaming. He was looking for a way to break into the house. Now I was terrified. My head felt as if it had grown. I was struck dumb. I took out my machete. I was going to chase him, but I could no longer find him. I shouted, but

---

* Throughout Central America, owls are ill omens.

because of my fear I couldn't shout loudly. When he disappeared, my fear passed a bit.

Later, a black cat came in and found me in my bed.[*] Before I realized it, it was curled up on top of me, asleep. I caught it and threw it outside, but it kept coming back in. Then I caught it and pulled it by the legs. I cut off its head. All its guts came out. It was dead. I went to get rid of it outside, but it bit my fingers. It still fought back.

When I woke up, I was terribly scared. I couldn't get back to sleep until I lit my lamp to guard me. I was so terrified in my dream because of all the resentful people behind me, beside me. They want me to get sick. They want to leave behind a little sickness.

Shit on Him and Shit on Me

I, Romin Teratol, dreamt at dawn, Tuesday, the 12th of February. God, My Lord, I had a terrible dream. I was going to San Cristóbal with my compadre, Lol Brinko.[†] On the other side of Ventana, where the Chamula road forks, a table was standing in the middle of the road, and a Ladino was sitting there writing. There was a privy at the side of the road and my compadre, Lol, went to take a shit. But when he finished shitting he didn't know how to put his pants on anymore. He put the front side in back.

There was a Ladina girl there, and she told my compadre that his pants were on wrong. So he turned his pants around, but his fly was covered with shit. The Ladino who was sitting there writing saw it and scolded him. I was standing nearby. And afterward I went to shit, too, but when I had finished, my shit jumped up and landed smack on my chest.

Maryan Chiku' and Maryan Martinis were standing there now. Maryan Chiku' removed the shit from my chest. He threw it at my mouth and it landed with a smack on my cheek. I removed it and was going to throw it at his face, but he told me to throw the shit away for good or else he would throw more at me. I got rid of it. Then I went to wash myself in a little gully. The spring was really beautiful. It wasn't a bit muddy. All the shit came off my hand and then I woke up. It was around three o'clock in the morning.

---

[*] Black cats are not generally considered ill omens in Zinacantán as they are in the United States.

[†] Lol Brinko (Lawrence Gringo) is the name by which I am known in Zinacantán. —R.L.

When I awoke I was terrified, because that is a very bad dream. It means accusations of carnal sin, false accusations. Maybe it will come true. But who knows when. Only Our Lord knows if the gods will still watch over me, will still stand up for me, because the resentful people beside me want to become more powerful.

I Stab My Wife

God, My Lord, I, Romin Teratol, dreamt at dawn today, the 9th of March. It seemed I lost my temper. I caught my wife by the door of don Chavel's house. I grabbed her. I threw her to the ground. I was going to hit her with a machete. But I couldn't because the machete was heavy. So I grabbed a knife and stuck it in her stomach. It was hard to get the knife in, but I was watching now to see if she was dying. When I tried to stick the knife deeper in her, I shouted.

And while I was in the middle of my dream, my wife was already up, grinding corn. She heard me shouting in my bed and came to wake me, "What's happening to you? What do you see?" she asked.

I told her, "It seemed as if I was killing you and I shouted when I stuck the knife in."

"Oh, how horrible! I shouldn't have woken you. I should have let your soul get a good scare. If only I had known it was me you were killing! It's probably just because you'll kill me one of these days," she said.

I Ride a Flying Cow

I, Romin Teratol, dreamt just before dawn, on Sunday, the 23rd of June. It seemed that I was at Ak'ol Ravol.* I was with some Chamulans there, at the church.

"Go, Romin," a Chamulan said to me, "Go, fetch this!" But it wasn't clear what I was to fetch. He just said, "Go, go and fetch it, because it is needed very badly right now." And he gave me a black cow. Quickly I mounted it. I went to fetch whatever it was that was needed. The black cow jumped over fences and tall trees. It flew high above the meadow.

Then on the return trip, the cow gored me. My leg was pierced, and the blood flowed. But the cow spoke to me. "I will cure your wound," she said. "It won't take too long to cure." And she began to lick my leg. It healed immediately.

And then I woke up and tried to figure out what my dream meant.

* The eastern section of Zinacantán Center.

97

I told my wife my dream. "Who knows what it means?" she said. Joking, she told me, "Probably it's because you are a witch. Why else would you dream of black cows?" But I think it's probably a bit of torment. That's what I tell myself.

I Am Chased by Women

God, My Lord, I don't know why I dream so often. Last night, around two in the morning, it seemed as if many women came to the house where I was sleeping. First they knocked on the door, but no one opened it for them. Then they broke in and came to the door to the very room where I sleep, and they knocked on it. I didn't open it, because I already knew they were evil people. I pushed against the door, but since there were more women, they won. But they didn't come in because I had turned the light on. I tried to shout to the landlord, but I was struck dumb with fear. Then I screwed up my courage. I went out and wrestled with the women. I couldn't see if they were Ladinas or our own people.

When they were about to kill me, I remembered what could be done to unnerve them. I took off my pants, turned them inside out, and threw them in their faces. And they were scared. All the women ran out into the street.

Now I wasn't afraid anymore. I found a stick lying by the door. I picked it up and whacked a woman's leg with it. Her leg broke immediately. But now I wasn't able to close the big door. When they came in to find me again, I hurried to the landlord's house and hid. Then I woke up, and that's how it ended. Maybe there are witches who are tormenting my soul. Or maybe the earth is dangerous, I don't know.*

Romin Tanchak

Romin Tanchak comes from a well-to-do family in Stzelejtik. He is the youngest brother of Romin Teratol's wife. When he told me his dreams, he claimed to be twenty-five, but barely looked twenty. Romin earned the funds to pay the bride-price† for his wife by working on a neighboring ranch, felling pine trees. Since

---

* If the earth is *kuxul* (literally "alive") or dangerous, this means that the place where the house is standing is next to the Earth Lord's door or in the middle of his trail. It is believed that we may unintentionally annoy the Earth Lord by constructing our house or choosing to sleep in his territory.

† Traditionally the groom gives gifts of food and a sum of money to the bride's parents to reimburse them for their expense in raising their daughter. To acquire these funds, the groom becomes indebted to his parents, assuring them of his support in their old age.

then he has devoted his energies to corn farming, in anticipation of his entrance into the Stewardship of Saint Dominic, a position in the first level of the religious hierarchy which requires considerable capital to provide for fiestas in honor of the saint. Our first encounters were guarded and formal. But despite his family's hostility toward gringo anthropologists, he always treated me with consideration and warmth.

My Sister Was Underground

My mother dreamt that my little baby sister was lost.

"Lolen!" she called. "Lolen!"

My baby sister was underground. She answered from inside the earth. My mother tried to see her, but she never found her. No!

"Come on out!" my mother tried to tell her. My sister answered back, but she didn't come out.

Three or four nights later, she got nausea and diarrhea. My mother brought a shaman, but the sickness didn't pass. My little sister simply died.

Dreams sometimes come true. If she couldn't be reached in the dream, she was lost forever.

Xun Min

Xun Min appears to be a gentle man of few words. Most often he wears an impassive face that grows even more wooden when he is making a joke. Xun's father died before he can remember. At an early age, he began working on a ranch at the edge of San Cristóbal, carrying garbage for one and a half pesos. When Xun was fifteen, his mother died. A widow took pity on him and proposed that he marry her daughter. After a courtship of only a month and a bride-price of a mere one hundred and sixty pesos, she became Xun's wife. Xun was then employed as a gardener by the National Indian Institute, did roadwork, and raised corn. He also learned to build houses and to play the fiddle, guitar, and harp. Xun is now a man of moderate prestige, having held office for a year as Justice of the Peace.

I Die and Am Buried

I dreamt that I was stretched out inside the house, my head to the west.*
I tried to move, but I couldn't move because I was dead. They were playing music for me. I was put into the coffin and taken to the graveyard. "The grave is deep enough now," they said. They lowered me in.

---

* A dead person is buried with his head to the west.

Xun Min.

"Son of a bitch, now I'm going to rot here, like this. But I'm not dead!" I said to myself. I was nailed up inside the coffin and I couldn't breathe. There was no more air. I tried hard. I scratched and scratched at my coffin so they would hear me. I couldn't even yell.

"There's noise coming from the coffin. I think he's alive," they said. They opened it up and took me out.

"I'm alive," I said to myself. All the men and women who had been burying me were already crying and crying. They took me out again and I came back with them.

"I thought he was dead!" they kept saying.

I was frightened when I awoke. But I haven't died.

How We See Whether It Will Be a Boy or a Girl

When a child is about to be born to my pregnant wife, I dream I am given a water jug. "Take this!" I am told. "Set it aside. Treat it well." It is a deep tortilla gourd. Yes! Then it will surely be a girl.

If I am given a hoe, if I am given a billhook, if I am given a digging stick: they are a boy's soul. Yes! "Probably it's going to be a boy," I say to myself. That's what I dreamt when my eight-year-old boy was born. It came true.

Tonik Nibak

Tonik Nibak is about seventy-seven years old. Her father died when she was an infant and her mother when she was seven. She was adopted into a Ladino household in San Cristóbal, paying her board by doing small chores. Two years later, she returned to Zinacantán and learned to weave. Engaged to be married, Tonik rebelled and rejected her suitor, and was then obliged to return to San Cristóbal and work as a maid in order to repay her suitor's courtship expenses. Tonik's younger sister then jilted her fiancé and skipped town, forcing Tonik to take the marriage vows in her stead. During their twenty-eight years of marriage, she bore her husband ten children, only five of whom survived into adulthood. In recent years, Tonik has carried on an adventurous flower trade, selling her products to far-off Tuxtla. Her sharp wit is both feared and relished by the men she works with. It is also evident in all her dreams. Even the ancestral gods take offense at her forwardness.

Tonik Nibak.

I Am Naked, My Skirt Disappears

I went to the river to soak my laundry. I changed my skirt. I tied my sash. I finished washing my clothes. Then I climbed up the riverbank and reached the trail, and I saw that one side of my skirt was torn and flapping.

"Why is my skirt like this?" I said to myself. I felt my waist. No skirt now! Then I saw that I was naked. "Thank God my blouse is long! The awful men will look and look at me, naked as I am, My Lord," I said to myself. I tried to pull my blouse down, but my blouse was too short. My left breast was showing. I wrapped my shawl around me to cover myself, because I was ashamed.

Then my old godfather came along. "Lord, why in the world are you like this, daughter? It isn't the proper way. Why are you naked all of a sudden? Could you not have seen who stole your skirt from you? Or didn't you notice where it went? Go on, then. You probably have an old skirt at home. Is this the time to be walking around like that? You'll meet people. Don't you see it's late afternoon? I'm going to bring in the mules," my godfather told me.

I hurried home. I spread out my wash. I combed my hair. I had an old skirt, covered with patches. The trouble was, I had no sash. I picked up my son's little sash. It was too short. "I'll simply go to Mother Loxa's house and ask her to weave me a sash. How could I get along like this, without my sash?" I said as I left.

Then my husband woke me. "What are you saying? Gabbing away, you loafer! Get up! It's growing light," he told me. One of my children had died recently. "What are you doing, gabbing away? Get up! Grind the corn!" my husband told me. I got up to light the fire. I was crying now about being naked.

"What could this mean, My Lord? Are my children going to die? Why was I like that, without my skirt?" I said to myself at dawn.

"Hurry up, you bitch, with tears streaming down your cheeks! I'm going to gather firewood," I was told. He asked for his tortillas. He ate before he left. Then I was left to cry by myself. Sitting at the foot of my metate, I cried.

Then my crying subsided.

"Never mind," I said to myself. I went to feed my chickens.

I Am Getting Married and Leave Him on the Trail

I was getting married. I had a fine new feathered robe. My outer skirt was brand new. But the skirt I wore on the inside was old and faded.

"Oh, My Lord, if the hem of my outer skirt turns up, people will see that my inner skirt is faded. This isn't good at all. It's better if I don't walk."

"Stop!" I told the man I was supposed to marry. I didn't recognize him. "Stand aside!" I said. I left him standing in the middle of the path. I hoisted up my robe and arrived home in a rush. My mother wasn't there. I was alone. How could I imagine that my mother would be there, since she was already dead?

I called my neighbor. "Mother Akux, please come and unbind my hair for me. My head is terribly tired being bound up like this."

"Why is your hair bound? Who are you marrying? Where is your husband?" she asked me.

"He's gone to work," I said. "I don't know why I need to marry someone else. How many men do I want? I'm just so disgusting!"

"That awful husband of yours is just skin and bones, daughter. Is your nose still as pink as a baby's that you are looking for another man? And you with two children!"

Now I was worried about the children. I had put them to sleep in the place where I was getting married. I unbraided my hair. I took off my headdress. I wrapped it up in a white cloth. I took off my robe. I folded it and put it away. I took off my outer skirt and kept the faded one on. My husband-to-be was left standing in the middle of the path, in his new pants, his new shirt, his black hat, his shawl.

They say it's bad if we dream we are getting married. "Why do you dream such awful things?" my neighbor said. "Who knows if you won't get divorced some time." It was thirty-two years ago when I had that dream. That husband of mine had gone to the lowlands. I was sleeping alone with my children. And I was getting married to another man!

Mikel Tzotzil

I remember Mikel Tzotzil squatting every morning in the dusty street in front of his brother-in-law's store at the entrance to Zinacantán Center, shooting marbles with a bunch of schoolboys. By the age of thirty, he had fathered seven children. Three were already buried. He seemed hesitant, bemused, strangely innocent and soft for a Zinacantec. He stuttered.

Unique to Mikel's narrative is the towering influence of his late father, whose ghost appears regularly in his dreams. As a younger man, Mikel had traveled with his father, selling salt. At that time, his younger sister was being courted by the son of a shaman. Mikel's father rejected the suitor and returned the bride-price. In revenge, the shaman sold Mikel's father's soul to the Earth Lord and, when Mikel was eighteen, his father died. Mikel then became a shopkeeper in his brother-in-law's store and invested money in his brother-in-law's truck (the first in Zinacantán). His investment was never returned and he soon became addicted to cane liquor. The store was sold, and now Mikel raises flowers at home and plants corn in the lowlands. These dreams predate his financial difficulties.

I Am in the Graveyard and My Boy is Alive Again

One time this happened to me: My boy died this past May on the 17th, as I told you. It seemed as if I was in the place where I buried him in the graveyard. I didn't know what to do. I was with my wife and my other children. My boy had gone to get his older sister at home and it seemed as if he hadn't died.

"What can he be thinking?" I said to myself. "He is still nursing."

I don't know what it means. My boy was already dead. Who knows. Sometimes I see myself carrying corpses. I'm going to a burial and I'm carrying the dead person. Or my late father has just died and I go to bury him. But he died long ago. Maybe it's devils who are upsetting our souls.

I Am a Shepherd, I Am Cut Open

I was walking along by the highway. It seemed as if I had some sheep with me and I was watching over them as they grazed. Then an awful highwayman appeared. Or could it have been just an innocent passerby? I tried to flee. I tried to take his machete away from him. Quickly he sliced me. My ass was cut wide open. My arms had shooting pains. I felt terrible. I jumped out of the way so that I wouldn't die.

Then I woke up. I still felt the machete slicing me. I felt a sudden chill. "In the name of God, could it be that I am going to be murdered?" I said to myself. Who knows if maybe a devil is tricking me a bit? Then I prayed to Our Lord. I couldn't get to sleep before morning came.

I Am Offered Tassels by a Pretty Girl

There are many bad dreams. Have you ever dreamt of sleeping with another woman besides your wife? That's what I have done. It seems that

Zinacantán Center, circa 1959.

I slept with women. It seems that they really desire us. They seem to be beautiful and our wives seem to be less attractive.

The girl was really beautiful. I had seen her in Zinacantán Center. She came by my house to talk to me. I was inside my house, with a worker of mine, a Chamulan, flailing my corn.

"Won't you buy tassels for your tunic?" she said.* "Won't you buy the cords? Won't you buy some?" she said.

"I'll buy some," I said. "Where are they?" I hugged her. I gave her a little kiss. Yes! She was laughing and laughing. She gave me three cords for my tunic.

"How much are they?" I asked.

"You'll find out later," she said. "My sister doesn't know what price to ask." She left. I went in to flail my corn again.

"Eh, she's a pretty sexy girl! She wants to be taken. Why else would she come purposely to give me the fastenings for my tunic?" I said to myself. "The cords for my tunic mean she wants to be taken. I'll speak to her. I'll see if she wants to be taken."

Then I woke up. "Could it be that she loves me?" I said to myself. "Or could it be a devil?" I didn't tell my wife. If I had told her she probably would have gotten upset. She probably would have said, "She's your mistress."

My Father is Dressed in Red

By our house is a hill and a steep path. There was a horse and my father was riding it.† His clothes were entirely red from head to toe. They were different—like those worn by the Great Spanish Lord in the Fiesta of Saint Sebastián. He was holding a banner aloft and he rode over the hill to our house.

I told him my dream. "Maybe it means that I'll die," he said. That wasn't long before he died. It came true. He hadn't been sick. He was just fine, like us. Two days later, he was dead. His clothes were red from head to toe.

He just died.

---

* The tassels for a man's tunic are usually made by the man himself.
† Riding horseback in a dream can signify death.

GÖSTA ÅGREN

The Return of Orpheus

No poet can endure
being dead, a sojourn without
rhyme or reason. He needs
order and rhythm. His poems
are indeed laws. He
always turns back
from the underworld, which resembles
the everyday.

The darkness hides the screams
around him, when
the walking begins. The sun is
only black heraldry, only
a cavern in the sky
of stone, and he sees
it, without being blinded.

Then he goes, through the walking's
immobile, invisible lattice
from horizon to horizon.

An occasional tornado
of consciousness moves
through the journey, which is
what will remain.

The figures he meets
are shadows remembering
all that could have been.
Broken illusions are the name of
the only space in which we
are always free, can
always breathe, but those who
do not give up for lost what they have lost
will never attain it. He passes
a gateway, and continues in its
long, invisible arm. A gateway
never ends; it waits.
The darkness expands until it is
obscurity, no longer threat but
depth for all. Orpheus is like
a lonely child in a poem.
He is afraid. Perhaps there are
no dangers. But then there is
no protection against them
either.

But then there is only
this.

That is why he is not afraid
when the smiles begin to gleam
in the darkness, a swarm of knives,
slowly approaching. He knows
that he must go toward them
in order to escape from them. In that
way we flee from all
that we cannot flee from:
by seeking it out.

In vain do we ask for names.
Only the myth can answer.
The particular is too
general. Orpheus runs
through the crowd of indistinct
demons, created by that
reality whose innermost,
subatomic particle's name
a scientist's trembling hand
will one day write: Emptiness.

Now he is threatened by the total
consciousness which exists
in the darkness in his body.
They strike him as
hatefully as though they
were striking themselves, his image
within them. He flees

by enduring. For
he must write his
poems. Only thus can he
silence them. When he
at last lies alone
by the roadside in the underworld
he rises up once and for all,
as though he were abandoning
the figure lying there,
and continues, continues
the journey.

The wordless autumn wind
puts people's grief
into words. They themselves cannot
do it, for it is existence
that grieves, a nothingness
inside us all that compels us
to torment, and be tormented,
and thus exist so
intensely that being
drowns out the grief. Orpheus
sees the enemy, one
who is helpless, and strikes him
in order to be freed from the blows
he himself has had to accept.
It was thus he became
their prisoner.

To walk through the north wind is
like pushing one's way forward
between the ice-cold atoms
in a knife blade. What is it called,
the helpless voice that shouts
in the cold without doing so?
Love? No, love is never
helpless. It is an immense
sponge that sucks everything
into itself, and thus, imperceptibly, becomes
everything. The one who holds fast
to his name cannot
accept life in any
other way than by
hating it. Orpheus is
helpless, but he is
Orpheus, and while

the sun thunders against the rock face
he meets Christ, here
and now a beggar
whose task is to
save people from
the insight that nothing
can save them. The kindness
his misery compels them to
shows that something else is
possible, if only

as the void in which it
does not exist. Thus may a haze
of mercy be wrapped
over facts. The ragged
figure walks slowly
onward, as absolute as a blind
judge. But Orpheus knows
that kindness is only part
of suffering, and they pass
each other without a word
while the sun burns
above the centuries.

His footsteps echo in the silence,
a monotonous leitmotif that
has got stuck. To
continue demands weakness.
His heart beats without resistance,
but Orpheus himself is strong.
He stops, he
turns around.

Who is she who is dimly seen
and vanishes inside
his gloom?
Now he knows: She is
a legend which no
narrator will tame. The

form he loves
he has himself sculpted.
Only if she becomes
real can he become
free. When one has waited long
the meeting
is a farewell.

The night closes society
and opens the stars.
Even in the underworld,
whose starless night
surrounds Orpheus's brain,
fatigue can grow
into grace. That is why the
sparse crowd of people
he meets is peaceful
as a landscape,
but stubbornly, mechanically
as a series of copies
of himself, Orpheus
walks in the opposite
direction.

The gateway's vault of clouds
and pillars of pines are
invisible. One sees only clouds
and pines. He walks out

into the unproven theory
that is called reality,
into the village where the faces
turn toward him like
lanterns in the gloom. He
thinks of a poem about what
he is thinking of: these
people who move
through the village, dragging long,
impassive shadows. Now
once again they know the result
of today's work: tomorrow's
work awaits. To endure
is a way to get strength
to endure. So

he thinks, and that is why
he does not shout that the one
who has walked long through
the underworld can only reject
everything, even this
meaningless gesture of
rejecting everything.

Instead the poem ends
like this: He comes home.

The air is motionless in the cottage.
Slowly, with movement after
movement, mother peels potatoes.
Is it poverty and illness
that stand still in here?

No, but she is choked
by an unsung song
of sorrow, our chance
to live.

That song aches like a child
without words. It is so hard
because sorrow demands love,
that immense hand
in our breast which no one
can reduce to fate.

The evening's black, swaying
trees are the horns of slowly moving
herds. Inexorably
everything journeys.

Orpheus sings
of sorrow.

Translated from the Swedish by David McDuff

116

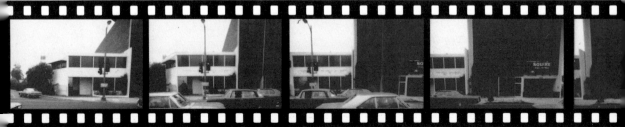

Fragments

Enduring Dream: She walked along the country road. I didn't see her, I only noticed how she moved as she walked, how her veil flew, how her foot rose. I sat on the edge of the field and looked into the water of a shallow brook. She walked through the villages, and children stood in doorways, watching her approach and then watching her leave.

I stood on the balcony outside my room. It was very high— I counted the rows of windows; it was on the seventh floor. Down below there were several gardens in a small courtyard, which was enclosed on three sides. It was obviously in Paris. I went into the room and left the door open. It seemed to be only March or April, but the day was warm. In a corner stood a small, very light writing table; I could have lifted it with one hand and swung it around in the air. For now, however, I took a seat. Quill and ink were all laid out, for I wanted to write a postcard. Uncertain whether I had a

card, I was reaching into my pocket when I heard a bird and noticed, as I turned around, a bird cage out on the balcony. I went out again at once. I had to stand on my toes to see the bird. It was a canary, which cheered me immensely. I pushed the lettuce which was lodged between two bars farther into the cage and let the bird nibble on it. Then I turned again to the courtyard, rubbed my hands, and leaned carelessly over the balustrade. On the other side of the courtyard, someone appeared to be watching me with opera glasses from his garret—probably because I was a new tenant. It was indeed petty, but perhaps it was an invalid whose world consisted entirely of the view from his window. Having found a card in my pocket, I went back into the room to write on it. There was, however, no picture of Paris on the card. Instead there was a painting titled *Evening Prayer*. There was a tranquil lake, a few reeds in the foreground, in the middle a boat, and in it a young mother with her child in her arms.

Hail the great swimmer! Hail the great swimmer!" the people shouted. I was coming from the Olympic Games in Antwerp, where I had just set a world record in swimming. I stood at the top of the steps outside the train station in my hometown—where was it?—and looked down at the indiscernible throng in the dusk. A girl, whose cheek I stroked cursorily, hung a sash around me, on which was written in a foreign language: *The Olympic Champion*. An automobile drove up and several men pushed me into it. Two other men drove along—the mayor and someone else. At once we were in a banquet room. A choir sang down from the gallery as I entered and all the guests—there were hundreds—rose and shouted, in perfect unison, a phrase that I didn't exactly understand. To my left sat a minister; I don't know why the word "minister" horrified me so much when we were introduced. At first I measured him wildly with my glances, but soon composed myself.

To my right sat the mayor's wife, a voluptuous woman; everything about her, particularly her bosom, seemed to emanate roses and the finest down. Across from me sat a fat man with a strikingly white face, whose name I had missed during the introductions. He had placed his elbows on the table—a particularly large place had been made for him—and looked straight ahead in silence. To his right and left sat two beautiful blond girls. They were cheerful and constantly had something to say, and I looked from one to the other. In spite of the more than ample lighting, though, I couldn't clearly recognize many of the other guests, perhaps because everything was in motion. The waiters scurried around, dishes arrived at the tables, and glasses were raised—indeed, perhaps everything was too well illuminated. There was also a certain disorder—the only disorderly element, actually—in the fact that several guests, particularly women, were sitting with their backs turned to the table and, further, in such a way that not even the backs of their chairs were between them and the table, but rather that their backs were almost touching the table. I drew the attention of the girls across from me to this, but while they had otherwise been so garrulous, now they said nothing, and instead only smiled at me with long looks. When a bell rang, the waiters froze in their positions and the fat man across from me rose and delivered a speech. But why was he so sad? During the speech he dabbed at his face with a handkerchief, which was quite understandable in light of his obesity, the heat in the room, and the strains of the speech itself. But I distinctly noticed that the whole effect was merely a clever disguise, meant to conceal the fact that he was wiping tears from his eyes. Also, although he looked directly at me as he spoke, it was as if he weren't seeing me, but rather my open grave. After he had finished, I, of course, also stood up and delivered a speech. I felt compelled to speak, for there was much that needed to be said, both here and probably also elsewhere, for the public's enlightenment. And so I began:

"Honored guests! I have, admittedly, broken a world record.

If, however, you were to ask me how I have achieved this, I could not answer adequately. Actually, I cannot even swim. I have always wanted to learn, but have never had the opportunity. How then did it come to be that I was sent by my country to the Olympic Games? This is, of course, also the question I ask of myself. I must first explain that I am not now in my fatherland and, in spite of considerable effort, cannot understand a word of what has been spoken. Your first thought might be that there has been some mistake, but there has been no mistake— I have broken the record, have returned to my country, and do indeed bear the name by which you know me. All this is true, but thereafter nothing is true. I am not in my fatherland, and I do not know or understand you. And now something that is somehow, even if not exactly, incompatible with this notion of a mistake: It does not much disturb me that I do not understand you and, likewise, the fact that you do not understand me does not seem to disturb you. I could only gather from the speech of the venerable gentleman who preceded me that it was inconsolably sad, and this knowledge is not only sufficient, in fact for me it is too much. And indeed, the same is true of all the conversations I have had here since my return. But let us return to my world record."

I sharpened the scythe and began to cut. Large, dark clumps fell before me, and I stepped through them without knowing what they were. Voices of warning called out from the village, but I took them for words of encouragement and went on further. I came to a small wooden bridge. The work was finished and I gave the scythe to a man who was waiting there. He reached out with one hand for the scythe and with the other stroked my cheek like a child. In the middle of the bridge I suddenly doubted whether I was on the right path and called out loudly in the darkness, but nobody answered. Then I went back to the solid ground to ask the man, but he was no longer there.

H ow did I get here," I cried. It was a fairly large room, lit only by a soft electric light. I inspected the walls. There were actually several doors, but upon opening them, I discovered a dark, flat stone wall, which was set back by perhaps only the width of a hand from the doorway and extended straight up and to both sides into the infinite distance. There was no way out here. Only one door led into another room, and the prospect there was more hopeful, but no less unsettling than that of the other doors. I looked into a royal chamber, decorated in shades of red and gold. There were several wall-size mirrors and an enormous chandelier. But that was not all.

I was granted permission to enter a strange garden. There were several difficulties to overcome at the entrance, but finally a man behind a table stood up and fixed a dark green piece of paper to my lapel with a pin. "That is, of course, a medal," I said jokingly, but the man only patted me on the shoulder as if to reassure me— but why should I be reassured? I learned from his knowing glance that I could now enter. After a few steps, however, I remembered that I had not yet paid. I wanted to turn around, but just then I saw a tall woman in an overcoat made of a coarse, yellowish-gray material bending over the table, counting a number of tiny coins. "That is for you," the man called out to me over the woman's head, as she stooped very low. "For me?" I asked in disbelief, and looked behind me to see if indeed someone else had been intended. "Always the same pettiness," said a gentleman who had come across the lawn, passed on the path directly in front of me, and then walked away again. "Yes, for you. For who else then? Here one pays for others." I thanked him for this information, reluctantly as it had been provided, but also drew his attention to the fact that I had not paid for anyone. "And for whom should you then pay?" said the gentleman in parting. I wanted in any case to wait for the woman and come

to some sort of an understanding with her, but she turned down another path, swishing off in her coat. A bluish veil streamed gracefully behind her majestic figure. "You admire Isabella," a stroller beside me said as he likewise watched her. After a while he said, "That is Isabella."

I sat up and saw, framed by the small rounded window of the boat's cabin, a hand stretched out in greeting, and the strong face of a woman enveloped by a black scarf. "Mother?" I asked, smiling. "If you wish," she said. "But you are so much younger than Father?" I said. "Yes," she said, "much younger. He could be my grandfather and you my husband." "You know," I said, "it is astonishing how one sails along alone in a boat, and suddenly a woman is there."

Those prepared to die lay on the ground, leaned on the furniture, and, with teeth chattering, groped along the wall without leaving their places.

Translated from the German by Daniel Slager

Dreams

[1] I WAS DRIVING IN MIDLAND LOOKING FOR A PARTY THE ADDRESS OF WHICH I'D NEGLECTED TO BRING WITH ME. I SAW A MUSCULAR WOMAN DOING EXERCISES IN HER FRONT YARD, EVEN THOUGH IT WAS 10 PM. I FOUND THIS ODDLY MODERN APARTMENT & THOUGHT IT WAS THE PLACE. INSIDE IT WAS A THEATER & THE PARTY WAS FOR A GAY, HIV-POSITIVE ARTIST FRIEND SO I PULLED OUT A PAGE OF MY DAY-AT-A-GLANCE THAT HAD LOTS OF BEEFCAKE STUFF ON IT & GAVE IT TO HIM SINCE I'D FORGOTTEN IT WAS HIS BIRTHDAY. IN A FLASHBACK, STRAIGHT JOCKS FROM HIGH SCHOOL WERE THINKING ABOUT THEIR SECRET DESIRES. ONE GUY WANTED TO FUCK A CUTE GUY, WHO COMMITTED SUICIDE OR SOMEHOW DIED SHORTLY THEREAFTER. THE OTHER GUY WANTED TO STICK A BOTTLE ROCKET UP THE CUTE GUY'S ASS & WAS SHOWN BOTH FLYING INTO A TREE BECAUSE OF THE EXPLODING ROCKET, AND FLINGING IT OUT OF HIS BUTT. THEN I SAW INCOMPLETE DRAWINGS I'D DONE OF THE PREVIOUS DREAM AS COMICS SET IN SLATE CAVES & SOME OLDER DREAMS WITH BATMAN. [2] 2 GUYS WERE SITTING ON A VINYL COUCH WITH A DISEMBODIED WOMAN'S BREAST BETWEEN THEM. THEY CONSIDERED ITS AESTHETICS. [3] I WAS IN A STUDIO WITH THAD & SARAH & DAVID PAGEL & I HAD A TABORET WITH A PLASTIC LITE-UP TROLL ON TOP WHICH I COULDN'T TURN OFF. I WAS WORKING ON A PAINTING OF ME WITH ERASERHEAD HAIR. MY BODY GOT SMALLER AS IT WENT AWAY FROM MY HEAD & I HAD AN ERECTION. I SAID I WANTED TO WORK ON PASTICHE PAINTINGS & WENT TO THE BATHROOM WHERE I INTERRUPTED SOMEONE. [4] I WAS SUPPOSED TO BE AN EXPERT IN COURT ON HOW WITNESSES COULD USE THEIR DREAMS TO IDENTIFY PEOPLE BUT MY BRASS TREE WAS USED YEARS EARLIER SO I WAS DISQUALIFIED.

—1995

[1] USING A COMPUTER YOU COULD VISUALIZE SOUNDS. ON THE LEFT WAS THE FORM OF AN ORGAN BURST. I IMAGINED A CITYSCAPE THAT REPRESENTED THE SOUNDS OF A SYMPHONY. [2] IN A HILLTOP HOUSE COLLEGE KIDS WERE REMINISCING ABOUT THEIR INNOCENT DAYS BEFORE THEY STARTED SMOKING POT. THEY HAD A PILE OF STUFF THEY NEEDED TO HIDE FROM A COP WHO WAS LURKING NEARBY. A KID WATCHED FROM A CAR BELOW & WHEN THE NARC SHOWED THEY HELD UP A GIANT OCTOPUS TAROT CARD TO BLOCK THE COP'S VIEW. [3] WE WERE HAVING A CONTEST WITH VICIOUS WEAPONS. A GUY WAS TRANSFORMED INTO THIS HOOK SO I THREW IT OUTSIDE BEFORE ANYONE GOT HURT. [4] WE WERE AT THE SAN DIEGO BIENNIAL & THIS PALE YOUNG ART COLLECTOR WAS BOWING ON THE TOP OF A STAIRCASE. WE WERE ON A PLATFORM ELEVATOR & WHEN WE GOT CLOSE HE TURNED OUT TO BE A HEADLESS OPTICAL ILLUSION. THERE WAS A PYRAMID OF PHOTOS SURROUNDED BY PINK & BLUE TEXT ON THE WALL & A MOBILE OF JOINED CARTOON CHARACTER HEADS. [5] I RAN INTO AN OLD BOSS OF MINE & HE IGNORED ME FOR A WHILE, TALKING TO SOME CIGAR-SMOKING GUY, FINALLY TURNING TO ME & TELLING ME "YOU KNOW WE REALLY DON'T LIKE YOUR WORK." LATER I HEARD SOME OF MARNIE'S NEW CD, WHICH WAS QUITE GOOD, & SAW SOME PAINTINGS SHE'D DONE OF JUNGLE ANIMALS ON GOLD PAPER. [6] A TV-HEADED FIGURE. [7] I SAW MYSELF, EMACIATED, SITTING IN A LOINCLOTH WITH A CRUCIFIXION TIE & 2 JESUS PICTURES IN SMALL FRAMES HANGING BY CHAINS FROM MY NECK.

—1995

THE OCTOPUS

[1] I'M WITH MIKE & ANITA IN AN OLD, DARK WOOD HOUSE & WE'RE PICKING UP INTESTINES & ORGANS & I'VE GOT 2 KIDNEYS WHICH I SEE ARE CONNECTED TO HIS GROIN SO I PUT THEM DOWN. 3 GIRLS COME UP & ASK IF HE'S MIKE KELLEY & HE SEES THAT ONE IS THE HEAD OF THE N.E.A. WHICH HE CALLS THE N.W.A. AT THE BOTTOM OF THE STAIRCASE I FIND AN ODD MAP WITH GIRLS' HEADS AS ISLANDS. [2] DENNIS HOPPER/ANDERSON'S GALLERY IS THE SITE OF A TV COMMERCIAL WITH CHRISTMAS CAROLERS SINGING ABOUT PEPSI IN A FASCIST WORLD. IT'S A COKE AD. [3] I WAS DRIVING THROUGH THIS SMALL MIDWESTERN TOWN WHERE TORNADOES STOOD STILL. THERE WERE BAROQUE COLUMNS OF ICE COMING UP FROM THE GROUND & A FUNHOUSE WITH STATUES OF DWARVES ALL OVER ITS GOTHIC COLUMNS. [4] IN THE BACK OF THE ENQUIRER THERE WERE 2 ADS WITH THE SAME LAYOUT—2 STAMPS OF A MAN IN PROFILE & HEAD ON. THE FIRST WAS REALISTIC & SAID "THIS GREEDY MAN WILL SHOW YOU HOW TO MAKE MONEY TRADING STAMPS" & THE SECOND WAS AN EARLY DUCHAMP & SAID "THIS MAN CAN EXPLAIN THE SECRETS OF HIS ART TO YOU." [5] A JAPANESE MAGAZINE WITH PAGE AFTER PAGE OF IMPRESSIONIST PAINTINGS OF BOUND OR BEATEN WOMEN. [6] I WAS HAVING SEX IN AN UNCLE SCROOGE COMIC WHEN MY FOLKS CAME IN.

—1995, DREAMED 1988—1992

[1] WE WERE SHARING A HOUSE WITH JODY ZELLEN & I FOUND A CUT-OUT FOAM-CORE CARTOON
HEART & IN A MICROSCOPE I LOOKED AT SOME FLAT BREAD & SAW INTERESTING & UNEXPECTED
GEOMETRIC FORMS. THEN THERE WAS A STAGE SHOW WHERE A WOMAN WHO COULDN'T SING WAS
GETTING WILD APPLAUSE, WHILE A PERFORMANCE BY ANITA OF PRECISE COMPLEX MOVEMENTS
(WHILE MIKE WORE A FOAM-CORE KIPPER KID-LIKE MASK, GIVING UNINTELLIGIBLE ORDERS)
GOT A POOR RESPONSE & I SAID "SEE, THEY LIKE IT BETTER IF YOU CAN'T SING." THEN
I RODE A CHAIR ALONG THE EDGE OF THE STAGE, NEARLY FALLING INTO THE ORCHESTRA PIT.
A PILE OF JUNK THAT FILLED THE STAGE AT AN ANGLE INCLUDED A SOFT METAL PIECE LIKE
A GIANT KIDDY BAND-AID. [2] I AM IN A RESTAURANT WHERE I NOTICE A LARGE BOTTLE OF
"MARTYR" PERFUME THAT LOOKS LIKE A COMMEMORATIVE WHISKEY BOTTLE IN THE SHAPE
OF A PILLAR & STONES & I NOTICE I'M WEARING A POLYESTER SHIRT WITH A SIMILAR
PILLAR ON IT. I LEAVE MY DRAWINGS THERE & GO TO A FIREHOUSE WHERE A WEDDING WITH
HORSE-DRAWN CARRIAGES IS TAKING PLACE. BEYOND I NOTICE IT BECOMES A CLASSY CASINO.
IN THE UPSTAIRS I SEE A STUDENT LEAVING AN AREA DECORATED WITH DECO VERSIONS OF
HER FACE. I'M LOOKING FOR AN ART SUPPLY STORE.

—1995

DANNA RUSCHA How did your dream drawings come to be?

JIM SHAW I originally just wanted to make a show of art I had dreamed of, and the idea behind doing the drawings was to fix the artwork in my mind. The first drawings were of dreams in which I was showing the painter Peter Saul some artwork. It was kind of embarrassing work, and he wanted to see some more mature stuff—which I have yet to do.

DANNA RUSCHA What did those drawings look like?

JIM SHAW Sort of like teenage testicular neosurrealism. The first thing you do when you're a teenager.

DANNA RUSCHA Do you consider the drawings to be a form of surrealism?

JIM SHAW You can't disassociate yourself from surrealism if you're working with dreams. When surrealism came out, Americans did their trickle-down version of it, which involved a lot of typical Daliesque spaces with Greek columns and other stuff thrown in. That became what dreams looked like in the popular world—if they ever showed a dream in a comic book, it always looked like Salvador Dalí.

DANNA RUSCHA How do you manage to have such vivid dreams? When you and I first worked together doing that frame-by-frame animation work, I'd go home and dream about looking for light leaks to spot.

JIM SHAW I think dreams become more entertaining when you start remembering them. It turns out that drawing a nightmare is more interesting than drawing a happy, bouncy dream.

DANNA RUSCHA Are these drawings all nightmares then?

JIM SHAW Not all, but the nightmares are more amusing. It's rare that anything happens even in the most horrible dream that scares me. Somewhere in me I know I'm going to draw it, even when I'm having the dream.

DANNA RUSCHA   Are you ever afraid that you're not going to dream? Dreamer's block?

JIM SHAW   I think that once you start drawing dreams, you're on a slippery slope to some other realm. At times I wake up and have some inane piece of music running through my head and I realize it's my subconscious trying to block me from remembering my dreams. By making the artworks I'd dreamed of, I felt I could make them come true.

DANNA RUSCHA   Do you consider that fabricating or drawing your dreams makes them come true?

JIM SHAW   Making these objects *is* having the dreams come true—the little part of them that I can control. Most of my dreams are about frustration anyway. There isn't much wish fulfillment in them—here, in this drawing, I am dressed up as the Flash and I have a pot belly and poor posture.

—December 1995

The Songs Of Those Who Are On The Sea Of Glass*

A hospital room in near silence
Men in beds in varying degrees of pain
A clutter and the color white
The bright January sun
illuminating . . .
the beige of the building opposite
The arrangement of buildings   so beautiful
Clouds and white puffs of smoke from unseen chimneys
reflected in the black windows

Waking to see this   from on high
across the morning courtyard
It's amazing

•

The bright vision fades

---

* Title of a volume of Welsh hymns by William Williams, published circa 1750:
  Caniadau y Rhai Sydd ar y Mor a Wydr.

A battered piece is put back
on the game board
whose endlessly complicated contradictory rules
. . . . . absurd and with no purpose

The box chipped and coated in dust
Jamaican cigars long gone
into the blue haze

•

Osip Mandelstam calls this earth
"a God-given palace"   "the happy heaven
. . . the boundless house in which we live our lives"

•

The living dead plod across the ice to
stare through thick glass walls
"Let me in!"   "Let me out!"

As though floating.   Couldn't care less.
Which side.   Outside.   Down there.

The ice window
(that's a metaphor)
Climbing over the bones

(that's a metaphor)
Aquarium walls

Grotesque gawping fish
Nightmare stuff

A new moon high in the sky over the sea

•

Suddenly keeling over
A blur
Dream ambulances, rooms, people, tubes

Back and forth over the river

Never come back. The right time to die.
But love and duty call and pull,
Stoic virtues make it amusing,
the whimpers and begging—a story.

•

Talking in code?

•

A rawness. The rediscovered face in the mirror
"I know you?"   Mid-morning.
Washed and shaved
A body stitched and wired together.   The Creature.

"The monster! The monster!" fleeing villagers yell
in black-and-white Transylvania.

"I don't need, I don't need . . ."

Emptiness would soothe
A bare room   no clutter

•

The sea was frozen as we approached Esbjerg
the crunch and crack of ice beneath the ferry's bow
as it plowed on towards a gray line in the whiteness

Inland a fox trotted nervously
across snow-covered fields and streams

The warmth of the cabin bunk, of the den,
of the sun when it breaks through
and, wrapped up, you skim stones across
a small frozen pool in the mountains,

the ricochet ringing, whining,
a high singing.

●

black glass windows
across the courtyard
reflections of clouds, columns of smoke
Bright January sun
a glitter in the air
that fills rooms
(a gold-leaf annunciation)

As though reborn
not racked with loss, past if-onlys
To walk at ease with the ghosts
(not a club member yet)
warm and open and thankful

with care
it seems possible

sat up in bed in bizarre pajamas

and Other Tastes

From the unpublished screenplay *Tough City*, 1983.
p. 156

Terry Southern at his home in East Canaan, Connecticut, 1972.
p. 157

Notes on *Easy Rider*, written shortly before Southern's death
in October 1995, in preparation for an interview
with the BBC. Text reads:

"The story of the disintegration of an entire culture (the American culture
in the 1960s) through alienation and despair—a culture so ravaged
by hatred and paranoia that like birds of prey or even a flock [of] ordinary
barnyard chickens they are compelled to dishonor their own kind if
the least difference or trace of individuality is discerned/noticeable in any
one of them. The story reaches its inevitably grotesque resolution/conclusion
when the two gentle and free-spirited protagonis[ts] are blown
away for no better reason than a Newt Gingrich type objecting to their
long hair. I think it is still the most [illegible]…"
p. 158

Terry Southern and Other Tastes was coordinated by Nile Southern, head of the
Terry Southern Estate/Terry Southern Archives.

TERRY SOUTHERN

It used to be that the Young Writer -- or the young person who wanted to become A Writer -- was instructed, first and foremost, to "develop a style". On the broad and more pervasive 'art-appreciation' levels -- creative writing courses and the like -- *this notion* still obtains; perniciously so, because preoccupation with 'style' is surely the greatest jeapordy (more so than booze or dope) that exists for the serious writer. One must take care, as the English novelist, Henry Green, so aptly put it, "not to become trapped in one's own clichés"; and he went on to illustrate how the work of Henry James, for example, through an *ever* more relentless refinement of style, finally became quite meaningless. *informative*

An unfortunate analogy may be recognized, I believe, when considering the work of a great actor -- Brando or Olivier, for instance. Each has scrupulously tried to run the gamut of style. Brando has played a *New Orleans* Polack, a cowboy, (a Mexican Bandit), Marc Antony, a song-and-dance-man, a Japanese houseboy, a German lieutenant, an American diplomat, etc., etc. And Olivier has played Othello. *an old Italian hood*

143

RUSSELL & VOLKENING, Inc.

Literary Agents

551 FIFTH AVENUE
NEW YORK 17, N. Y.

DIARMUID RUSSELL
HENRY VOLKENING
CANDIDA DONADIO

MURRAY HILL 2-5340

June 22, 1962

Mr. Terry Southern
Blackberry River
Canaan, Connecticut

Dear Mr. Southern:

Yes, William Gaddis did tell me of your interest in
reprinting a piece of his novel in the antholgy you're doing
with Dick Seaver. The pages you suggest--78-100 of THE RECOGNITIONS
is a satisfactory, to Gaddis, excerpt.

Am I to tell you that I'd like to have $250 for
the use of the excerpt, or are you going to tell me how
much of the $2000 advance (in both editions) is to be applied
to William G?

I had a note today from Algren, who's about ready
to ship out to Calcutta, and he asks me to send his howydo
to you if I happen to hear where you are.

Sincerely,

Candida Donadio

Candida Donadio

Blackberry River
Canaan, Conn.

1 July 1962

Miss Candida Donadio
Russell & Volkening, Inc.
551 Fifth Avenue
New York, N.Y.

Dear Miss Donadio:

Many thanks for yours of 22nd June.

Nels off to Calcutta! What the devil!?! Did you arrange that?
I spent an evening with the grand guy before he left and he spoke
of you, almost incessantly, for something like two hours. I have
heard of, read of, and seen, certainly, in real life, cases of in-
fatuation, love, obsession even to a point of insanity, but never
have I come across a devotion to compare, intensewise, with his
for you, professionally -- some say (and I would be less than can-
did if I didn't tell you) that it goes considerably beyond that
 -- and now, when you speak of "$250" for the Gaddis piece, I be-
gin to understand at least one aspect of his childlike reverence.
$160 is the highest we have paid, for lengthy selections of ESTAB-
LISHED MASTERS, even when dealing with some arch money-nut like
Blanche Knopf. Try to realize, Miss D., that $2000 divided by 400-
450 pps. is $5 or less per page. Money however is not the immedia-
te concern; bringing to the fore neglected and deserving work is
the goal. . .fame, prestige (and can fortune be far behind??) is
our aim here. Again may I ask you to dig the l. of c. in that vol.,
Miss D. -- Hesse! Baud! Beck! Cel! Iones! Etc! All tops in the
quality-lit game, and it will be very good for your boy, Bill, to
be seen with that high-stepping crowd.

Since each selection is still in its original format, thus varying
as to words-per-page, it is not possible to accurately prorate the
selections -- which can be done only when the book is in page-proofs.
I stress this point because it is on the basis thus established that
any future monies (and there is such a possibility, with small book-
-clubs, etc.) will be shared. If you absolutely must, due to some
queer psychic quirk which you'd rather not discuss, have a specific
sum guarenteed in front, the highest we could possible go would be
$100, and would probably be "out of pocket" because of it. However,
due to the excellence of Mr. Gaddis' work, and not wishing to
see him miss this boat as it were, I would be willing to take that
chance.

I do hope you may be able to look upon this offer favorably in the
light of the aforementioned.

                    With best regards,

P.S. I shall be working at Esquire magazine, July 15 - Sept 15,
during the absence of R. Hills, and in that very capacity. I would,
of course, like to use something by Gaddis, and perhaps by other young
swingers of your stable. Our rates are competitive, Miss D., and
 -- also we might have lunch one day; utilizing both our expense
accounts we should be able to put away quite a repas.

NAKED LUNCH

Introduction
by
Terry Southern

In life there is that which is funny, and there is that which
is politely supposed to be funny. Literature, out of a misguided
appeal to̲ₐ imaginary ᵖᵒᵖᵘˡᵃʳ̲ taste and the caution of self-
distrust, generally follows the latter course, so that the humor
found in books is almost always vicarious -- meeting certain "tradi-
tional" requirements, and producing only the kind of laughter one
might expect: rather strained. Burroughs' work is an all-stops-out
departure from this practice, and he invariably writes at the very
top of his ability.

The element of humor in Naked Lunch is one of the book's great
moral strengths, whereby the existentialist sense of the absurd is
taken towards an informal conclusion. It is an absolutely devastating
ridicule of all that is false, primitive, and vicious in current
American life: the abuses of power, hero worship, aimless violence,
materialistic obsession, intolerance, and every form of hypocrisy.
No one, for example, has written with such eloquent disgust about
capital punishment; throughout Naked Lunch recur sequences to portray
the unfathomable barbarity of a "civilization" which can countenance
this ritual. There is only one way, of course, to ridicule capital
punishment -- and that is by exaggerating its circumstances, increasing
its horror, accentuating the animal irresponsibility of those involved,
insisting that the monstrous deed be witnessed (and in technicolor, so
to speak) by all concerned. Burroughs is perhaps the first modern
writer to seriously attempt this; he is certainly the first to have

done so with such startling effectiveness. Social analogy and
parallels of this sort abound in Naked Lunch, but one must never
mistake this author's work for political comment, which, as in
all genuine art, is more instinctive than deliberate -- for Burroughs
is first and foremost a poet. His attunement to contemporary language
is probably unequalled in American writing, and one must suppose that
its translation would be as elusive as rendering Part II of Faust
into French or English. But anyone with a feeling for English phrase
at its most balanced, concise, and arresting cannot fail to see this
excellence. For example, in describing the difficulty of obtaining
narcotics-prescriptions from wary doctors in the southwestern United
States, he writes:

"Itinerant short con and carny hyp men have burned down the croakers
of Texas . . ."
None of these words are new, but the sudden freshness of using "burned
down" (to mean 'having exploited beyond further possibility') in this
prosaic context indicates his remarkable power of giving life to a dead
vernacular.

Or again, where the metaphysical finds expression in slang:
"One day Little Boy Blue starts to slip, and what crawls out would
make an ambulance attendant puke . . ."

And, psychological:
"The Mark Inside was coming up on him and that's a rumble nobody
can cool . . ."

Imagery of this calibre puts the use of argot on a level considerabl;
beyond merely "having a good ear for the spoken word." Compared to
Burroughs' grasp of modern idiom in almost every form of English -- and
his ability at distillation and ellipsis -- the similiar efforts of

Ring Lardner, and of Hemingway, appear amateurish and groping.

The role of drugs is of singular importance in Burroughs' work, as it is, indeed, in American life. In no other culture in the history of the world has the use of narcotics, both legal and illicit, become so strange and integral a part of the overall scene. And reviviscent addiction has reached such prevalence and intensity that, in the larger view, it can no longer matter whether it be considered a 'crime' or a 'sickness' -- it is a cultural phenomenon with far more profound implications than either diagnosis suggests.

Burroughs' treatment of narcotics, like his treatment of homosexuality, ranges from that of personal psychology, through the sociological, and finally into pure metaphor. And he is perhaps the first writer to treat either with both humor and humility.

Although Naked Lunch, and his second novel, The Soft Machine, have not been available (except clandestinely) in either America or England -- ostensibly because of the preponderance of 'obscene words' -- they have had, in their Paris editions, an extremely wide reading among the creatively inclined of both countries. No one writing in English, with the exception of Henry Miller, has done so much towards freeing the reader of the superstitions surrounding the use of certain words and certain attitudes. And it is safe to add that for the new generation of American writers the work of William Burroughs is by far the most seriously influential being done today.

. . .

▆▆▆▆▆▆▆▆▆▆▆▆▆▆▆▆▆▆▆▆▆▆▆▆▆▆▆▆▆▆▆▆▆▆▆

About three months ago, ▆▆▆▆▆▆ had lunch with one ▆▆▆▆▆▆ on the West Coast for the ▆▆▆▆▆▆ said that TERRY SOUTHERN, who received screen credit for the controversial film "Dr. STRANGELOVE", written in conjunction with others, had written one of the current best sellers, "CANDY", which, in the opinion of ▆▆▆▆▆ "is pure pornography".

▆▆▆ also advised that TERRY SOUTHERN has one of the finest collections of pornographic films in the country. ▆▆▆ explained that this is not the ordinary type of pornographic film but is high quality, the best made, including some made for KING FAROUK.

No further information was available from ▆▆▆▆▆ other than that set forth above.

On 2/1/65 ▆▆▆▆▆ contacted ▆▆▆▆▆▆ of the Writers Guild of America West ▆▆▆▆▆▆▆ who advised that as of May 1963, TERRY SOUTHERN resided at RFD E, Canaan, Connecticut and could be reached in care of Sterling Lad Agency, 75 East 55th Street, New York, New York. SOUTHERN received joint screen play credit for "DR. STRANGELOVE" along with STANLEY KUBRICK, Producer-Director, and PETER GEORGE, who wrote the book. Columbia Pictures Corp., released the film. SOUTHERN has no local address, past or present, in Los Angeles, and is a member of the Writers Guild of America East, New York.

In view of the fact prior ITOM investigations pertaining to paperback books has included the identifying of the author, knowing of his credit and criminal background and, in most cases, interviewing the author as to his contractual relationships with the publisher, this is set forth for informational purposes for all offices receiving copies of this communication.

However, it is believed that the Bureau should furnish the investigative direction of this particular individual as to whether he should be directly interviewed as to any work he has done on the book "CANDY", which of the publishing houses employed him to do such work, if any.

With reference to the pornographic library of films which SOUTHERN allegedly has in his possession, it is not known to this office whether it is a local violation in Connecticut to display films to "guests" and it is therefore left to the discretion of the Bureau as to whether such information should be made available, strictly on a confidential basis, to a local law enforcement agency covering SOUTHERN'S place of residence.

- 2 -

> COUNSEL
>
> Your honor, the Defense wishes
>
> to call to the stand at this time our
>
> distinguished <u>poet</u> <u>laureate</u>, Mr. Allen
>
> Ginsberg.

APPLAUSE. The Judge raps vigorously for silence, eyes the Counsel
narrowly.

> JUDGE (his expression changing to one
> of sly shrewdness)
>
> '<u>Poet-deviate</u>'? Did you say '<u>poet-</u>
> <u>deviate</u>', Mr. Kunstler?
>
> COUNSEL (with emphasis)
>
> I said,'poet laureate', your honor, and
>
> I must take the most serious exception
>
> to your uncalled for---
>
> JUDGE (interrupting furiously)
>
> Just one minute, Mr. William Counselor!
>
> Are you trying to tell the court that
>
> this witness -- this <u>Jehovah's</u> <u>witness</u> --
>
> is not, in actual fact, a self-avowed
>
> PREVERT?!?
>
> COUNSEL (cooly)
>
> Your honor, I would suggest to you that
>
> the sex-life of the witness is not rel-
>
> event to the substance of his testimony.
>
> JUDGE (menacingly)
>
> And I would suggest to <u>you</u>, Mr. William
>
> A. Kunstler, that you are on the verge
>
> (MORE)

JUDGE (CONTD.)

of being in contempt.

COUNSEL (bewildered)

In contempt, your honor?

PROSECUTOR (chuckling with good-
                                 natured drunken joviality)

That's a little town just outside of

Scranton, P.A.
                           (continues chuckling, starts coughing
                           has a nip)

His laughter is joined by that of the Judge, and the weird chortle

of the Reporter.

COUNSEL (impatiently)

Your honor, may we please call the

witness?!?

JUDGE (exasperated sigh)

All right...call the witness.

REPORTER

Yes, your honor.
                           (sternly to the Guards)

All right, men, if he tries any preversion

there on the stand -- you know what to do.

GUARDS (with grim relish)

(1)   Yer fuckin' A!

(2)   Yer fuckin' A-rab!

(3)   We'll waste the mother!

(4)   Smoke that turkey!

(5)   Light him up!

                    GUARDS (CONTD.)
    (6) Blow 'im away!

    (1) Hot damn, Viet-Nam!

    (2) San Ann-tone!
                          Etc.
                REPORTER
                        (calling)
        Mr. Allen Ginsberg!

Ginsberg steps to the stage amidst sustained applause. while the

Judge RAPS. for silence, and the Reporter avidly switches the dir-

ection of the mike from Judge to Spectators---back and forth,

grimacing madly the while.

                (ALLEN GINSBERG)
Ginsberg finishes his poems, and leaves the stage, during sustained

applause and the Juge's RAPPING gavel.

                REPORTER (muttering)
        Completely irrelevant. . .

                PROSECUTOR
        Immaterial. . .

                JUDGE

        Inadmissable!

        (to Counsel)

        Perhaps I should remind you, Counsel, that

        this is a court of law -- not a lunatic-

        asylum! And not a massage-parlor!

        Just what is your purpose with this

        parade of ne'er-do-wells?

HI THERE TOURISTS!
GET WITH IT!

TOUGH CITY TOURS

TAKES YOU WHERE THE ACTION IS!
SEE!
RAPE!
RIOTS!
MUGGINGS!
SHOOT-OUTS!
GANG-FIGHTS!
TENEMENT-FIRES!
ROBBERIES IN-PRGRESS!
DOPE-DROPS AND PICK-UPS!
ALL MANNER OF GAY WEIRDNESS!
DRUG-CRAZED JUNKIES MAIN-LINING IT FOR KICKS!
and more
SEE ALL THIS TOUGH CITY ACTION IN PERFECT
SAFETY FROM THE AIR CONDITIONED COMFORT
OF OUR **TOUGH CITY TOUR** BUSES ROCK, BOTTLE
AND BULLET-PROOF! TOURS INCLUDE:
HARLEM! BELLVUE!
GREENWICH VILLAGE!
and
...THE INTERNATIONALLY FAMOUS
HELL'S KITCHEN!
(immortalized by the late Humphrey Bogart in "dead end"
and soon to be re-released as a major motion picture!)
DEPARTURES AT: 10:00, 1:00, 5:00, AND 8:00...
$10 PER PERSON

The story of the desintegration
of an entire culture (the American culture
in the 1960's) through alienation
and despair — a culture so
ravaged by hatred and paranoia
that like a flock birds of prey
ever an ordinary barony and chickens
they are compelled to destroy
their own kind at the least
difference or trace of individuality
in any one of them.

This story reaches its inevitable grotesque
resolution in which the two gentle
and free spirited protagonists
are blown away for no
better reason than a Newt
Gingrich type objecting to
their long hair still the most convenient

Possessives and Apostrophes

Today's air despite its
intermissions's become
a semblance of its self
when without lemons it
cooled everybody human's hot teeth
including the animals', flowers',
fireflies' & praying mantises'
plus the luna moths' and
jacks-in-the-pulpits' & arachnids',
that is at that time in the past's
whatever-it-was when there were
still wooden statues whose
authors'd remained unknown
to our every impulse toward
history's frame's musculatures
or muscles like languages' wanting
to be the brain's spokespersons
in some of our physiology's ways.

The Screaming Cheetah Wheelies

Once I finished with my etymology class
I went to see ron sunshine & the smoking
  section followed by choosey mothers
Then we had some coffee & heard
Pain killers & crash test dummies &
Even later after red red meat, the
  afghan whigs came on
We slept and saw think again & were
  inspired by trenchmouth
plus scarce wider jawbox saturnine
& also railroad jerk & psychic penguin
  & the maul girls
Next day chrome cranks & the authority
  appeared
with venus for breakfast & screaming
  headless torsos
Zen tricksters made us hungry, we ate
  goats & went to special head,
  lunachicks, voodoo dolls, morning
  glories
and friends, romans & countrymen all
  in one night

our downstairs neighbors were giving us
    a hard time
So we went back out to vice royals
    & pork chops followed
by lobster of hate, oral groove &
    knockout drops
it wasn't eight hours later till we
    saw professor spoon & hyperactive
and when cool aid temple appeared
    with serious pilgrim & thin lizard
    dawn we saw
girls against boys that same night
far beyond driven, halcion speedball
    babies as we are
we tsunamied back to subdudes
& sugar-beared our tea between
stone soul picnic around with
the flying neutrinos & nine below zero
I don't know how you feel but if
    you've seen all this
cold sweat, true love, the titans
    and meters are in order
along with of course a roomful of blues
you couldn't help but back that up
with mr. thing and the professional
    human beings opening for
    loup garou zydeco

& by that time you're ready for
 the late show & jane doe too
now i'm going to see sisters grimm
 & rats of unusual size
tomorrow amazing cherubs, thrust
 & blush
I'll be at entombed on sunday,
 loretta's doll & prong on tuesday
 & schooly d on thursday
smashed gladys & killer lipstick
 will have to wait
but not as long as falafel mafia
& psychedelic thursdays versus sleeper
I want to see courtney & western too

St. Martin

W e were caretakers for most of that year, from early fall until summer. We had to look after a house and grounds, two dogs, and two cats. We fed the cats, one white and one calico, who lived outside and ate their meals on the kitchen windowsill, sparring in the sunlight as they waited for their food, but we did not keep the house very clean, or the weeds cut in the yard, and our employers, kind people though they were, probably never quite forgave us for what happened to one of the dogs.

We hardly knew what a clean house should look like. We would begin to think we were quite tidy, and then we would see the dust and clutter of the rooms, and the two hearths covered with ash. Sometimes we argued about it, sometimes we cleaned it. The oil stove became badly blocked and we did nothing for days because the telephone was out of order. When we needed help, we went to see the former caretakers, an old couple who lived with their cages of breeding canaries in the nearest village. The old man came by sometimes, and when he

saw how the grass had grown so tall around the house, he scythed it without comment.

What our employers needed most from us was simply that we stay in the house. We were not supposed to leave it for more than a few hours, because it had been robbed so often. We left it overnight only once, to celebrate New Year's Eve with a friend many miles away. We took the dogs with us on a mattress in the back of the car. We stopped at village fountains along the way and sprinkled water on their backs. We had too little money, anyway, to go anywhere. Our employers sent us a small amount each month, most of which we spent immediately on postage, cigarettes, and groceries. We brought home whole mackerels, which we cleaned, and whole chickens, which we beheaded and cleaned and prepared to roast, tying their legs together. The kitchen often smelled of garlic. We were told many times that year that garlic would give us strength. Sometimes we wrote letters home asking for money, and sometimes a check was sent for a small sum, but the bank took weeks to cash it.

We could not go much farther than the closest town to shop for food and to a village half an hour away over a small mountain covered with scrub oaks. There we left our sheets, towels, table linen, and other laundry to be washed, as our employers had instructed us to do, and when we picked it up a week later, we sometimes stayed to see a movie. Our mail was delivered to the house by a woman on a motorcycle.

But even if we had had the money, we would not have gone far, since we had chosen to live there in that house, in that isolation, in order to do work of our own, and we often sat inside the house trying to work, not always succeeding. We spent a great deal of time sitting inside one room or another looking down at our work and then up and out the window, though there was not much to see, one bit of landscape or another depending on which room we were in—trees, fields, clouds in the sky, a distant road, distant cars on the road, a village that lay on the horizon to the west of us, piled around its square

church tower like a mirage, another village on a hilltop to the north of us across the valley, a person walking or working in a field, a bird or a pair of birds walking or flying, the ruined outbuilding not far from the house.

The dogs stayed near us almost all the time, sleeping in tight curls. If we spoke to them, they looked up with the worried eyes of old people. They were purebred yellow labradors, brother and sister. The male was large, muscular, perfectly formed, of a blond color so light he was nearly white, with a fine head and a lovely broad face. His nature was simple and good. He ran, sniffed, came when we called, ate, and slept. Strong, adept, and willing, he retrieved as long as we asked him to, running down a cliff of sand no matter how steep or how long, plunging into a body of water in pursuit of a stick. Only in villages and towns did he turn shy and fearful, trembling and diving toward the shelter of a café table or a car.

His sister was very different, and as we admired her brother for his simple goodness and beauty, we admired her for her peculiar sense of humor, her reluctance, her cunning, her bad moods, her deviousness. She was calm in villages and cities and would not retrieve at all. She was small, with a rusty brown coat, and not well formed, a barrel of a body on thin legs and a face like a weasel.

Because of the dogs, we went outside the house often in the course of the day. Sometimes one of us would have to leave the warm bed at five in the morning and hurry down the cold stone steps to let them out, and they were so eager that they leaked and left a pattern of drops on the red tiles of the kitchen and the patio. As we waited for them, we would look up at the stars, bright and distinct, the whole sky having shifted from where it was when we last saw it.

In the early fall, as grape pickers came into the neighboring fields to harvest, snails crept up the outside of the windowpanes, their undersides greenish gold. Flies infested the rooms. We swatted them in the wide bands of sunlight that came through the glass doors of the

music room. They tormented us while alive, then died in piles on the windowsills, covering our notebooks and papers. They were one of our seven plagues, the others being the fighter jets that thundered suddenly over our roof, the army helicopters that batted their more leisurely way over the treetops, the hunters who roamed close to the house, the thunderstorms, the two thieving cats, and, after a time, the cold.

The guns of the hunters boomed from beyond the hills or under our windows, waking us early in the morning. Men walked alone or in pairs, sometimes a woman trailed by a small child, spaniels loping out of sight and smoke rising from the mouths of the rifles. When we were in the woods, we would find a hunter's mess by the ruins of a stone house where he had settled for lunch—a plastic wine bottle, a glass wine bottle, scraps of paper, a crumpled paper bag, and an empty cartridge box. Or we would come upon a hunter squatting so motionless in the bushes, his gun resting in his arms, that we did not see him until we were on top of him, and even then he did not move, his eyes fixed on us.

In the village café, at the end of the day, the owner's young son, in olive-green pants, would slip around the counter and up the stairs with his two aged, slinking, tangerine-colored dogs, at the same time that women would come in with the mushrooms they had gathered just before dusk. Cartridge cases peppered the ground across a flat field near the house, one of the odd waste patches that lay in this valley of cultivated fields. Its dry autumn grass was strewn with boulders, among them two abandoned cars. Here from one direction came the smell of wild thyme, from the other the smell of sewage from a sewage bed.

We visited almost no one, only a farmer, a butcher, and a rather pompous retired businessman from the city. The farmer lived alone with his dog and his two cats in a large stone house a field or two away. The businessman, whose hyphenated name in fact contained the word "pomp," lived in a new house in the closest village, to the west of us

across the fields. The young butcher lived with his childless wife in town, and we would sometimes encounter him there moving meat across the street from his van to his shop. Cradling a beef carcass or a lamb in his arms, he would stop to talk to us in the sunlight, a wary smile on his face. When he was finished working for the day, he often went out to take photographs. He had studied photography through a correspondence course and received a degree. He photographed town festivals and processions, fairs and shooting matches. Sometimes he took us with him. Now and then a stranger came to the house by mistake. Once it was a young girl who entered the kitchen suddenly in a gust of wind, pale, thin, and strange, like a stray thought.

Because we had so little money, our amusements were simple. We would go out into the sun that beat down on the white gravel and shone off the leaves of the olive tree and toss pebbles one by one, over-hand, from a distance of ten feet or so into a large clay urn that stood among the rosemary plants. We did this as a contest with each other, but also alone when we were finished working or couldn't work. One would be working and hear the dull click, over and over, of a pebble striking the urn and falling back onto the gravel, and the more reso-nant pock of the pebble landing inside the urn, and would know the other was outside.

When the weather grew too cold, we stayed inside and played gin rummy. By the middle of winter, when only a few rooms in the house were heated, we were playing so much, day and night, that we orga-nized our games into tournaments. Then, for a few weeks, we stopped playing and studied German in the evenings by the fire. In the spring, we went back to our pebble game.

Nearly every afternoon, we took the dogs for a walk. On the cold-est days of winter, we went out only long enough to gather kindling wood and pinecones for the fire. On warmer days, we went out for an hour or more at a time, most often into the government forest that spread out for miles on a plateau above and behind the house, sometimes into the fields of vines or lavender in the valley, or into the meadows, or across to the far side of the valley, into old groves of olive trees. We were surrounded for so long by scrub brush, rocks, pine trees, oaks, red earth, fields, that we felt enclosed by them even once we were back inside the house.

We would walk, and return with burrs in our socks and scratches on our legs and arms where we had pushed through the brambles to get up into the forest, and go out again the next day and walk, and the dogs always trusted that we were setting out in a certain direction for a reason, and then returning home for a reason, but in the forest, which seemed so endless, there was hardly a distinguishing feature that could be taken as a destination for a walk, and we were simply walking, watching the sameness pass on both sides, the thorny, scrubby oaks growing densely together along the dusty track that ran quite straight until it came to a gentle bend and perhaps a slight rise and then ran straight again.

If we came home by an unfamiliar route, skirting the forest, avoiding a deeply furrowed, overgrown field, and then stepping into the edge of a reedy marsh, veering close to a farmyard where a farmer in blue and his wife in red were doing chores, trailed by their dog, we felt so changed ourselves that we were surprised nothing about home had changed: for a moment the placidity of the house and yard nearly persuaded us we had not even left.

Between the forest and the fields, in the thickets of underbrush, we would sometimes come upon a farmhouse in ruins, with a curving flight of deep stone steps, worn at the edges, leading to an upper story that was now empty air, brambles and nettles and mint growing up inside and around it, and sometimes, nearby, an ancient, awkward, and shaggy fruit tree, half its branches dead. In the form of this farmhouse, we recognized our own house. We went up the same curving flight of stone steps to bed at night. The animals had lived downstairs in our house, too—our vaulted dining room had once been a sheepfold.

Sometimes, in our walks, we came upon inexplicable things, once, in the cinders of an abandoned fire, two dead jackrabbits. Sometimes we lost our way, and were still lost after the sun had set, when we would start to run, and run without tiring, afraid of the dark, until we saw where we were again.

We had visitors who came from far away to stay with us for several days and sometimes several weeks, sometimes welcome, sometimes less so, as they stayed on and on. One was a young photographer who had worked with our employer and was in the habit of stopping at the house. He would travel through the region on assignments for his magazine, always taking his pictures at dawn or at sunset when the shadows were long. For every night he stayed with us, he paid us the amount he would have paid for a room at a good hotel, since he traveled on a company expense account. He was a small, neat man with a quick, toothy smile. He came alone, or he came with his girlfriend.

He played with the dogs, fondling them, wrestling with them overhead as we sat in the room below trying to work, while we spoke against him angrily, to ourselves. Or he and his girlfriend ironed their clothes above us, with noises we did not at first understand, the stiff cord knocking and sliding against the floorboards. It was hard enough for us to work, sometimes.

They were curiously disorganized, and when they went out on an errand, left water coming to a boil on the stove or the sink full of warm, soapy water as though they were still at home. Or when they returned from an errand, they left the doors wide open so that the cold air and the cats came in. They were still at breakfast close to noon, and left crumbs on the table. Late in the evening, sometimes, we would find the girlfriend asleep on the sofa.

But we were lonely, and the photographer and his girlfriend were friendly, and they would sometimes cook dinner for us, or take us out to a restaurant. A visit from them meant money in our pockets again.

At the beginning of December, when we began to have the oil stove going full blast in the kitchen all day, the dogs slept next to it while we worked at the dining-room table. We watched through the window as two men returned to work in a cultivated field, one on a tractor and one behind a plow that had been sitting for weeks growing rusty, after opening perhaps ten furrows. Violent high winds sometimes rose during the night and then continued blowing all day so that the birds had trouble flying and dust sifted down through the floorboards. Sometimes one of us would get up in the night, hearing a shutter bang, and go out in pajamas onto the tiles of the garage roof to tie it back again or remove it from its hinge.

A rainstorm would last hours, soaking the ruined outbuilding nearby, darkening its stones. The air in the morning would be soft and limp. After the constant dripping of the rain or wuthering of the wind, there was sometimes complete silence, minute after minute, and then abruptly the rocky echoes of a plane far away in the sky. The light on the wet gravel outside the house was so white, after a storm, it looked like snow.

By the middle of the month, the trees and bushes had begun to lose their leaves and in a nearby field a stone shed, its black doorway overgrown by brambles, gradually came into view.

A flock of sheep gathered around the ruined outbuilding, fat, long-tailed, a dirty brown color, with pale scrawny lambs. Jostling one another, they poured up out of the ruin, climbing the tumbledown walls, the little ones crying in high human voices over the dull clamor of the bells. The shepherd, dressed all in brown with a cap pulled low over his eyes, sat eating on the grass by the woodpile, his face glowing and his chin unshaven. When the sheep became too active, he grunted and his small black dog raced once around the side of the flock and the sheep cantered away in a forest of stick-like legs. When they came near again, streaming out between the walls, the dog sent them flying again. When they disappeared into the next field, the shepherd continued to sit for a while, then moved off slowly, in his baggy brown

pants, a leather pouch hanging on long straps down his back, a light stick in one hand, his coat flung over his shoulder, the little black dog charging and veering when he whistled.

One afternoon we had almost no money left, and almost no food. Our spirits were low. Hoping to be invited to dinner, we dropped in on the businessman and his wife. They had been upstairs reading, and came down one after the other holding their reading glasses in their hands, looking tired and old. We saw that when they were not expecting company, they had in their living room a blanket and a sleeping bag arranged over the two armchairs in front of the television. They invited us to have dinner with them the next night.

When we went to their house the next night, we were offered rum cocktails by Monsieur Assiez-de-Pompignan before dinner and afterward we watched a movie with them. When it ended, we left, hurrying to our car against the wind, through the narrow, shuttered streets, dust flying in our teeth.

The following day, for dinner, we had one sausage. The only money left now was a pile of coins on the living-room table collected from saucers around the house and amounting to 2.97 francs, less than fifty cents, but enough to buy something for dinner the next day.

Then we had no money at all anywhere in the house, and almost nothing left to eat. What we found, when we searched the kitchen carefully, were some onions, an old but unopened box of pastry-crust mix, a little fat, and a little dried milk. Out of this, we realized, we could make an onion pie. We made it, baked it, cut ourselves two pieces, and put the rest back in the hot oven to cook a little more while we ate. It was surprisingly good. Our spirits lifting, we talked as we ate and forgot all about the pie as it went on baking. By the time we smelled it, it had burned too badly to be saved.

In the afternoon of that day, we went out onto the gravel, not knowing what to do now. We tossed pebbles for a while, there in the boiling sun and the cool air, saying very little because we had no answer to our

problem. Then we heard the sound of an approaching car. Along the bumpy dirt road that led to our house from the main road, past the house of the weekend people, of pink stucco with black ironwork, and then past a vineyard on one side and a field on the other, came the photographer in his neat rented car. By pure chance, or like an angel, he was arriving to rescue us at the very moment we had used up our last resource.

We were not embarrassed to say we had no money, and no food either, and he was pleased to invite us out to dinner. He took us into town to a very good restaurant on the main square where the rows of plantain trees stood. A television crew was also dining there, twelve at the table, including a hunchback. By the large, bright fire on one wall, three old women sat knitting: one with liver spots covering her face and hands, the second pinched and bony, the third younger and merrier but slow-witted. The photographer fed us well on his expense account. He stayed with us that night and a few nights after, leaving us with several fifty-franc notes, so we were all right for a while, since a bottle of local wine, for instance, cost no more than one franc fifty.

When winter set in, we closed one by one the other rooms in the house and confined ourselves to the kitchen with its fat oil-burning stove, the vaulted dining room with its massive oak table where we played cards in the thick heat from the kitchen, the music room with its expensive electric heater burning our legs, and, at the top of the stone stairway, the unheated bedroom with its floor of red tiles so vast there was ample time for it to dip down in the center and rise again on its way to the single small casement window that looked out onto the almond tree and the olive tree below. The house had a different feeling to it when the wind was blowing and parts of it were darkened because we had closed the shutters.

Larks fluttered over the fields in the afternoons, showing silver. The long, straight, deeply rutted road to the village turned to soft mud. In certain lights, the inner walls of the ruined outbuilding were as

rosy as a seashell. The dogs sighed heavily as they lay down on the cold tiles, closing their almond-shaped eyes. When they were let out into the sunlight, they fought, panting and scattering gravel. The shadow of the almond tree in the bright, hard sunlight flowed over the gravel like a dark river and lapped up against the wall of the house.

One night, during a heavy rainstorm, we went to the farmer's house for dinner. Nothing grew around his house, not even grass; there was only the massive stone house in a yard of deep mud. The front door was heavy to push open. The entryway was filled with a damp, musty smell from the truffles hanging in a leather pouch from a peg. Sacks full of seed and grain lined the wall.

With the farmer, we went out to the side of the house to collect eggs for dinner. Under the house, in the pens where he had once kept sheep, hens roosted now, their faces sharp in the beam of his flashlight. He gathered the eggs, holding the flashlight in one hand, and gave them to us to carry. The umbrella, as we started back around to the front of the house, turned inside out in the wind.

The kitchen was warm from the heat of a large oil stove. The oven door was open and a cat sat inside looking out. When he was in the house, the farmer spent most of his time in the kitchen. When he had something to throw away, he threw it out the window, burying it later. The table was crowded with bottles—vinegar, oil, his own wine in whisky bottles which he had brought up from the cellar—and among them cloth napkins and large lumps of sea salt. Behind the table was a couch piled with coats. Two rifles hung in racks against the wall. Taped to the refrigerator was a photograph of the farmer and the truck he used to drive from Paris to Marseilles.

For dinner he gave us leeks with oil and vinegar, bits of hard sausage and bread, black olives like cardboard, and scrambled eggs with truffles. He dried lettuce leaves by shaking them in a dishtowel and gave us a salad full of garlic, and then some Roquefort. He told us that his first breakfast, before he went out to work in the fields, was a piece of bread and garlic. He called himself a Communist and talked about the Resistance, telling us that the people of the area knew just who the collaborators were. The collaborators stayed at home out of sight, did not go to the cafés much, and in fact would be killed immediately if there was trouble, though he did not say what he meant by trouble. He had opinions about many things, even the Koran, in which, he said, lying and stealing were not considered sins, and he had questions for us: he wondered if it was the same year over there, in our country.

To get to his new, clean bathroom, we took the flashlight and lit our way past the head of the stairs and through an empty, high-ceilinged room of which we could see nothing but a great stone fireplace. After dinner, we listened in silence to a record of revolutionary songs which he took from a pile on the floor, while he grew sleepy, yawning and twiddling his thumbs.

When we returned home, we let the dogs out, as we always did, to run around before they were shut in for the night. The hunting season had begun again. We should not have let the dogs out loose, but we did not know that. More than an hour passed and the female came back but her brother did not. We were afraid right away, because he never stayed out more than an hour or so. We called and called, near the house, and then the next morning, when he had still not returned, we walked through the woods in all directions, calling and searching among the trees.

We knew he would not have stayed away so long unless he had somehow been stopped from coming back. We began to think he had been stolen by a hunter, someone avid for a good-natured, handsome hunting dog, proud to show it off in a smoke-filled café. He could have wandered into the nearest village, lured by the scent of a female in heat. He could have been spotted near the road and taken by a passing motorist. But we believed first, and longest, that he lay in the underbrush poisoned, or caught in a trap, or wounded by a bullet.

Day after day passed and he did not come home and we had no news of him. We drove from village to village asking questions, and put up notices with his photograph attached, but we also knew that the people we talked to might lie to us, and that such a beautiful dog would probably not be returned.

People called us who had a yellow dog, or had found a stray, but each time we went to see it, it was not much like our dog. Because we did not know what had happened to him, because it was always possible that he might return, it was hard for us to accept the fact that he was gone. What made it worse was that he was not our dog.

After a month, we still hoped the dog would return, though signs of spring began to appear and other things came along to distract us. The almond tree blossomed with flowers so white that against the soft plowed field beyond them they were almost blue. A pair of magpies came to the scrub oak beside the woodpile, fluttering, squawking, diving obliquely down.

The weekend people returned, and every Sunday they called out to each other as they worked the long strip of earth in the field below us. The dog went to the border of our land and barked at them, tense on her stiff legs.

Once we stopped to talk to a woman at the edge of the village and she showed us her hand covered with dirt from digging in the ground. Behind her we could see a man, leading another man back into his garden to give him some herbs.

Drifts of daffodils and narcissus bloomed in the fields. We gathered a vase full of them and slept with them in the room, waking up drugged and sluggish. Irises bloomed and then the first roses opened, yellow. The flies became numerous again, and noisy.

We took long walks again, with one dog now. There were bugs in the wiry, stiff grass near the house, small cracks in the dirt, ants. In the field, purple clover grew around our ankles, and large white and yellow daisies at our knees. Bloodred bumblebees landed on buttercups

as high as our hands. The long, lush grass in the field rose and fell in waves before the wind, and near us in a thick grove of trees dead branches clacked together. Whenever the wind died, we could hear the trickle of a swollen stream as though it were falling into a stone basin.

In May, we heard the first nightingale. Just as the night fully darkened, it began to sing. Its song was not really unlike the song of a mockingbird, with warbles, and twitters, and trills, warbles, chirps, and warbles again, but it issued in the midst of the silence of the night, in the dark, or in the moonlight, from a spot mysteriously hidden among the black branches.

RACHEL HECKER

Almost Heaven

Buttermilk, 1994.

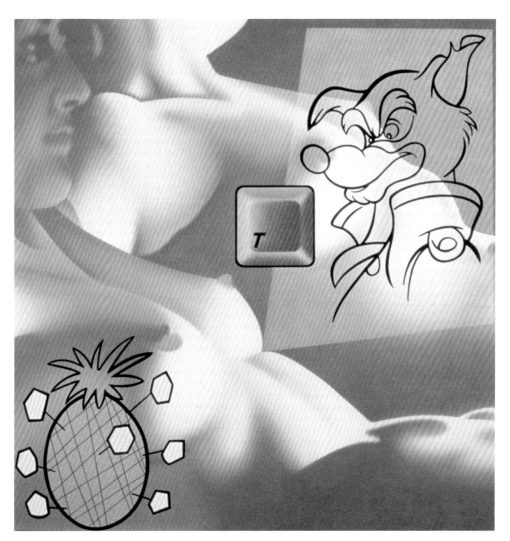

History Painting, 1994.

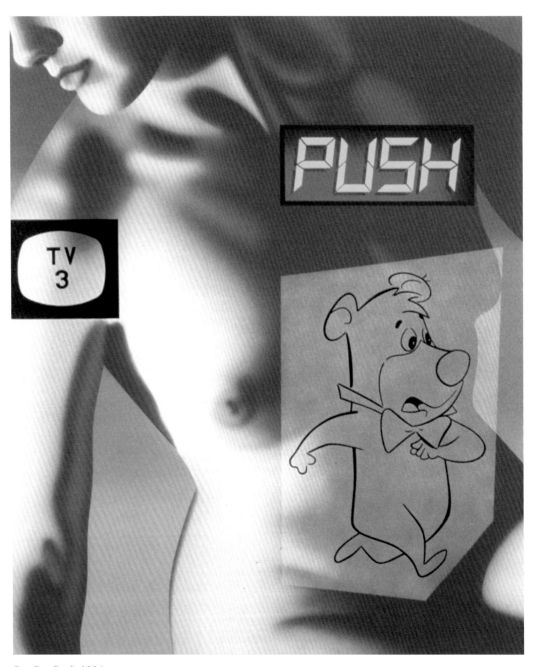

Boo Boo Push, 1994.

34% Off, 1994.

Bait, 1995.

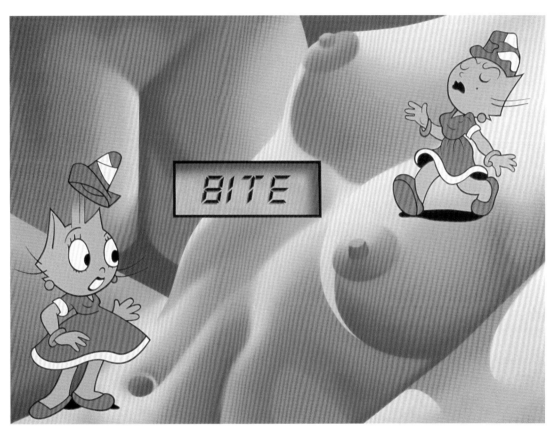

Bite, 1995.

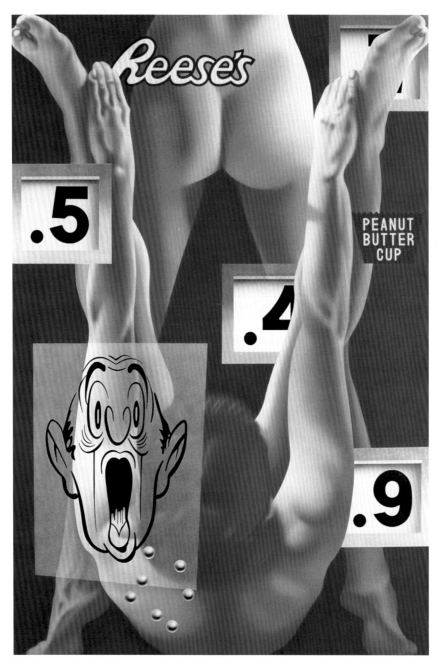

.5.4.9, 1994.

Rachel Hecker's paintings explore the profound ambivalence at the heart of mass consumption, an ambivalence that appears most conspicuously in the female consumer's response to mass culture's troubling and fantastic images of women. By daring to appropriate quasi-pornographic images of women to produce pleasure as well as to question or disrupt, Hecker establishes a new point of departure for feminist cultural critique.

Hecker's most recent series, *Almost Heaven*, borrows from art-instruction manuals of the 1950s, a genre in which the textbook meets soft porn, and one that, like so many forms of post–World War II American popular culture, now possesses considerable camp appeal. She remakes the original photographs with acrylic paint, cropping and enlarging the images on larger-than-life canvases, then uses airbrushing techniques to emphasize photography's illusions and conventions. These female bodies are further transformed by the images that Hecker superimposes onto them—word captions in the form of LED readouts, and commercial icons, and images borrowed from another popular-culture genre, cartoons—as she uses the power of montage to create new meanings. Long a vehicle of fantasy because of their freedom from the conventions of realist representation, cartoons are an especially rich resource: Hot Stuff, Miss Kitty, Felix the Cat, and other childhood favorites appear to frolic across the bodies of the women, turning them into playgrounds. The cartoon figures' power is illusory, however, since their two-dimensional world never meets the plane on which the female figures reside in pictorial space. Never quite touched by the childish antics of the cartoon characters, the female figures preserve a serene and monumental presence.

Hecker's originality does not rely on an independence from mass culture's anonymous and ghostly agency. Rather Hecker insists that, for better or for worse, part of what animates mass culture is her own desire, whose contradictory qualities preclude any simple choice between loving it and leaving it. To produce pleasure as effectively as the Disney empire and the Hollywood studios—or the pornography industry—is to possess power indeed. Hecker makes both this power and this pleasure her own.

—Ann Cvetkovich

The North End

True to the harbor surrounded by lookouts
You peed I deigned to be a pier till you found me
In the mistness no rust hulk ducked
near, we hurried off in hand
Hockey game crowd let out we swam
counter, the only open liquor store
on our way's clerk turbaned & fingers wrapped
under the register had a gun we imagined
Pair making out in pockmarked car curbside security
guard in bright light at front desk dozing
The night really swung because after the wine
we unscrewed the Jim Beam
under overpass over canal past pedestrian bridge
tombstones row homes stairs to light
& squares, to be free as car doors
valuables open to, we weren't scared.

Sullivan Square

O Libertine! I was laughing at my credit line
when you called! They extended it
they ascend my rent to what I
can't afford to be tethered to
by bribe alone, heaven

She goes I look at
painting toward her dream of
vessels filling & a blue dress I can't seem
to get off he goes a succulent lawyer evicts me
while I wait for the unrated doctor in his office
where if you didn't absently pinch your nipple
once in a while, how would you know you're alive?

I run for the bus I search the margins of dust
for the dime that would make me
on time but I have to make change
before the orgy & audit
of everything
easy & inclusive as the universe

Anniversary

You won't let me publish the roof
because of images of your insulation

I had my boyfriend & my girlfriends
but you insisted on airplanes

so the mustard's french flag could give me dreams
& gratitude toward you moved the boxes

Then we could not agree on the proper subscriptions
I hung from the mercy of your bicep

Gladly in your disheveled address book I lolled
Persian & melodious you returned

heads where feet were on the bed & vice versa
shared of your books, your codeine, your drumsticks

One string for the light & one for the fan
& one off your guitar to lure that

cherished horse that rode between book & dream
regnant with disorder

I shake a thermometer
you break the chalk

so abstemiously but completely do we
share the names of our fathers & a street

The Rifles:
from *The Atlas*

Montréal, Québec, Canada (1993)

They caught baby birds and held them. One bird they passed too many times among them and it ended up with a broken wing. They threw it repeatedly into the air to see if it could fly but it only tumbled crazily down into the moss, flapping its good wing in desperate silence. Finally they dropped it into the campfire. They did that where life was green and muddy and stony in late July; they did it on their low brown mass of island with its pale-eyed lakes and skinny long wispy streaks of snow across gullies and mounds; they did it in their streaky whiteness between capes, but he'd done it down south with Reepah, picking her up one time too many so that she loved him and couldn't fly away, then dropping her and when her wing got better seizing her again. He'd never drop her, though, never. Besides, she'd started it.

He felt terribly nervous and gloomy as he waited for Reepah at the airport. She was now above the blue and green squares and rectangles of fields half hidden by bright northern clouds (small irregular puddles

of forest among them); now if she looked down she'd see the lovely indigo of the Saint Lawrence River mirroring clouds between the pincers of its islets where the river darkened between the flat gray bellies of thunderheads; it partook of the wide grace of rivers suddenly tinged by hot dark clouds.

Thank you for Montréal, she said.

It was a July day, a sunny day of rain in Montréal. The maple trees sparkled. Red trucks were so red and the fresh girls as bright as wet stones, striding umbrellaless in the rain.

She wanted him to buy her cigarettes. She said: Secrets is my best friend.

She didn't really want to talk to him or be with him. When they met a drunken Inuk lady on Rue Sainte-Catherine, Reepah talked with her for hours. Him she ignored.

She wanted him to buy her beers until she got drunk. He didn't want to. She looked at him with a hard and nasty viciousness he'd never seen before and shouted: You want to fuck me tonight? If you want to fuck me, I want drunk. I want *drunk*!

Fine, he said. You don't have to fuck me at all. I'll get you drunk and you can do whatever you want.

After her second or third beer she got louder and happier and she said: I like you. 'Cause I'm drunk.

Every few blocks some spectacle would come out of the summer darkness, like the fantastically roofed houses shooting steep and narrow above the dark street. Purple-plumed clowns mimed by candlelight. They passed the fountain where Reepah had wanted to swim in the afternoon, and she didn't remember it. Everybody was sitting around it; its water fell with a glow; and people sat on the grass listening to musicians and smelling the sweet summer night. Reepah dipped her hand in and wanted to go get drunk. Fullbreasted girls in sundresses floated on the grass's emerald darkness. On the lighted cobblestones a pancake-made-up twelve-year-old was singing humorous

French ballads in an exaggerated mincing voice while her father played the guitar; then suddenly the songs grew serious and he could tell that she had a magnificent voice. Reepah smiled faintly for the first moment. Then she sat scratching and staring at her empty beer.

The musicians (who were really astoundingly good) got everybody clapping, so she clapped; in those marble mirrored morgues of blue-lit soundproofed sex bars at first she smiled with naughty delight to see naked boys and girls but soon enough she sat picking her teeth morosely between beers (each of which lasted seconds), and her lower lip gaped slightly wider at the flash of genitals or the applause of the other drinkers but then her black eyes would gaze into some particularly monotonous version of zero. And then a beautiful dancer might move in beautiful ways and she would stare steadily, leaning forward, maybe trying to be beautiful in the way the dancer was (the dancers usually thought that Reepah was a boy), trying to learn what made this other soul the center of attention in a way she could never be. When she was happy, when he bought her another beer, she cried: *Aw-riiiiiiiiiiiiiiiiigh'!*

If you don't like me, it's okay, he said. I'll give you some money for the hotel and then go away. Yes or no?

I don't know, she wrote on a piece of paper.

Reepah, I love you.

Same here, she wrote.

Reepah, I want you happy. I want everything for you.

I like Montréal. I am sad I don't have money.

Don't be sad. I don't have much money but I'll give you a little bit.

I want some beer, please.

In our room at the hotel, he said, not wanting to have to get her at the police station.

Way not read now? I am sick. I am tired.

They went walking late after midnight down to Chinatown and then back up the hill to Sherbrooke Street and she cried: Wow! Look at those lights! Just like good orange Inukjuak berries!

That was about the only time she sounded happy over anything but beer. He had wanted to give her something good and she had wanted to come there, but nothing that came from him could reach her, not even Montréal's streets, which were a guitar of light.

Inukjuak, Québec, Canada (1990)

Thirty or forty feet high, and therefore up in the clouds, a small lake had been set in rock by God. The rapids from this made a foamy white fall as soft and pure as caribou hair. Crowberries, grasses, and lichens grew on and between the rock shapes around the pool, so that the grayness of the place was softened by green, red, and yellow. A cool wind blew away some of the clouds like smoke, leaving zones of blue as sweet as anything in Italy. It seemed here above the bog of caribou skulls (the place so lovely with grass-antlers nodding even on foam-sprayed rock) that the foreverness of the Barren Lands was something lovely like the eternal echo of a bell—something secret, too, like whatever sensibility she had—her consciousness or integrity, both of which were either eroding or else withdrawing from his like those shrinking clouds.

In the lake itself, just where the falls commenced, rose a low rock-island, faceless like an irregular crystal (in other words, shaped just like any other rock mass hereabouts), and it was close enough to the bank that a strong man might be able to leap onto it. He was not a strong man but he wasn't weak, either. On that day when he had walked away from Reepah's house because they loved each other in a sad and terrible way that made her steal his blue pills until she passed out snoring while the baby cried and shat on the floor, he proposed a contest with himself to see if he could reach that rock with a running lunge—the loser being by definition he who missed and was therefore whirled down the rapids. He landed on the rock, had no sensation of winning, paced a while, turned, jumped back, and missed of course. For an instant, just

before the cold water got him, he saw Reepah's face shining as if in darkness, watching him with hurt black eyes, her lips slightly parted as if she were about to scream in pain and terror. Then the falls had him, and every stone he grabbed slipped out of his hands, and he was thumped and choked and chilled and bruised all the way down. It was a warm and windy day, so when he got out he didn't shiver much. He walked back to Reepah's house, squish-squish-squish. . . .

Montréal, Québec, Canada (1993)

Reepah?

Reepah, why did you come to Montréal with me?

I don't know.

Reepah, today you don't talk to me. So I get afraid you don't like me.

I want drunk.

You don't like me. You only like drunk.

She was clapping all by herself on the balcony, smiling and nodding, and in the street below her people were beginning to jump up and down in the happiness that the music gave them and the musicians were stamping their feet and dry ice smoked in all colors from the stage and the musicians whirled their arms and everyone went: *Aaaaaah!*

Aah, whispered Reepah on the balcony, not looking at him.

The next morning she slept until checkout time, and when he woke her up so that he wouldn't have to pay for another day she cried: *Aaah!* Doan' wake up me! I'm hot. I doan' like you.

Eureka Sound, Ellesmere Island, Northwest Territories, Canada (1988)

Before he ever met Reepah he'd been farther north at summer's end where the ripples in the leads flowed like chevrons, like herringbones. At the edge of a gray ice-islet, slush crumbled steadily into the water with a hissing noise.

In the evening there was a pencil-thick line of clear sky across the fjord, and he could see the white streak of ice in the middle and the white and brown land to the south, amputated miraculously flat and even by the fog-knife, and a steady steam noise came from the weather station, the buildings and petrol towers standing silhouetted in the fog like a great city. A streetlight glowed in front of the dome of the H building, and other lights glowed behind it. A truck rolled across the red and blue pontoon bridge and it was the Inuk handyman again taking him and many friendly soldiers to the dump to feed slops to the wolves, but there was only one fox and one seagull and the soldiers stood with their cameras dangling in disappointment. They were scheduled to fly to Alert on the thirteenth and back to Ottawa on the fifteenth. They worried about the pastries, wishing that they could lose twenty pounds. (Shivering in his tent, he wished that he could gain twenty pounds. It was very gray in there and he could see his breath and his iron-frozen boots hurt to touch.)

He was at the end of a long journey, waiting for the supply plane to come and take him home. He'd been far from the soldiers in a country that began with a lake which was a gray mirror the color of the sky, with nothing else but a low ridge-horizon. From this lake he'd walked up the ridge that was very snowy and white and gently treacherous because he could not see the top of it in the fog (although he kept thinking that he could), and half-frozen tussocks burst out of it, half-soft, but crushed hard and slippery so that his feet glided off and fell hard in an ankle-deep snow-hole, over and over, every few steps. A low ridge of cloud circumnavigated him. Pastel-white mountains pulsed in the yellow light. It was 26°F. Half a month later he'd come back and the lake was frozen. He'd wanted to drink from it before. It was suppertime, and he was thirsty so he chopped a piece out and melted it on his stove. It tasted like burned desolation. He was lonely but not yet thinking of Reepah because he didn't know her, and he wasn't thinking of the lake in Inukjuak because he hadn't

been there; later he'd say to himself: those two lakes were the same. They were one lake, the lake of my wrongdoing. What did I do wrong?

Montréal, Québec, Canada (1993)

I love my Reepah.

I love you, too. I want more beer, please. Thanks for beer. I want boyfriend in Montréal.

I'm your boyfriend in Montréal.

I want it.

Montréal, Québec, Canada (1993)

The night before she went back home she sat with him on the hotel balcony gazing down into nothing and when he asked her if she liked the parade that was going on below them she worked her lower lip and nodded and that was all; she'd virtually given up speaking. Only in the middle of the night when she woke up drunk would she say anything; usually she'd laugh and say: I want to kill myself.—Why? he'd say.—Because I hate myself.—Why?—I don't know.—Then they had another fight because she wanted him to buy a bottle of vodka for her to take back and he'd said okay but since it was Sunday all the *Sociétés des alcools* were closed and the grocery stores didn't have it. She didn't understand, and blamed him. He'd bought her a six-pack of beer as a consolation prize but that wasn't good enough anymore although she'd been drinking nothing else the whole time except for ginger ale; every night at about two or three she'd wake him up by tickling him and then demand one beer, one cigarette, and one ginger ale; all she'd enjoyed doing was going to more sex clubs, getting drunk, and wishing she were beautiful enough to be a stripper too. No, the six-pack wasn't good enough. She kept saying in that new hard and angry voice: *You stupid. You stupid.*—For the first time in the years he'd known her he felt rage. He opened one of the bottles and poured it down the toilet.—Don't call me stupid anymore, he said.

You stupid.

He poured out the second bottle. So it went with the third, the fourth, and the fifth. She looked at the last bottle and her thirsty greed momentarily overmastered her pride, so she said: Okay. I'm sorry okay.

Then a moment later she looked him full in the face and said: You stupid. I hate you.

He poured the bottle out.

She took her suitcase and went into that Montréal midnight with the intention of leaving him forever, and he sat in anguish worrying about her because she didn't have any money; she'd come without money and he'd doled it out this time so she couldn't get crazy drunk and cause more trouble; what would happen to her? But she was free; she didn't want him; she had to make her own way. She came back because she'd forgotten something; then she went out again. Through the window he glimpsed her down on Saint-Denis between the giant grinning green plastic monster heads where the music went whirling crazily like a Russian orgy, singing up over the street of those shouting, jigging heads from which she had previously curled timidly back; she vanished there now.

He stood at the window and saw chess-chested kicking girls and blue-haired green-footed drummers.

An hour later she came back quietly, her face screwed up by weeping, wearing those same low brownish wrinkles he'd seen in the indigo sea salted with ice.—My friend went away, she explained. He said I can't go with him.

Okay, he said. Let's go to sleep.

They turned out the light and he rolled tight against the wall to avoid annoying her. She said very softly: Please don't come to the Inukjuak anymore.

His heart almost exploded. For a moment he could not speak.— I'll go where I want, he said finally.

Please. Please.

Okay. I won't go to Inukjuak anymore.

Then she laughed with relief and touched him and made love to him and said she loved him. That was the worst.

He lay awake thinking how the previous night she'd gotten drunk and said: I want to go to Inukjuak, so I can see my boyfriend in Heaven.

How did he die?

From rifle. He killed himself.

When will you kill yourself?

When I go to Inukjuak.

Early the next morning he took her to the airport and the last he saw of her she was walking away, wiping his good-bye kiss off her mouth with the back of her hand, a gesture he recognized from somewhere, although she'd never unkissed him before; then, as he went to get his bus, he realized that it had been with that same slow forcefulness that she used to squash mosquitoes against the wall of the tent.

In Coral Harbour a boy had asked him why Reepah would meet him in Montréal but not in a northern town.

Maybe the south is more interesting for her because she doesn't live there, he said. Maybe she's ashamed to be seen by other Inuit when she's with a *Qaallunaat**.

Don't worry, the Inuk said kindly. Lots of our girls have ugly boyfriends and we don't mind it. One girl even goes with a man with a wooden leg.

Later still, walking upon the tundra, he remembered Reepah stepping so easily and confidently from rock to tussock, never wetting her toe in any hidden puddle, never needing to look.

---

* White man.

Spirit Horses and Thunder Beings

Plains Indian Dream Drawings

My work was made for me and given to me
by the other world, by the Thunder Beings.
I am compelled to live this way that is not of
my own choosing because they chose me.
                    —Pete Catches (1912–1993),
              Pine Ridge Reservation, South Dakota

During the last third of the nineteenth century and the first third of the twentieth, men of numerous Plains Indian nations—the Lakota, Kiowa, Cheyenne, and others—made sense of their changing lives through drawing. Developing from the traditional pictography that had been painted on hide robes, these artworks grew in new directions through the use of novel materials such as pens, pencils, and the discarded ledger books from trading posts and Army personnel. Plains men often carried small drawing books, and shared them with their cohorts in discussions around the campfire. Primarily historical in nature, the drawings chronicled the traditional male world of hunting and intertribal warfare, as well as the various new cultural calamities that befell Indian peoples during the inexorable conquest of the Great Plains by Euro-Americans.

A smaller number of drawings reveal interior or spiritual landscapes. While individuals in these tribes generally sought solitude to experience the sacred—which was usually revealed in a dream or vision quest—cultural mores dictated that the contents of the vision be shared with others, either through narration, drawing, or reenactment. In his youth, the Lakota holy man Black Elk (1863–1950) experienced a vision in which spirit horses gathered from all directions of the sky, wearing necklaces of elk teeth and buffalo hooves. Some were horned and neighed like thunder. In 1881, Black Elk conducted a public reenactment of the most spectacular portion of his horse-dance vision. The same year, another Lakota artist and holy man named Black Hawk portrayed his own visionary experience of Thunder Beings. These supernatural creatures combined aspects of horse, buffalo, and eagle, all powerful animals to which humans were profoundly connected in Lakota cosmology. Some years later, the artist Kills Two drew a performance of another horse-dance vision. Here, too, horned beings ride spirit horses painted with symbols of hail, lightning, and other celestial phenomena.

The iconography of sacred dreams is widely shared among Plains people. A year after Black Hawk's drawing, the Arapaho artist Frank Henderson also drew a thunder horse ridden by a winged spirit. This spirit offers a medicine shield painted with protective imagery. The power of the vision radiates like lightning to the artist lying prostrate below.

Plains Indian artists continue to record their visionary experiences through painting and drawing, many of them profoundly influenced by the century-old drawings in which their ancestors first used the artistic materials of an alien culture to inscribe intensely personal events.

—Janet Catherine Berlo

Kills Two (1869–1927, Oglala Lakota), *An Indian Horse Dance*, circa 1920. A drawing of ceremonially painted horses and their riders enacting a performance of a sacred dream.

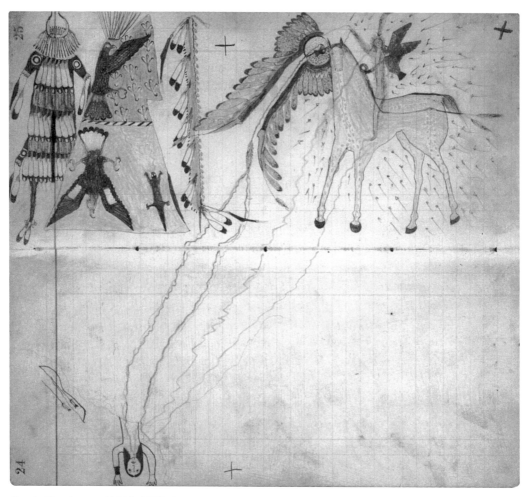

Frank Henderson (1862–1885, Arapaho), *Dream Shield*, 1882. The winged rider of a Thunder Horse presents a feathered shield to the artist. A painted tepee, lance, and horned headdress in the upper left complete the scene.

Artist unknown (Southern Cheyenne), *Dreamer and Visionary Animals*, 1895. Rising from his bed, the dreamer reaches toward a vision portraying a sandhill crane and two animals with stars encircling their necks—one with a ten-point collar, the other a black bear with a four-pointed star.

Artist unknown (Southern Cheyenne), *Vision Seeker and Buffalo Skulls*, 1895. In a portrayal of the sacred Sun Dance, the vision-seeker makes offerings of buffalo skulls to the directions of the world.

Artist unknown (Southern Cheyenne), *Dreamer Rises from Bed to Receive Sacred Images*, 1895. In this visionary scene, when the dreamer rises from his bed to receive his sacred vision, his feet have become eagle talons, and he sees a horned owl. A line of four grasshoppers and a bee fly above the scene.

Artist unknown (Lakota), circa 1880. Lines of power radiate from a spirit figure's hands and feet.

Artist unknown (Lakota), circa 1880. A horned figure holds up a sacred pipe to a spirit horse and a variety of winged beings, including a dragonfly, a swallow, and a hawk.

Black Hawk (circa 1832–1889, Sans Arc Lakota), *Dream or Vision of Himself Changed to a Destroyer and Riding a Buffalo Eagle*, 1880–1881. Black Hawk's elemental drawing of powerful spirit figures seen during a vision conveys the awesome power of the sky-dwellers.

Gesture

—for D.H.

Waiting to want to be physical
day to day seems more arbitrary
than the delegated soothing
and still there exists this difficulty.
Every morning I can wake up
with few exceptions
to see the quiet swaying
of your secondary colors
and in the halting breeze
its amazing equation.
My mural seems less likely
to forget these things.
Anchored, do you feel obliged
to place your hands in the spilling
of relentless adventure
still suspect and subject
to the arresting curiosity
of the intended danger.
Each irritation (sensual
or not) makes, for an instance,
a new announcement of things
never before seen & then understood:
a gesture resting idly for response.

animal speak

This is my favorite place in the park.
In some bays there is slow water
where the least current seems to dissolve
and not implements of produce,
the swarming nutrients,
plants in, on, over: fins and talons
making it a day; "I could very calmly go wild,"
and as I get closer to that thin stalk
of our being's presence, to our inheritance,
the prolonged exploration will be life
because and that is all.
It was this compromise of things,
the adaptation, that baffled our senses
and made identical the transient lives
that we most mutually agree are complications
and only beginnings. There is that consolation:
language: a literary nipple
and someone tells me from the fading
of that certain wilderness
you have forgotten reflection
and the simplicity of these captive failures
is a sad facility.
It rained again yesterday, all day,
the frozen pine appendages

are more evident than before
and as I get better, what was chore
became recognition, has become understanding
and covenant, and finally consciously
with this intervention, I am able
and so a nymph.
I have thought about what it might look like
to see a snowy owl eating like other owls eat;
I know what it should think is edible—
the soft domain would be the erotic
and the chartered erotic near a boundary
of genetically controlled journeys
where we only understand
the significant tutoring of the physical
and the easily understood.
(Eros does not resent the erotic,
nor the intent and regardless
preoccupied with its occasional delivery
I have been a hostage of its diluted caress
and the entire sex of it all
has become a perfect occurrence:
a reckless model, an attraction and a wreckage
with no redeeming affectids.)
Not what we may have chosen
from our seasons of choices.
There is baseball, the Midwest,
and there is animal speak—
any of which may or may not be accessible:
like an estuary and unlike sound.

Field Guide

To these people, the people I know from my books,
I know from my dreams, I am watching you, as if phallic.
Do these things make you feel reduced levels
of already accessible comfort: wet socks?
Who is your audience, are your protectors,
practitioners, and your facilitators of exploding stars,
and have you read carefully the Field Guide
to Hunted Beasts—the makeup and equally attractive
appeasing scents of the dead whale obliged
and wandering. Empty stare by empty stare,
feel the presence of the daunted symphony
immediately dismounted and aggrandizing.
Perhaps the preferred hoisting of one's transparent
and perfectly baleen tongue is less difficult
than we had imagined. Understand a thing—
belly-deep and ascending into the grains
of the damsel world: ironclad protection expelled
and the route to valuable departing indigeni—
above is an eternal gray.

Karlheinz Stockhausen

HELIKOPTER-STREICHQUARTETT

(vom MITTWOCH aus LICHT)

für
Streichquartett,
4 Helikopter mit 4 Piloten und 4 Tontechnikern /
4 Fernseh-Sender, 4 x 3 Ton-Sender /
Auditorium mit 4 Bildschirm-Säulen und 4 Lautsprecher-Säulen /
Klangregisseur mit Mischpult / Moderator (*ad lib.*)

Partitur
für szenische oder quasi konzertante Aufführungen

1992/93

Werk Nr. 68

For string quartet, 4 helicopters with pilots and 4 sound technicians / 4 television transmitters, 4 x 3 sound transmitters / auditorium with 4 columns of televisions and 4 columns of loudspeakers / sound projectionist with mixing console / moderator (ad lib.). Duration: circa 28 minutes.

E arly in 1991, I received a commission from Professor Hans Landesmann of the Salzburg Festival to compose a string quartet.

My first reaction was that I would not write a "string quartet." The "string quartet" is a typical genre of the eighteenth century and, for forty-five years, I had not written symphonies, sonatas, piano concertos, or violin concertos, as such. Each of my works has its own form, its own instrumentation and performance practice.

But then I had a dream: I heard and saw the four string players playing in four helicopters flying in the air. At the same time I saw people on the ground seated in an audio-visual hall; others were standing outdoors on a large public plaza. In front of them, four towers of television screens and loudspeakers had been set up: one on the left, one on the right, and two evenly spaced in between. At each of the four positions, one of the four string players could be heard and seen in close-up. The string players played tremoli most of the time, which blended so well with the timbres and rhythms of the rotor blades that the helicopters sounded like musical instruments.

When I woke up, I felt strongly that something had been communicated to me which I never would have thought of on my own. I did not tell anyone anything about it.

Since I did not have time right after the dream to compose, I wrote and drew several sketches and developed the *Helicopter String Quartet* as the third scene of *Wednesday* from *Light (Licht)*, the cycle of music dramas that I have been composing since 1977. Only in 1992–93 did I find the peace to compose the *Helicopter String Quartet.*

A performance of the *Helicopter String Quartet* is staged in the following way: The four string players enter the auditorium holding their bows (their instruments are already in the helicopters), step onto a podium in front of the audience, and stand in the same order as their transmission via the television monitors and loudspeakers: cellist, violist, second violinist, and first violinist.

The musicians are introduced by the sound projectionist (or a separate moderator), who briefly describes the technical process of the performance to come. At this time, cameras are already transmitting images of the musicians onto the television screens. The string players then walk out, followed by a camera (or several cameras) and their actions are transmitted to the television monitors, until they have—one after the other—arrived at the helicopters and boarded.

Each player seats himself in his helicopter, prepares himself and, from the moment of take-off, his image is transmitted to his assigned television monitors in the auditorium by the camera installed above him. The earth can be seen through the glass cockpit of the helicopter behind each player. First the turbines are ignited. Then, when the rotor blades start to rotate, each musician begins playing his first page, *Aufstieg (Ascent)*. The first line of the score is, therefore, not synchronous.

The *Ascent* lasts about three minutes—until the pilots indicate that they have reached the desired flight altitude, which will vary throughout the performance. The microphone transmission from each helicopter should be such that the sound of the rotor blades blends well with that of the instrument, and the instrument is heard *slightly* louder. To achieve this, at least three microphones per helicopter are necessary: one contact microphone on the bridge of the instrument, one in front of the player's mouth, and one outside the helicopter which clearly picks up the sounds and rhythms of the rotor blades. The twelve microphone signals are transmitted by twelve individual transmitters— possibly via satellite relay—and received at the concert hall, then balanced and mixed at the console.

The players are synchronized by a click-track which is transmitted up to them and which they hear over headphones. Since the four string players usually tremolo in criss-crossing glissandi, I had to draw their pitch lines and curves on top of one another in four colors, so that the melody trajectories could be followed. (The musicians each wear shirts in the colors of the score: first violinist red, second violinist blue, violist green, and cellist orange.)

Throughout the performance, the helicopters circle above the performance venue, individually varying their altitudes. They should fly high enough for the direct sound of the rotor blades to be much softer than that coming from the loudspeakers. During the flight, the face, upper torso, instrument with fingerboard, and all finger movements of the players can be seen close-up on the four columns of the television monitors.

At 21 minutes 37.8 seconds the musicians give the pilots a sign for the *Abstieg (Descent)*, and they continue to play until the rotors have been shut off. Followed by the cameras, they climb out and go with the pilots, one after another, into the auditorium. The string players position themselves as before on the podium, with their pilots next to them. The sound projectionist/moderator introduces the pilots. He then moderates a conversation with each musician, with the pilots, and finally with the audience.

In the autumn of 1993, I sent the score to Professor Landesmann in Salzburg, trembling a little at the possibility of him exploding in dismay. Amazingly enough, his response and that of the general director of the Festival, Dr. Gerard Mortier, were unexpectedly positive, inspired, and courageous. A long series of negotiations followed in order to obtain the necessary equipment from the Austrian army, radio and television stations, and local officials.

Despite their efforts, however, the performance planned for 1994 came to nothing. It was said that the Green political party had announced that it would be intolerable to the environment to allow four helicopters to fly over Salzburg just for the music of Stockhausen, and the general director of Austrian television and radio therefore set such astronomically high rental fees for the equipment that the production became unaffordable.

I then explained this story to Jan van Vlijmen, the director of the Holland Festival. At first, he didn't say anything, but he must have been infected by my dream. After trying several experiments, he told me in April 1995 that the *Helicopter String Quartet* would be definitively performed three times on June 26, 1995 in Amsterdam.

World premiere:
Alouette Helicopters of the Royal Dutch Air Force were flown by a display team called The Grasshoppers.
First helicopter: cellist Rohan de Saram and pilot Captain Erik Boekelman;
Second helicopter: violist Garth Knox and pilot Lieutenant Robert de Lange;
Third helicopter: second violinist Graeme Jennings and pilot Lieutenant Denis Jans;
Fourth helicopter: first violinist Irvine Arditti and pilot Marco Oliver.

Top and Bottom: Members of the Arditti Quartet prepare for take-off.

HELIKOPTER-STREICHQUARTETT

Stockhausen

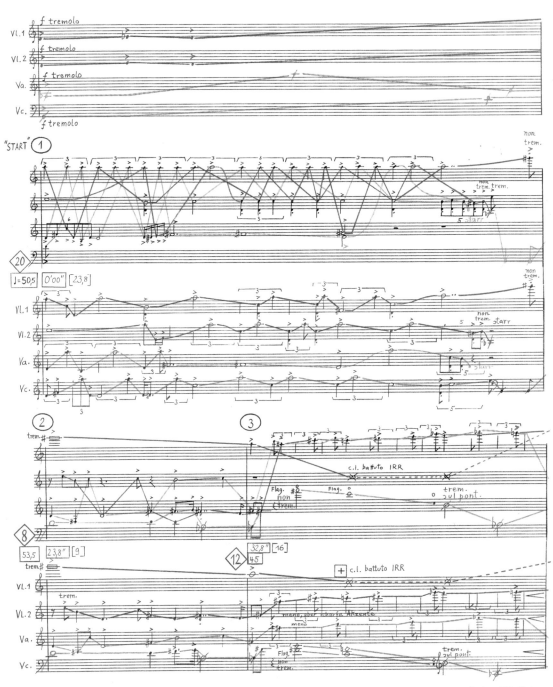

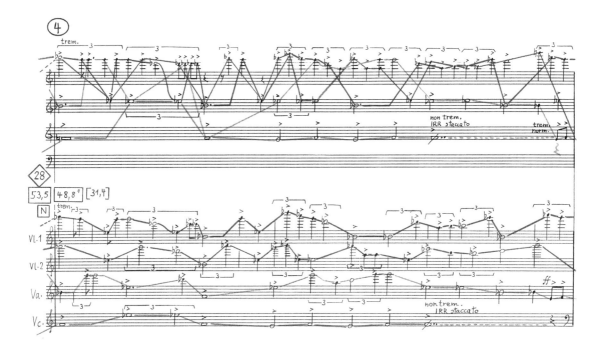

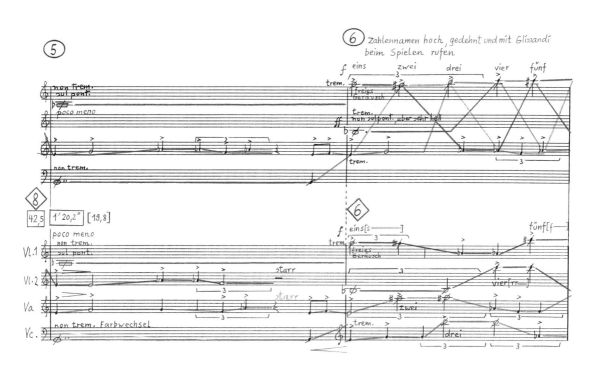

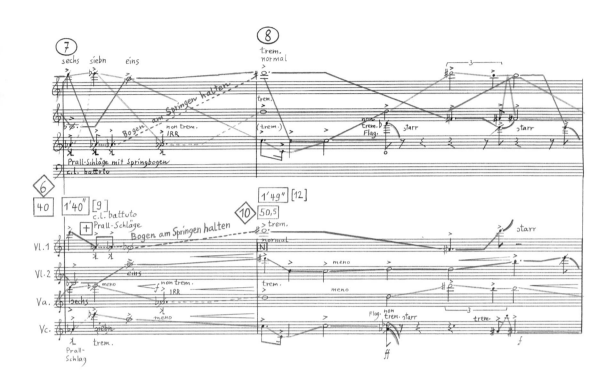

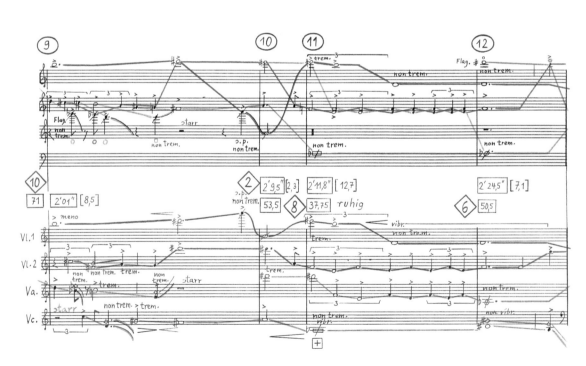

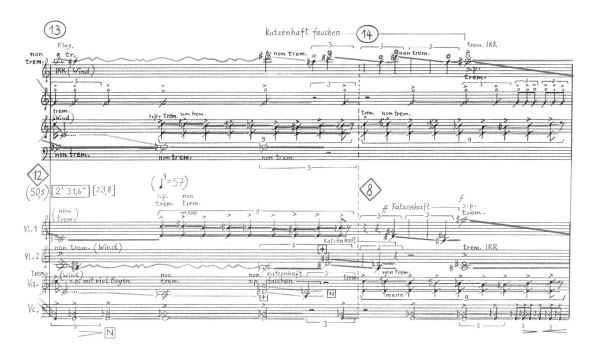

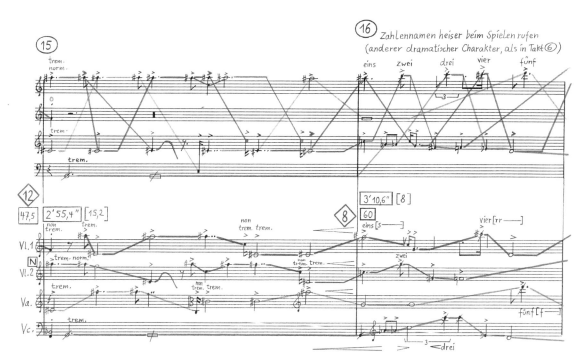

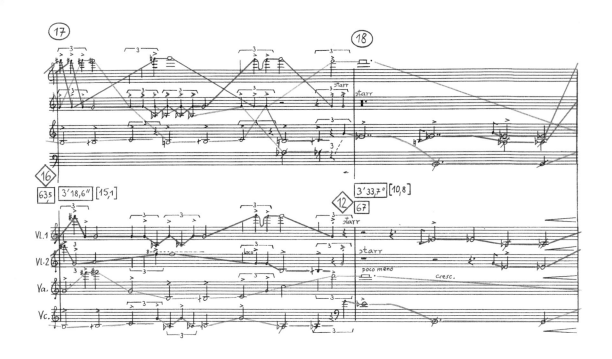

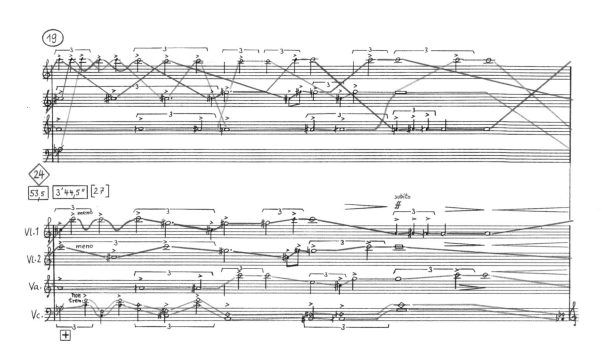

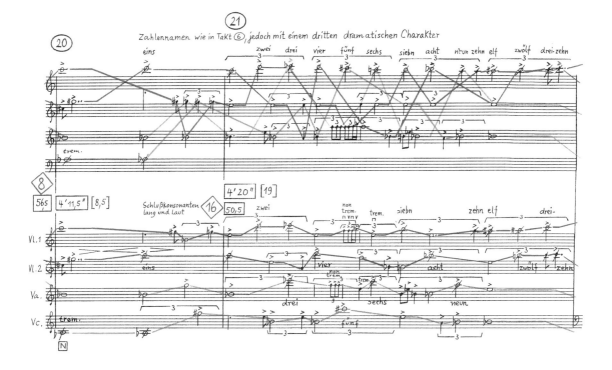

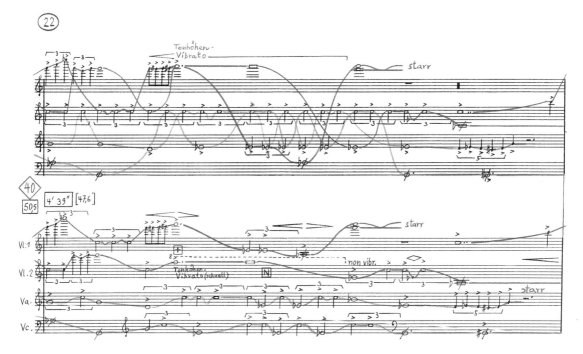

Top: The helicopters in descent. Bottom: The musicians return to their audience and are introduced by Stockhausen (center, in white).

Notes to the Score

World première:

For about 1½ hours during the testing on the day before the world première, I tried out the transmission of the sounds with the rotors running. During this, I filtered the 4 x 3 channels as follows, in order to be able to hear clearly distinguishable timbres in the 4 groups of loudspeakers. I read the frequencies on continually changeable control knobs, so they are approximate.

Filters		Violoncello Voice	Violoncello Instr.	Violoncello Rotor	Viola Voice	Viola Instr.	Viola Rotor	4 VCA Faders Vc.	Va.	Vl. 2	Vl. 1	2nd Violin Voice	2nd Violin Instr.	2nd Violin Rotor	1st Violin Voice	1st Violin Instr.	1st Violin Rotor
high	Hz	12000	10000	10000	8000	9000	10000					6800	5800	5500	6500	6200	5600
	dB	+5	+2,5	-2,5	+4	+2,5	+2,5					+7,5	-3	+2,5	+4	-2	+6
medium	Hz	3000	3000	3000	3000	3400	3000					5500	2000	1200	4000	2500	1200
	dB	+2,5	+4	+5	+4	+3	+8					+6	+5	+5	+7,5	+5	+5
	Hz	250	300	550	800	800	750					800	280	1000	700	450	900
	dB	+6	+8,5	+7,5	+5	+4	+5					+5	+6,5	+4	+3	+5	+6,5
low	Hz	100	140	160	110	/	170					80	120	100	80	110	110
	dB	-7,5	+7,5	+5	-7,5	/	+4					-5	-15	+4	-5	-15	+5
low frequency rejection filter	Hz	20	20	20	20	150	20					200	100	20	100	100	20

Notation

Tremolo is constantly played (more or less dense), with the exception of the places where *non trem.* is indicated. The speed of the *tremoli* should be varied according to the different intervals and durations, to the melodic changes of direction, and **in reaction to the changing rhythm of the rotor blades** including their *accelerandi* and *ritardandi*.

Various simultaneous speeds should be aimed for, and agreed upon. Each player is asked to study the sequence of the single notes and note groups which he has to play **as a continuation** of the preceding player and **as a preparation** for the following instrument playing **the same melodic line**. The upper four staves with crossing glissandi indicate the **relationships** by the four colours. Changing speeds of the *tremoli* should elucidate these **connections**.

Vibrato when indicated is played conspicuously, otherwise *ad libitum*, but not during the glissando.

The overall **volume** should always be full, yet not forced. The work should be rehearsed in such a way that the individual dynamic levels are balanced. Wherever a weak timbre occurs (e. g. *flageolet* sounds, or "wind" noises like *sul ponticello mit viel Bogen / with much bowing* or *katzenhaft "fauchen" / "hissing" cat-like*), the timbres of the other players should be reduced in dynamic level. In certain places, *meno* (= *meno forte*) is prescribed.

In addition, the **sound projectionist** should **amplify** an instrument **more** than the others when it has a weak timbre (in particular at *col legno battuto*):

[+] = amplification more than normal, [N] = amplification again normal.

[23,8] = 23.8 seconds: duration of a section.

An accidental ♯ or ♭ applies only to the **one** note it directly precedes; ♮s serve only as aids to reading.

♯ = ¾ tone higher, + = ¼ tone higher, ♭ = ¼ tone lower, ♭ = ¾ tone lower.

 = noise timbre. Sometimes *sul pont.* or *col legno* is explicitly prescribed. Even when *sul pont.* or *col legno* is not notated, it can be used nonetheless in conjuction with various degrees of bow pressure, distorting the sound but never completely losing the pitch. When a note **without** crossline follows , *sul pont.* or *col legno* is no longer valid.

IRR = irregular (**irregular rhythm**, not too fast: it must be possible to count the individual notes).

 = Glissando in the range prescribed. The glissandi are usually drawn with a straight line, however, may be played with various curves, depending on the duration and context of the glissando.

 = Bouncing-beats: Allow the bow to rapidly bounce *c. l. battuto* (like clicks). The beats should be artificially prolonged with a stiff right wrist in order to produce a quasi regular repetition of attacks **without** *diminuendo*.

[s] = with the instrument, produce a noise similar to a sharp [s].

starr (rigid) = motionless like a doll (in rests).

① = Bar number (blue). On the *Stockhausen-Verlag* **click-track**, the bar numbers are spoken in English and marked by a high click.

⟨20⟩ = Number of beats in the bar (violet). On the *Stockhausen-Verlag* **click-track**, the beats in each bar are counted in German and are marked by low clicks.

The Clever Daughter

After a misericord in Worcester Cathedral

For six hundred years I have traveled
to meet my father. *Neither walking nor riding,*
I have carried your heartbeat to him
across marble, to the sound of singing,
my right hand growing to horn.

Your head droops in a stain of windows
as we come closer. The man who made us—
hare and girl—can barely recognize
the lines his blade left: six centuries
have darkened our shallow footprint.

Clothed and unclothed, we reach him, netted
at his cold feet, our eyes clouding
as he unwraps us. But I release you,
caught under my cloak, your pent flutter
of madness. And we shall see you

run from his hands and vanish,
your new zigzag opening the cornfield
like the path of lovers, the nights of journey
falling from your long ears, my gift to him
given and yet not given.

The Wave

A narrow path runs below an overhanging rock on the northern side of the headland. It is a place where feral goats can often be found sheltering. Battered by waves during storms, the great dark rock face beneath the overhang plunges abruptly and precipitously into the sea. Oedipus and Clius have come to examine the cliff face that Oedipus has carved in his dreams. Oedipus runs his hands over the stone, heaves himself precariously up onto the rock face. Pressing against the roughness of the stone, he examines it, explores it with slow heavy movements like a half-submerged swimmer. Clius declares: "The rock looks like an enormous wave rising up, ready to engulf everything as it falls."

Oedipus is satisfied. "The wave is there, we must somehow prevent it from sweeping us away. One man can't do this alone, we'll need a ship and oarsmen."

Searching with his body in the intrinsic complexity of the cliff for the position of the oarsmen and the boat he feels should be there, he suddenly finds it—he becomes the boat—using his body he outlines it

in the stone. He wants to sculpt it. Clius wants to know why. Because of his dream, because of the three of them, swept away by the sea. Clius cannot see how it is possible to escape the wave.

"We must fashion the cliff," Oedipus says, "and uncover what it is trying to reveal."

"That's an enormous undertaking!"

"We must begin right away. Get some tools. Antigone can help us, she creates excellent bodies and faces."

Exhilarated by the project, Clius goes down to the village to find Antigone and ask the fishermen for some tools. Left alone, Oedipus continues to explore the rock, to familiarize himself with the wave. Sometimes he slips and cuts his hands. It is almost a pleasure to mark the cliff with his blood for the wave is there as well as within him; just as the sea was, when he was lost, contemplating it. But the sea was compliant as he gazed at it contentedly, immersed in its featureless immensity. Not so here where everything is hard, unequivocal, like the fishermen of Corinth he loved so much when he was a boy.

Remembering his early childhood, he sees himself in the port amongst the giant-like sailors and enormous ships. Queen Merope holds his hand as they go to the quay to buy fish. When she comes to a ship whose mast has been ripped off in a storm, she stops. The fishermen had managed to bring the ship back, the catch intact, for the fish glisten in the hold. Merope is horrified when she sees the damage inflicted by the sea, but the master of the vessel has survived many storms and demonstrates how he steered her through the swell. Up, down, constantly on the lookout for the next wave and, more importantly, keeping a cool head. He laughs in a self-assured manner, and today Oedipus finds comfort in the recollection of his merry laughter and steadfastness.

Their first obstacle is Antigone, who refuses to help them. She finds the project—so attractive to the two men—absurd, preposterous. She is not prepared to give up her work in the village to return to her life as a beggar. The next day, Clius goes down to the port and Oedipus begins the task of carving the wave alone.

Antigone has a dream where she sees a child standing at the foot of the immense cliff, his diminutive tools in his hands. It is Oedipus, full of confidence, calling to someone. Despite the howling wind she eventually catches his cries: *sister, sister!* She wakes in tears. It is the middle of the night. She opens the door, the moon is bright. Dressing hurriedly she runs to the headland. She longs to throw herself into Oedipus's arms, but he and Clius are asleep and she does not want to wake them. Instead she lies down next to them, thinking that she can refuse her father's request to contribute to this colossal task, but how can she do that to her brother, a brother struck down by misfortune, whom she followed, pursued, when he left Thebes?

The men wake up to find Antigone preparing a meal. Without any explanation, Clius hands her some tools. When they attain the foot of the rock, Oedipus shows her what to do. It soon becomes apparent that Antigone is the most skilled at doing detailed work. She will not need to beg, for when the villagers hear about Oedipus's project, they offer to feed them while the work is in progress in the belief that the wave will protect their ships.

From morning to night they hew the cliffs, only pausing at midday to bathe and eat. The stone is hard but, as their arms and hands strengthen, Oedipus has to warn them not to strain the rock. The wave exists. It is just a question of helping it to emerge. Although Clius and Antigone cannot see it yet with their eyes, they feel its presence beneath their hands. Whenever they lose confidence, they call Oedipus over. He permits his hands to glide over the stone. He listens to it, tastes it with his lips and tongue, flattens his body against it. "Let yourselves be guided, transported by it." Then they are reassured that the wave exists. It has entered their lives with a vengeance, submerged them, and might submerge them again, but the knowledge does not prevent them from feeling alive.

They begin to feel the wave, but not the ship. Oedipus has located its position, but dares not attempt to give it a shape. Storms and erosion have blackened the stone. As they dig into it, it becomes white and the foaming outline of the wave emerges bright on the dark background of the cliff face.

While he is working, Oedipus sometimes releases two or three melodious notes. The other two hope he is about to sing, but no, and this saddens Antigone. So she stops working and launches into a sea chantey she was in the habit of singing in Thebes, a time so remote it is hard to believe it ever existed. When they hear her, Clius's hands and feet dance on the narrow path and Oedipus takes out his flute and plays. There should be a song to follow but either Oedipus cannot or is reluctant to sing and they become dejected.

Leaving the other two to work on the wave, Oedipus marks the outline of the ship in the rock, its slender stem pointing toward the yawning chasm. Already the wave is beginning to curve back over the poop. The boat takes its rhythm from the exertions of the three oarsmen. There is a man standing behind them at the rudder. The ship plunges into the depths. As her prow begins to right itself, she skips under the wave. It is a breathtaking spectacle and only when it is certain that she will overcome the obstacle does relief set in. The wave looks invincible but the more subtle craft uses its adversary's incredible strength to elude it.

The outline is done. Oedipus asks Antigone to concentrate on the oarsmen and the man at the helm, as her hands are delicate enough to do this without disturbing the natural lines of the stone. Oedipus will fashion the boat to resemble either those he knew in Corinth which sailed the high seas, or those from here described to him by Clius. But this one will be sharper, similar to those first shapes that emerged one day from the sea. As he sculpts, his thoughts are on the Sphinx who, like the wave, was infinitely more powerful than he. He used her strength to dispose of her, plunging the knife of his replies into her abstruseness.

The Sphinx faded in the same way that waves do. He accepted responsibility, embraced his victory, the queen and the kingship, oblivious to the fact that another wave, this one much higher, was already rising up in front of him ready to sweep him away. Not so these oarsmen. They will know that this is not the only wave, that it is not solely a question of conquering it but that the full force of the storm with its succession of waves will have to be faced before they reach port.

For a while Antigone scrutinizes the oarsmen and pilot Oedipus has outlined and then gets down to work. Something is troubling her, she feels Oedipus has made a mistake, that he has not followed the invisible line of the rock. She calls him over, makes him touch the stone and feel the real position of the oarsmen. They are not pitched forward, their heads bowing beneath the spray. They are at the apex of their effort, bodies and heads pulled back, exhaling the air from their lungs, eyes fixed on the enormity of the wave before them and on the pilot, his valor, skill, his voice even, an inspiration to them.

At dusk, Oedipus tells his companions to go and rest, but he works on for several more long hours and it is already night when he joins them. White, slim, graceful, the stone ship has emerged triumphant, projected forward like an arrow by the wave.

Antigone focuses on the three sailors. With powerful strokes, they row, preserving their energy, for they still have a long struggle ahead of them. These oarsmen, she thinks, are the three of us, battling to help the cliff bring the wave into the world; as Oedipus says: helping the cliff in its act of creation. The first is Clius: handsome, intent, but without that ferocious expression, that cruel hunted smile which appears all too frequently. With those magnificent eyes, his mouth forming a smile of defiance, he watches the pilot and not the wave as he gives rhythm to this dance in the storm. The androgynous body of Antigone sits behind him, the natural lines of the rock creating a head of foaming hair that floats in the wind. Her face she cannot do, for she is unaware of who she is or what the rock wants. Oedipus can do it if he can.

Oedipus who in a dream compelled her against her will to join them on this cliff, calling her *my sister*, in that harrowing way. Unable to bear it any longer, she picks up her tools and runs off.

Oedipus, who has been smoothing over the front of the boat, stops, and for some time explores the face of the first oarsman with his hands. He calls Clius over. Clius is overwhelmed, at once full of admiration and fear. So this is how Antigone sees him, how she wants to see him. Angry, he says: "This is what she wants me to be like."

"She has made you as you are," declares Oedipus. They return to their work—Clius, rejecting the statement and yet deeply moved by it. Oedipus moves on to the second oarsman. He feels the stone, examines it, and with light blows begins to chisel the face. By the time evening falls, Clius cannot see well enough to continue. He calls Oedipus, goes over to him, speaks; but Oedipus is so absorbed in his work that he does not hear, just as he did not hear on the headland when he was lost in contemplation of the sea.

Exhausted, Clius leaves. He lights the fire and prepares a meal. As Oedipus does not return, he lies down and falls asleep. At dawn he opens his eyes long enough to see blind Apollo glowing above him. The light radiating from the god is weak, for he is broken by his night's work. Dropping off again, Clius feels him lie down next to him.

Two days spent resting in the village and Antigone is pleased to return to the headland. The sun has dispersed the mist; the fishermen, with their red sails billowing in the head wind, have set out to sea. Before joining the men, Antigone goes to lay flowers at the statue of the local god—protector of the village. The statue has been marked by time and rain; it has been rubbed smooth by the many hands that have touched it, the hands of people hoping for protection or a cure. She can just make out a head rising delicately from the plinth which she presumes represents the trough between two waves or the furrow of a field. The head is faceless and yet there is the hint of a smile in its shape—humble, self-contained like the village. This eternal little

rustic god will always exist. The place where he stands will be sacred long after the wave, through the action of the weather and storms, has crumbled into the sea, as Oedipus knows it will. As she knows Oedipus wants it to.

The onset of autumn is beginning to color the leaves; recent rains have turned the fields and hills green again. From the cliff, they can hear shepherds calling and dogs barking. Antigone can feel the earthenware jar pressing on her neck and shoulders as she ascends the coastal path. It weighs down on her, giving her strength while at the same time helping her keep her balance. She knows how her body must respond beneath its burden; she feels it guiding her, encouraging her. She thinks: *my body is made to carry, one day it will carry a child*, and she smiles to herself. Placing her pitcher at the entrance to the cave, she sees Oedipus steadily and confidently walking into the setting sun. As he reaches the edge of the abyss, she is about to shout a warning when he stops, offering up his body and face to the rays. He is practically naked, still young, still handsome, bearing the invisible yet ever-present scars of misfortune and exhaustion. She admires his strong, lean body, but has difficulty connecting this picture to the wonderful mental image she had of him as a child, when laughter, speech, and ever-changing expressions constantly animated his face.

He has heard her and half turns the way he used to when she came into his room in Thebes. She is a small girl running toward him. Kneeling to be the height she once was, she clasps him around the knees and waist as she kisses him. She snuggles up to him—she must, for it is the other one, Ismene, who is always petted without seeking to be. Antigone has to do something, to ask, before she is noticed. Ismene just waits. Maybe she does call out, does ask—but who knows since even she does not know why it happens. Ismene may be the more skilled, but it was she, Antigone, whom he summoned with his heart in Thebes; it was she who heard him. She buries her young girl's head in the hollow of Oedipus's hip. He catches her by the waist and with amazing strength

and ease lifts her in his outstretched arms. Head and torso arched back, he raises her above him. To Antigone's astonishment and shame, she hears herself gurgling with delight like a small child. How could she be so self-indulgent? Oblivious to this, Oedipus twists her round and presents her to the sun, dedicating her to him. Unable now to look at her as he used to, he entrusts her to the gaze of this other living body. Once he has set her down, she tries to recapture the feeling of her tiny hand slipping into the great warmth of his. But her hand has grown, her lips too: she is tall. With agonizing regret, she kisses the scarred, callused hand which has shrunk in relation to hers and which will never again be the giant hand she loved. He strokes her hair and looking up, she receives full face the imperious glare of the sun as if it were his.

She moves down into the shade and cool light of the cliff. She sees the brilliant white ship emerging from the gigantic rock and how, over the last two days and nights, Oedipus has personified his daughter Antigone in the stone. Around her forehead and long hair, whipped by the wind, the line of the stone has formed a crown of foam. So this is how Oedipus sees her, how he wants her to see herself, infused with a beauty quite unlike Jocasta's or Ismene's. A vibrant, determined beauty, suffused with confidence. Although this face understands the power of the wave's crushing weight, it remains undaunted. The stone wanted it to look enlightened and solid, like the body she herself has carved and is astounded to discover. Oedipus has accentuated the bold outline of the body which could belong to a strong boy or a slim young girl, more intrepid than the young girls of Thebes. Their bodies united in their efforts to survive, her body adds its muscle to that of the other two oarsmen. Oedipus has achieved this effect through the amazing, unsmiling face he has sculpted, in which everything concentrates on physical exertion and correct breathing. And yet, like the village's little worn god, her whole head and body have been imbued with a smile, the transparent light of which emanates directly from the stone. What she finds so striking and what moves her more than anything else in this outline born of

Oedipus's vision is its clarity. And this is how—through her confusion, her uncertainty—he has loved her with his soul and with his hands. She embraces the hidden smile he has given her, here in the stone. She feels more reconciled to herself, feels that maybe one day, as Diotima has told her, she will at last truly become Antigone.

Oedipus and Clius advance down the path together. Oedipus is looking tired and thinner. But he refuses to rest, despite the colossal work he has just completed. He pauses in front of the second oarsman and runs his hand over his work as far as the curve of the brow. With a brief smile, he says: "It's good." He looks dazed, as though, having just woken up, he is still attempting to separate what the day has in store from what belongs to the subterranean world of sleep.

Antigone leans over, takes his hands and kissing them says: "Thank you."

A tender, teasing expression appears on Oedipus's face: "Now you have found the shapeless little god's smile." She is speechless. How does he know? He chuckles as though he were saying: *I know, I know who you are, much better than you ever will.*

They resume their work. Oedipus finishes the boat which bounds upward, propelled more by the booming trough of the waves than by the oarsmen. Clius works on the crest of the wave that must turn and fall back into the depths. The ladder he made is not high enough, so he brings a ship's rope from the port, attaches it to a protruding rock and lowers himself to within reach of his work. Antigone is frightened when she sees him swinging above the void. Sometimes, when she raises her head, she sees him watching her with that strange smile— part tender, part ironic—on his lips. The smile of a man who knows all there is to know about women and what they are really like when they give themselves to a man who loves or desires them, as Clius has so often done, and still does—for they have told her so in the village. He knows everything she does not know. What Jocasta knew so well, as each one of her movements revealed. It gave them their warmth, their

essence, and that unusual majestic quality. She is not like that and never will be. She is just tall, thin Antigone whom that man up there on his rock—with his handsome, anxious face and dancer's body—respects and desires with an unwieldy longing. She begins to sculpt the third oarsman, aware of Clius's gaze following each of her body's movements beneath her dusty, worn clothes. When the sensation ceases, she raises her eyes and sees he is absorbed in his work, no longer preoccupied by her. Relieved at first, she feels a dull, penetrating grief the longer it continues. Then, she too becomes engrossed in the shapes her chisel is creating. The third oarsman is Oedipus, not the one she once knew— Zeus incarnate to the citizens of Thebes and to Jocasta's eyes and body. She wants to carve him as he was before that time, the savage boy—conqueror and victor—who beat the Sphinx with his sharp but youthful intelligence, who rode the first wave only to fall at the next. He who, with the help of the others, must now avoid being drowned.

She is oblivious to the passing of time, only half-aware that evening is approaching, when she hears a shout. Clius has detached himself, slid down the rope and is dangling high above her; he drops without losing his balance, audaciously and effortlessly landing next to her on the narrow path. Examining her work, he bursts out laughing: "Still the little girl in love with the once handsome Oedipus!"

She is offended: "Is he not still handsome?"

"Yes. In a way. But he's not as you see him, any more than you are still how he's represented you."

He pulls on a tear in her dress, making it worse; as Ismene used to whenever she was caught in the kitchen helping the servants.

"Look at you! Filthy, dusty, scruffy! Covered in fleas no doubt. The village is crawling with them!"

"And what about you! Aren't you dirty at the end of a day's work?"

"Yes, but I do as I'm told, especially when the master is his usual silent self, but you are his daughter, his younger sister!" Then instantly: "In a way, Antigone, you are beautiful, unique, fortunately you are quite

unaware of it. Maybe I'm in love with you, sometimes I think I am, but that's not what we're here for. Come, you need food and rest. Leave the old fool to kill himself if that's what he wants. He'll find his own way back."

She follows him, so upset that she leaves her tools behind. She turns back and sees the one he called the old fool bent over his work, completely absorbed in it.

She runs and catches up with Clius. The evening is no different from any other. He lights the fire; she prepares the meal and washes as best she can, for there is very little water. She changes into her other patched and darned dress which is relatively clean. It is late, too late she feels to go back to the village, so Clius rearranges the cave for her. Oedipus returns. The moon is high and casts a diffuse light over his tall frame and dusty clothes and hair. He is tired and preoccupied. Never has he seemed so tall or so noble as today, in his poverty and weariness. How could Clius have had the gall to call him an old fool?

She tries to eat, but suddenly disheartened and overcome by an unexpected rush of nausea, in full view of the two men she leaps up and, filled with shame at her groans, vomits behind a rock.

She returns to the fire. How magnificent, how complete—like the rocks—they are. She is acutely conscious of her fragility, her pain, her vulnerability. How she wishes Jocasta were there so that she could rest her cheek against her beautiful shoulder. If only Ismene were not so far away, or if she could be in the safety of Diotima's company. But first they must finish the wave, and that is difficult, too difficult for someone like her, as soft and malleable as the earth itself. She is weeping, shedding bitter tears of exhaustion, then honeyed tears, as they put their arms about her and lay her down in the cave.

When she wakes, the fire is lit and the food ready. Clius appears and today he is in a good mood: "Come on. We have a surprise for you." Like an excited child she rushes out. Oedipus is mixing flowers and herbs into two pitchers that Clius has filled with water from the spring.

The water smells exquisite, its fragrance familiar. It is what Jocasta used to call her enchanted water. So many plants were needed for its preparation and an expert hand to pick them, that she rarely used it. But whenever she did, she would feel invigorated and attractive. As a treat, the little girls would be given a few drops in their cupped hands to pat over their faces and necks. So it was Oedipus who prepared the enchanted water, but this time he has done it for her. The men leave. Very slowly, she pours the contents of the pitchers over her head, as she had watched Jocasta do, and massages the streaming water into her whole body, starting and jumping and squealing with pleasure as she did when she was young. Then, shivering, she stretches out in the sun totally relaxed, looking up at the sky, losing herself in it, the aroma permeating her whole being.

She stands up and dresses, experiencing a sensation of lightness, the like of which she has not felt for a long time. She joins the others; the meal is ready and tastes good. She eats with a hearty appetite. To have picked so many plants, Oedipus and Clius must have set out before dawn. After a hard day and a short night, the one guiding the other, they had carried out this difficult task to assuage that moment of incomprehensible pain she had experienced the previous evening. Clius is watching her. With an almost imperceptible gesture he apologizes, indicating that that is how he is, as she knows only too well. They consider the work to be done over the next few days; Oedipus asks her to concentrate on the master of the boat. "Do the outline and I'll carve the rest. When you've done the pilot, the third oarsman will be easier." She is reluctant to abandon the third oarsman, but realizes they have already discussed it between themselves, man to man. Why? Why not? She agrees—she will do the master next. She can sense they are pleased. They must have debated at length.

They return to their work. Antigone searches to find the pilot's position. Suspended from his rope, Clius becomes increasingly frustrated with the crest. He loses his grip, then his footing. The rope

swings him vertiginously along the cliff face and he lets out a fearful laugh. Antigone shouts up to him to climb back up and rest. Instead he climbs down, lands near her, and sits down exhausted. Oedipus joins them, picks up his flute, and plays an ancient tune which at one time could be heard on feast days throughout the poorer districts of Thebes. The enchanted water is taking effect, Antigone feels carefree, scented and confident; she sings and Clius periodically joins his voice to hers. He leaves, no doubt going back to the cave to sleep, and this gratifying moment comes to an abrupt end.

Antigone scans the stone where the pilot will surface. She was right, the outline marked out by Oedipus is not large enough; it is out of proportion in relation to the oarsmen. The stone cries out for different dimensions. He had not detected the majestic sweep that leads up toward the top; he could not see the shadow where the rock straightens, nor the expression of hope on the faces of the oarsmen enlarging it. But to where? Confronted by the stone she is alarmed to discover that even her new delineation is too restrained. The master of this craft must be tall, extremely tall. The discovery of this lack of moderation scares her. She runs over to Oedipus: "The stone is turning the pilot into a giant!"

"Well then, the stone must be right."

She is on the verge of tears: "But I've never seen a giant."

"Yes, you have. Think back, everyone was a giant to you when you were small."

She works on the contours and proportions of the body. Once again the enchanted water works its magic, making her lighthearted and self-assured. The outline begins to take shape. The pilot seen in profile will be tall but not too tall—like Oedipus and Jocasta were in the sacred kingdom of Thebes. She is satisfied but it is time she returned to the village. The fire in front of the cave has gone out. Clius is waiting for her: "I'll walk down with you." He looks preoccupied.

Half-hidden behind the clouds, the sun casts an uneven light over the coastline. Boats are returning to port, their sails hoisted, the sailors

resting on their oars. Clius holds her back: "I have to talk to you." A thrill of anticipation and wild hope races through her. He goes on: "I can't do the crest, I'll never manage it." She cannot disguise her deep disappointment. Fortunately, Clius has not understood. Angry, he grabs her roughly by the arm, hurting and alarming her: "That wave is Oedipus's folly and mine. I've managed to make it rise, but it must turn and fall back into the sea. But I can't, there is no way I can hold it back. Do you understand? It will crash onto the headland and drown us all."

"But Clius, it's made of stone."

"That's what you think, Antigone—but let me tell you, the wave's impossible to control. Completely impossible."

She is appalled when she sees the full implication of what he has said. They must find an immediate solution. Disengaging her arm, she asks: "Do you want me to take over?"

"You, hanging from a rope! Never, never!"

Delighted, she murmurs: "Why?"

"For my sake," he replies.

She is conscious of her blushes as elation replaces delight. Then the significance of Clius's words hits her: "You want Oedipus to finish the wave?"

Decisively, he replies: "Yes."

"My blind father hanging from a rope!"

"He must. Otherwise the wave will engulf us all. You must tell him!"

This last directive fills her with dread and she protests: "Why me?"

With a smug yet disarming grin, he adds: "For my sake." He has turned and gone, bounding up the slope like a goat or the dancer he is. He returns to the headland, lights a fire, gives Oedipus his food and sees to his needs as he does every night; dances perhaps, if the stars are auspicious.

At the port all the villagers are there. The fishermen are bringing in their catch and sorting out their nets; the women are calling in their children for the evening meal. They have seen Antigone returning from

the headland and greet her. Many have already taken her into their homes but tonight it is Chloe's turn. She is the wife of an old fisherman; she lost a son at sea and two newborn babies. Her face is serene and dignified; she was obviously a girl and then a woman who enjoyed a good laugh and who still does when the mood of the sea allows her to.

Antigone asks an old sailor: "What's it like in a storm?"

He finds the question amusing and, scratching his head, replies: "Difficult to say when you're in it rather than on the outside."

Chloe has made room in her bed for Antigone, who falls asleep in the warm, strong, reassuring presence of her body. Next day, when the men have left, Chloe gives her a basket filled with flowers, fruit, and three fish wrapped in leaves. "I'll take back the basket when you've finished with it." Antigone thanks her and bending her knee gives her the curtsy of a Theban princess. Chloe beams and a network of delicate wrinkles flickers across her face. She goes into her house and watches Antigone climb the hill, her basket on her head, agile, barefoot, her sandals in her hand.

When Antigone arrives at the cave, Oedipus is seated at the top of the headland, his face to the sun and sea. She remembers how it was there that she shattered that unbearable state of ecstasy he had plunged into.

As she approaches him, he says without needing to turn round: "Antigone"; just that: "Antigone." It is enough, for in the syllables of her name she senses that he understands and loves her for what she is. Returning from the poverty of the village, her clothes are impregnated with the scent of Chloe's flowers and the smell of fried fish.

She sits next to him: "Clius can't finish the wave. He says he won't be able to make it curve back and fall into the sea."

"I know."

She is greatly relieved at not having to elaborate. He is covering up his eyes with the large white band he wears to protect them while he is working. When he has finished, he says: "Tell Clius to prepare the rope."

Clius appears and helps Oedipus into his working clothes. Antigone heats up the fish. The men eat; she had thought she would not be able to swallow a thing but, on an order from her father, she forces herself and feels better. Clius wraps a sheepskin around Oedipus's waist to soften the contact with the rope and binds the knot with cloth. He did not go to these lengths for himself. Antigone checks the knots. She wants to help him but Oedipus tells her to carry on as usual. The moment she has gone, he starts to shake and his teeth chatter.

Clius is concerned: "Will you be all right going down?"

"Yes. It's nerves. The abyss. Vertigo! You understand."

He understands. Slowly, he lowers Oedipus.

Oedipus searches for footholds in the cliff. Antigone can hear him cutting into the rock in front of where the wave must begin to unfurl. She listens to the normal, regular beat of Oedipus's hammer and feels half-reassured. Up above, Clius calls out his instructions. Suddenly she hears the notes of the flute demanding: *Bring me back up!* Oedipus clambers along the rock face. A piercing shout! He has slipped and fallen before Clius could take up the slack. He swings across the cliff face, his body smashing into the protruding rocks. He is still clutching his tools and making vain attempts to find a hold in the ridge; but each time he is frustrated by the overhang. He cries out, howls in anger, just as he must have done when he killed Laius and his guards. Clius will never be able to bring him back up alone; she must go and help. She passes beneath Oedipus, now groaning even though the slack of the rope has improved. She turns and stops, stunned. Writhing at the end of the rope, shouting between each spasm, Oedipus is sick several times. He has given up trying to find a foothold, he just dangles miserably from the rope like a stained object. His vomit runs down the stone and falls onto the path. She flees, too petrified to look round. As she runs up the slope, she hears that his groans have turned to shouts of rage. He still has not found a foothold but at least Clius has managed to help him right himself. Breathless and overwhelmed by the sounds coming from

Oedipus, she stops and realizes that they are different again—more like those he used to make when he was out training with his guards in the courtyard of the palace, when Jocasta, as she watched him from the balcony, would chase away her daughters if she surprised them trying to catch a glimpse of him in the frenzy of the fight.

Antigone has reached the headland; Oedipus is silent. It is not yet night but the sky is jet black. She rushes over to Clius who, having secured the rope around a rock, is flat on his stomach on the ground. Leaning over the abyss totally engrossed, he does not see her approaching. He does not look anxious, not even concerned—she has never seen him look like this. He seems drunk. She touches his shoulder, he turns and shouts: "He's done it!" She does not understand what he means; she has come to help but he does not need it. Then she also leans over and sees that Oedipus has cleared the protruding rock and found himself some deep footholds. His back against the overhang, he is chiseling with rapid, powerful strokes. "Everything is fine," says Clius. "Go and take shelter. A storm is on the way."

She does not want to take refuge. Like him she wants to watch, she wants to know: "How did he do it?"

"He turned on the offensive and that was it."

"I saw him being sick."

"There was a sudden change," says Clius, "and now nothing can stand in his way. Listen. It's as though the wave itself were carving."

It is true, the rhythm of his blows is not patient and restrained but relentless, sending chunks of stone flying out in all directions, as though the sea had unleashed its energy or the storm were hurtling toward them. In the distance—the rumble of thunder and now the first drops of rain. The storm breaks. The waves roar up to the cliff and crash down again. Sheets of rain hammer down. Frightened, Antigone shouts: "Come up, come up quickly!" Oedipus's cries of elation ring out to be answered by Clius's ecstatic laughter. Then Clius roars out between two claps of thunder: "The wave's rising! It's rising! He's going to force it,

turn it!" Oedipus pulls himself up onto the end of the rock and sits astride it, both hands free to wield his enormous tools. Blinded by the rain and lightning, Antigone can still hear the rock shattering beneath the frantic blows of chisel and hammer.

He is like a giant striking, molding the cliff. Clius laughs, yelling out messages as he regularly adjusts the tension of the rope. Oedipus's jubilant peals of laughter rise in reply. Antigone feels crushed by the torrential rain, wind, and crashing thunder. Lightning flashes; will it strike Oedipus? No—it hits an enormous tree on the shore that bursts into flames—the eye of the storm has not yet come.

Clius hollers into her ear: "He's done it, the wave's fallen back!" Afraid and chilled to the bone, she does not understand. Clius is now virtually naked, whooping with glee as he continues to maneuver the rope. Antigone knows the sea will have washed away Oedipus's vomit; it will have gone, leaving no trace of that terrible moment which she alone experienced.

A few rays of hazy sunlight pierce the retreating clouds but already a second squall is on its way. Another clap of thunder, but at least the rain no longer blinds her. She leans over to warn Oedipus. Sparks shoot out around the massive shoulders and head with its shrouded eyes. With deadly accuracy, he is striking into the base of the overhanging rock, forcibly wrenching out the wave, turning it under him and sending it back, furious and foaming, to unfurl into the sea. Can Clius see this? He does not seem to find it alarming, quite the opposite: he is flushed, elated, and when Oedipus calls out in his deep resonant voice, he echoes him with all the power of his own lungs. He turns toward her, compelling her to look, to understand, to copy him and lend the full power of her own voice to what is taking place. She cannot refuse. Sibyl or pythoness, reduced to no more than a voice, forcing from her body her loudest cries, she screams back in response to Oedipus, or Zeus, as he and the sea roar out together. And in the meantime with his hallowed tools and magnificent shoulders, he makes the cliff quake.

The rain increases; flashes rend the sky and bolts strike in several places. Trees burn on the cliff and she thinks: "Let's hope the fishermen are back." She has become disoriented by the turbulence of the elements.

All of a sudden, Clius strains at the rope and shouts: "All is well; he's coming back up."

Two massive hands grip the edge of the cliff, brace themselves, and instantly the giant is there, still surrounded by sparks. Laughing, he snaps the rope attached to his waist and with one superb movement he is up, towering above her. Handsome, blind, radiant, exuberant even. How he glows, iridescent, as with a sweeping and careless gesture he throws his enormous tools into the sea.

Standing before her with arms open wide, his mouth, brow, and—concealed behind their white band—eyes radiate his consummate goodness. She runs to him, wraps her arms around his leg, then rests her forehead against his mighty knee, level with her mouth. Cheerful or tearful, what bliss to sink to your knees, to catch hold of and kiss those ankles and bare, wounded feet. Will this giant grow any more? Leap into the sea, be taken up into the sky by a blazing chariot drawn by fiery horses?

The rain is still falling and she is cold. *We need a fire*, she thinks, *they must be as frozen as me.* Perhaps the body she no longer dares look at is by now lost high up in the clouds. She turns and takes off through the torrential rain like a hunted animal. She gets back to the cave and tries to revive the fire. It is not easy and the billowing clouds of smoke sting her eyes. At last a flame. Frantically she starts throwing onto it all the wood Clius has stored. The torrents of rain make the fire sizzle, but nevertheless it springs to life. The wind drives the flames into the shallow cave. She flattens herself against the rock, convinced that she will burn to death. She is so numbed by fear she cannot even scream. All is well; Clius is there. Leaping over the flames, he kicks back the fire and rolls the logs out of the cave. She thinks he is going to pick her up and carry her but all he does is clear a path and lead her out, helping her jump over the embers. He tries to make her rest on a tree stump but she refuses. After what she has just been through she must have fire, more fire, with its incredible light. She picks up the logs Clius rolled out to save her and throws them into the flames. Stunned at first, Clius is seized with the same impulse, the same ebullient rage. They throw onto the blazing pile all the wood so carefully amassed since they have sheltered there. The heat and great flames feed their exuberance and shield them from the sea mist creeping along the headland.

Had Oedipus not taken over, thinks Antigone, *the uncontrollable wave would now be engulfing us, separating us.* Through the thickening smoke and mist she can just make out Oedipus. Now his normal height, he is standing a short distance away in his rain-soaked clothes. He looks exhausted and yet she can still detect in his features traces of his giant's gentleness and euphoria. He stands there, silent. She would like to run over to him but, like Clius, she feels she must respect his need for solitude. She takes a few logs from the fire and starts to prepare some food; for, whatever the heart might feel, the body continues to make its unrelenting demands.

Oedipus draws nearer, picks up his flute, and plays one of those simple, elementary tunes he is so fond of, reminiscent of the sea. Then his voice rises, weak, timid, shaky, like that of a child's. On hearing it, Clius weaves around singer and fire the exquisite movements of one of his dances. Antigone understands neither words nor phrases in Oedipus's song, but she senses a feeling of jubilation beyond its actual meaning. She would like to glorify it like Clius but alas, she is not lithe, she is earthbound. Neither does she have his passionate nature, nor his ability to improvise movements; so she goes and stands next to her father and is content to follow the inflections of his voice that seem as though rusted after a long winter.

Oedipus falls silent. Clius, swept along by his enthusiasm, yells: "You turned it, you bent it back!" Oedipus chuckles and Clius rushes at him, embraces him, swamps him with whoops of glee and they end up collapsed on the ground with Clius repeating: "You did it! You saved us!" and Oedipus, the blind man, the supplicant, responds with a mute yet noisy laugh that is new to Antigone. Experiencing a pang of jealousy, she is drawn into their exhilaration, this mad yet sober intoxication. She throws herself onto them, hugs and kisses them in turn, shouting, ecstatic, jubilant. She hears their voices, their laughter resonate in the distance with the thunder, while deep inside her a hushed, rather nebulous voice whispers: *Yes, we have all been saved, just a little—a tiny bit saved.*

Antigone insists that Oedipus sit by the fire on the tree stump. He is shivering; his teeth chatter; he has cramps in his hands and feet: he has reverted to the human condition. Gently but firmly, Clius removes Oedipus's wet clothes, dries him, rubs him down, puts dry clothes on him, and massages his hands while Antigone busies herself with the meal. Clius may look after him but it is she who gives him the hot drink and biscuits she has cooked on the embers. As they eat, Clius looks first at Antigone then at Oedipus: "Your daughter looked very beautiful when she was overcome by it all. Rolling on the ground, smelling of fire and smoke, shouting and kissing us the way boys in the stadium or soldiers after a victory do. How lovely she was, slightly burned, slightly singed by the blaze!"

Suddenly conscious of how tired she is and how painful her burns are, Antigone stands and leaves their comforting warmth and ring of light. As she nears the village, she turns. Their stockpile, used up in one go, still illuminates the headland with its flames. She pictures Clius, having settled Oedipus, circling around it, dancing.

By the time Antigone reaches the village, the fog has cleared. She is relieved; the ships are all back in port, without the storm having claimed any lives. The fishermen and many of the sailors' wives are there. They have obviously been waiting for her. To her amazement they come and thank her for the fire. "In that storm, we couldn't even see the ends

of our oars, the wind and fog were so bad. It's thanks to the fire that we all got back."

Chloe asks: "How on earth did you make such a huge blaze in that terrible storm?"

"I was careless. I lit it in the cave and almost caught fire myself with the wind blowing as it was."

A young woman touches her head: "Your hair's singed. You're lucky it was raining. Come to my house, I'll tend your burns and see to your hair. My name is Isis and I cut the hair of the loveliest women in the village." Antigone follows her. Some of the women are astonished, for Isis is a young widow with a bad reputation. She is considered to be a bit of a sorceress and, since her husband disappeared, sailors and shepherds have often visited her, some have fought—and even died—for her. As she walks into the house Antigone breaks into an icy sweat and is on the point of collapsing.

Isis lays her down, warms her, and removes her clothes. "I thought as much, you've burned your legs, arms, and shoulders. All your lovely hair could have gone up in flames." She washes her very gently. "You're lucky, it's not too serious. I'm going to apply clay, herbs, and Egyptian ointments. My mother was Egyptian, my father a pirate. He kidnapped her. He was a real tyrant but he did love her. He really did! Just like your Clius!" Although thrilled beyond belief when she hears this, Antigone realizes Clius has been a regular visitor. She rests for three days while Isis and Chloe take it in turns to look after her. They patch and wash her scorched dress.

On the morning of the fourth day, after they have eaten, she tells Isis she is going back up to the headland. Isis informs her that Clius, who has come each day for news of her, is waiting outside.

There he is, covered in dressings, head practically shaved, giving him an even wilder look. He laughs unkindly when he sees Antigone's singed strands of hair that Isis has not completely disguised. Despite her protestations he heaves a large bundle of wood onto his back and sets off in front of her, his body bent beneath its weight like a tree in a storm.

As they reach the headland, Antigone hears the regular rhythm of Oedipus's hammer and chisel. At last Clius speaks: "All the time you and I have been ill, he's continued working. The wave's coming along well." She is cross when she sees the load has dislodged and soiled his dressings. She insists he sit down so that she can attend to them. She notices that the cave has been restocked with wood and provisions and that half-burned logs smoulder on the fire. There is nothing left to remind them of the events of the storm save the rope, lying at the edge of the abyss, which was attached to Oedipus as he harnessed the wave. It is still there, not cut but visibly broken by some giant force. Taking an ax, Clius severs the fragment that is left.

They go down the path. Arriving at the place where the wave rises, Antigone is suddenly anxious. On the overhanging rock the wave curves back, twisting under the pressure of its own weight and falls, as Oedipus wanted it to, plunging back into the sea.

The next day, Clius works on linking the section of the wave that rises up with that which is breaking. Oedipus carves the body of the third oarsman. Antigone is struck by the control and delicacy of his movements—so unlike the violence and fury of the blows made by he who forced back the wave. For the first time she notices that his wonderful head of chestnut hair is turning gray. He turns his face with its bandaged eyes toward her, on his lips the smile that once conquered all hearts.

She says: "I'm slowing you down."

He replies: "You've got plenty of time."

She feels that despite the onset of autumn and winter, he is giving her a vast stretch of time, telling her that it is vital not to hurry. She settles herself in front of the outline she has marked out for the pilot and is momentarily daunted by the amount of work still left to be done. Because Oedipus is allowing her to take time, she stares at the stone, loses herself in it, rests her face on it, runs her hands across it. Beneath

her forehead she feels a center of calm. Finding inspiration there, she slowly draws it into her whole being and sets to work. By midday, the foot, ankle, and leg are delineated.

With wood and ropes, Clius builds her some scaffolding, enabling her to move easily along the giant body. First she works on the shape, the body's general stance, then Oedipus accentuates the relief; he smooths and polishes the stone, emphasizing the shadows and angles. They hardly speak, but when he senses that she is tired he tells her to sit, and draws from his flute tunes and sounds from a long time ago, a period predating Thebes, Zeus, and Prometheus, predating the discovery of fire, when men and women were like the eagle, in their original state of innocence and ferocity.

Clius completes the wave, then turns to the rudder. To take the pressure off Antigone, he takes charge of the cooking. He has moved some logs down to the path and builds a fire at the base of the scaffolding so the others can warm themselves whenever it rains or the wind blows cold.

In the evenings she goes down to Chloe's or Isis's where there is always a fire and a hot meal waiting for her. The two women talk of the giant pilot as though he were a sea god. Antigone is preoccupied, for although the body is almost finished, she still has to do the head. She says to Isis: "Up until now my hands and eyes have known what they were doing but I have no idea what the head should look like."

"Don't worry," Isis replies, "you're not alone."

What does she mean? She decides not to ask for an explanation. Indeed, tonight she is not alone in this restful house where, after Isis has massaged and bathed her, she is tucked into bed.

She has a dream that night that she is communicating with people who have taken refuge underground to escape annihilation by those living above. Endurance has become a skill and they move freely through rock, water, and earth, surviving on infinitesimal amounts of food. As they adapt to this subterranean existence, their minds unite,

enriching and improving the quality of their lives. Love is paramount and spreads beyond their world to the outside. From them comes man's craving for all that is beautiful and sacred. At one with matter, sight has become redundant; they no longer use their eyes and people might think they are blind. A perceptive inner vision has inspired them with a greater sense of justice and strength. It would appear that they have overcome death and if, like those who live above ground, they have their problems, then they are those of a higher plane.

Antigone wakes unable to decide whether it was a dream or something she experienced in a semiconscious state. It leaves her with the impression that these subterranean people are encouraging the three of them because they understand, perhaps because they are waiting for them.

Oedipus is already busy when she arrives at the headland. Clius looks at her with admiration: "Last night after you'd gone, we both spent a long time examining your sculpting with our hands, for by that time it was dark for both of us. Oedipus said: 'Antigone's inspired.'"

Despite her pleasure at hearing this, she says, "It's not me—it's my hands that are inspired."

"You are your hands," says Clius, "your hands are you. Oedipus also said: 'Antigone is no longer conceiving the stone, the stone is conceiving her. Her pilot is worthy to look out to sea.'"

She would like to tell him of her dream but she is frightened of undermining him by forcing him into the ambivalent fabric of words; apart from which, she must get working. They both walk down the path and find Oedipus kneeling on the scaffolding already hard at it. She kneels in front of him. Taking his face in her hands, she feels how thin and gaunt he has become since he has been working so relentlessly. Running his hand down the back he is polishing, he says: "A man with victory in his spine."

All three are on the scaffolding. The north wind blows harder, biting into them. Clius lights the fire and when Antigone is too cold to hold her implements, she goes down and warms herself while the other two sit nearby with hot drinks. The two men eat but she is incapable of swallowing anything. Occasionally she examines her hands, chapped and callused despite Isis's efforts to care for them. She surveys her patched clothes, conscious of her dusty face and body. Clius has stopped taunting her and calling her grubby and disheveled. On the contrary he now often suggests that she go and relax in the cave, but she always declines.

The brow and windswept hair are almost finished. She molds into the stone that lofty figure so familiar to her when she was a child. She searches and recalls her father's former radiant good looks. But she cannot ignore the bitter creases left on his face by the plague, his father's murder, and Jocasta's death, nor the scars of that long intro-spective road leading nowhere, and worse still, the loss of the vertiginous rapture he had found while contemplating the sea—that happiness which he had relinquished because she could not bear what she con-sidered to be an escape, an evasion, but which might have been no more than the crossing of the abyss. She does not regret what she did. She demanded from him, and was granted by him, a different fate. But what right did she have? Could one still talk of such a right? She was the strongest and summoned him to a different destiny, the one that led him to spend months sculpting the cliff, displaying the strength of a god and the tenacity of a laborer. The same fate which demanded that today she create on this faceless victorious frame a giant representation of him gazing out to sea.

One day, one evening, several evenings, Clius helps her clamber up the cliff, then down to the village as far as Isis's door, where he entrusts her to the care of the young woman, and that of the old woman as well, for come nightfall Chloe is there, ready to look after her, too. Antigone is exhausted. She allows him to kiss her hand or shoulder before he bounds away as usual. Every evening, she promises her friends she will take a day off but by sunrise she is up, ready to resume her work. Clius

is outside, waiting for her in the half-light. They go up the path in silence, watching the sun rise gradually from the sea. In front of the cave, there is but the fire, for Oedipus is already on the cliff. They eat and, as soon as it is light, make their way down the path together. As she pulls herself up the scaffolding, Oedipus turns and gives her one of his confident, shrewd smiles: one that understands the terrible power of the sea, and of fate, and which knows they can be vanquished. It is that fleeting, elusive smile that she must capture and extract from the cliff. She touches the stone, strokes it for a long time the way Oedipus does. She stares at it and receives a reply—trembling with new questions. Could it be a message from the rock-dwellers who appeared in her dream last night? She sees a smile; or could it be a mouth, emerging from among the shadows and indistinct signs occupying the space where the face should be? All she has to do is let it happen by carefully molding the stone. Determined, magnificent, the laughing mouth is taking shape, asking to be restrained, controlled, so that it can confront tremendous unleashed forces. All day she is absorbed in it; a whole day with the wind biting through her. Though cold and hungry, she cannot pull herself away from her place on the scaffolding. When the men call her down, she answers but does not move. Clius brings her soup and hot stones so that she can warm herself. Only when the face that will be is brightened by the laughing mouth, the smile; only when she is certain she can see it and hear it, does she decide to come down. Unable to descend on her own, she calls to Clius for help. In the light of the dying day, he looks at what she has accomplished: "That's the most exquisite thing you've ever done."

"It wasn't me, it was them!" Utterly exhausted, her voice is aggressive, hard, as though he had upset her. He guides her down; she feels heavy as if she is about to faint. He helps her get warm then accompanies her to Isis's house. She is so tired she has to keep stopping. He feels that part of her would like him to take her in his arms while the other would never forgive him if he did. As they stand in front of Isis's door, she says:

"I still have to do the eyes but I can't visualize them!" Taken aback, he remarks casually: "Never mind. Tomorrow you will."

She replies coldly: "No," and slams the door in his face.

Later, attending to Oedipus, Clius relates that although Antigone is pleased with what she has achieved, she is worried about the eyes as she cannot visualize them. Oedipus lies down, makes himself comfortable, and stretches several times, as he often does before falling asleep: "If there are no eyes, that is what will be depicted."

On her way to the headland with Clius in the half-light of the dawning day, Antigone is no longer preoccupied with the eyes. She consoles herself with the image of the gigantic face of the father of the sea. Just as she is about to go down to the cliff, Clius repeats what Oedipus said the previous night: "If there are no eyes, that is what will be depicted." Astounded she steps onto the path echoing: "If there are no eyes, no eyes . . ."

Oedipus has accomplished his work on the giant. Everything behind the pilot is finished. He is now turning his attention to the third oarsman. They are waiting for Antigone to complete the master of the ship. She goes up to Oedipus, takes him in her arms and blinds herself by pressing her eyes against her father's face. Indeed there are no eyes—that is what is so painful when the memory of what he used to look like returns. However, and she goes over it in her mind with the fragment of his phrase, perhaps he sees more now. Like that small invisible community of rock-dwellers, he continually watches you with his inner eye, and thus envelops you with a more perceptive organ. Closing her eyes, she spreads her hands over Oedipus's face. She feels the band that Clius carefully ties over his sockets each morning. She sees him every day and thought she knew him but it is only now, through her hands, that she feels him and knows him, as her father. Why didn't she think of it before? There are no eyes but she can depict this band which, since it is the blind giant guiding the ship, reveals the inner eye that is present through its absence and

abundance. She kisses Oedipus and scrambles up the scaffolding. Down below, Clius lights the fire which splutters merrily beneath the drops of a passing shower of rain.

She works all day. First she finishes the brow, then delineates the band. The feeling that she is being assisted by the subterranean people and by the trust and intense devotion of her two companions returns. From time to time, Clius obliges her to come down and get warm. Oedipus joins them, but neither speaks to her, aware that she is still up there gazing at the giant face who has entrusted his laughing mouth to posterity. She returns to her task and a hazy thought comes into her head: "The blind man singing." The forehead is vast, smooth, superb, above the slightly protruding nose. She completes the band, it is worn and frayed at the edges like the one Oedipus wears for work. She steps back to get a better view, returns to the stone, makes a few adjustments and steps back to look at the carving as a whole once more.

She cannot believe it. Everything tells her that she can do no more, for within the limits of her abilities she has done all she can. It is not finished and never will be. Abandoned, left to himself, the master of the boat is ahead of her, well ahead of her. With the action of the wind and that of the sea, he will continue to advance into the immensity of time and the distance between them will always increase.

She is tempted to call Oedipus and Clius over, to shout: "Look! It's finished. Come and see how magnificent, how much greater than us, our unfinished work is!" Yet she cannot and her whole body is gripped by a pain which becomes a crushing sadness.

It is done. She turns away and looks at the sea, black under a leaden sky. Encouraged by the two men, she has given birth to this giant on whom she now turns her back. Gazing at the waves beating up against the cliff, she is horrified to discover a desire to destroy herself as her mother had done. The alternative is that blind man confronting the storm, the action of starting again every morning

and a never-ending, unrelenting yearning. She is at the edge of the plat-form; she grabs the rope and leans out. It is born: she has done enough; they do not need her anymore.

Clutching the rope as she sways, mesmerized by the sea, she is on the verge of falling when a powerful hand seizes hers, and strong arms lift her up. Is it her child, the father of the sea, bringing her with unexpected ease down from the scaffolding? Who is infusing her with his strength and courage? Who, without obvious effort, is bringing her back up the narrow path? At the headland, the effortlessness, the omnipotence dissolve, leaving Oedipus staggering with her in his arms, his strength ebbing away. In a strangled voice, he calls to Clius for help. After having been carried by her child of stone, she finds pleasure in crawling alone, held up by the two men. Her child is big; he will have to live without her. All she must do now is gradually absorb the pain of having finished a task that was never meant to end.

Antigone has spent two days being nursed by Isis. Clius has come to tell her that Chloe's husband, the old fisherman, will take them out in his boat the next day so that they can see the wave from the sea.

"What's Oedipus doing?"

Clius tells her he has stopped working on the cliff, that he seems to think the wave is finished. He is cutting rocks; he wants to build a fire tower above the cave like the one he saw in Egypt.

The next day is cold. At sunrise, the headland is still shrouded in mist. Having rounded it, the two sons start rowing to the north face. At first it is indistinct but the mist lifts abruptly and suddenly the wave is there. Their hearts miss a beat when it appears. It is as though Clius and Antigone are seeing it for the first time. Little did they realize it was so immense, so very extraordinary, so much more terrifying than they imagined it to be when viewed from the path. The wave, dark at its base, becoming lighter as it rises, springs up out of the sea. Level with the overhanging rock, it unfurls the whole of its foaming mass, encircled by pillars of water that fall like arrows into a sparkle of fiery

drops. Nothing can stand up to it. It is about to fall back into the vast trough but the boat gets there first and uses the power of the wave and the gap it has created to project itself forward. White, slim, graceful, with its three oarsmen at the apex of their effort, it is guided toward the port by the blind man of the sea.

They get as close as possible to the cliff without endangering their lives so that they can get a good look at it. They admire the great, pale, and dark figures that imbue the cliff with a new meaning, sending out a message of hope to all sailors and to King Theseus.

Antigone is lost in thought. Clius turns to her: "We should add some colors, different shades of blue and gray, some brilliant white, a touch of red."

She is seduced by this colorful vision but does not agree with him.

"But the colors would exalt the stone," Clius argues.

"Oedipus doesn't want the stone to be exalted. He wants it to be visible."

"He wants to give it a meaning but it has no more meaning than do the sea, the headland, the cliff. They exist. And that's all."

The old sailor chuckles: "Whoever did that wave understands the sea. He has made a boat and fishermen who will get back to port with their catch. And that's what counts for us. The fish."

Time is pressing. They must return. From the top of the headland comes the steady sound of Oedipus's hammering.

That evening Oedipus and Clius eat in silence, listening to the sea beating tirelessly against the foot of the cliff. Clius builds the fire for the night.

Oedipus says: "You are now a potter and a sculptor, but color is your true vocation. It will develop alongside you and will take up an increasing amount of space. Clius will have to move over. People like us who have been steeped in crime can only escape from it through freedom, complete freedom, and the ceaseless struggle to achieve it."

"What about Antigone?" asks Clius. "She has committed no crime.

Is there no other way for her?"

"No. Freedom is never easy."

The following day when Antigone comes up from the village, Oedipus takes her down to the foot of the cliff. The third oarsman is incomplete. And yet there is no doubt in her mind that it is Polynices. Polynices with his princely ease, that incomparable grace inherited from Oedipus and Jocasta.

"Why? Why him?"

Oedipus offers no explanation; all he says before leaving is:

"Finish the face, the mouth . . ."

She stands there, confronting Polynices—the idea, the vision of her brother, formulated over the years since she was a child. And now she has to do this face which has weighed so heavily on her destiny. For it was Polynices who, instead of turning against Eteocles and Creon, shut the last door of Thebes on his father, condemning him to perish in some burrow or other. Which he would have done, had she not drawn around him those protective murmurings of compassion which she herself unwittingly instigated.

Is Polynices's face still capable of being endowed with hope? His inexcusable conflict with Eteocles and Creon's secret hostility cast doubt upon it. But as she has come to learn since she has been on the road, there is more than one path to choose from.

She goes back up the headland and fetches her tools from the cave where she had left them, thinking the work was finished. Clius waves to her, grinning. Oedipus does not raise his head. He is squatting on the ground, cutting rectangular rocks with a large hammer which Clius then prepares for assembly. And so he who once held the scepter and the royal bow, he who first had the idea of the wave and then accomplished it, does not find it unnatural to do the same work as a quarryman. She thinks: *It is all the same to him. Everything has become the same.*

For several days she works ceaselessly on Polynices's face. She is troubled by the smile she has given him—it is weak and supercilious. It seems to denote that his joviality, if joviality it be, has nothing to do with the outcome of this deed. To vanquish or perish, kill or be killed, are one and the same to this face, have the same sense or, as Clius would say, the same no-sense. She gazes for a long time at the boat as it escapes the storm, with its three glowing oarsmen and its blind pilot. This time she feels that the work, the adventure that has wrecked their bodies and united their minds, is complete. The product of their labors, their patience, their fascination with the rock-dwellers, has been yielded—yielded up to the sky, the sea, the stars, to cataclysms, insensibility, and finally to oblivion. It is no longer theirs and she understands what they have to endure up there, having finished—no doubt as planned—the task before her.

She runs back up the path, falls to her knees beside her father and calls Clius. She says: "I am filled with sadness. I have understood. I too am suffering." She puts her arms around their shoulders and weeps, her face pressed up against theirs, letting flow the tears they cannot release. Huddled closely together in the icy wind, they recreate for a moment the binding circle of their deed which has just been broken. Clius lights some brushwood at the center of the ring and spreads their linked hands over the tiny flame. He says: "Let us bless this moment and these tears with fire and ashes." They return to their work. Oedipus raises and lowers his hammer onto the stone. As Antigone makes her way to the village, she only thinks: "How fast the night is falling."

Translated from the French by Anne-Marie Glasheen

From *Hollywood Boulevard,* 1973/1995

Previously unpublished, these photographs were taken by Edward Ruscha on July 8, 1973, on the north and south sides of Hollywood Boulevard, in Los Angeles, California. Shooting from a moving truck, Ruscha used a motorized Nikon camera with a perspective control lens and 250-exposure cassettes. His filmlike, unedited sequential contact strips recreate the experience of driving down the infamous Boulevard of Dreams. The selection of frames printed here is contiguous as photographed, except where displaced by other portfolios of art or illustrated texts. *Hollywood Boulevard* exists as a companion to Ruscha's similarly continuous *Sunset Strip* (1966), a book of photographs in which the full length of Sunset Strip was reproduced on one long, folded, accordion-like sheet.

CONTRIBUTORS

ADOBE LA (Architects, Artists and Designers Opening the Border Edge of Los Angeles) was founded in 1992 as an activist collaboration of architects, artists, and theorists. Current members are designers Ulises Diaz and Gustavo Leclerc, and artists Alessandra Moctezuma and Leda Ramos. ADOBE LA takes the cultural landscape of Los Angeles, and in particular that of the Latin American community, as the point of departure for projects that address the values of Los Angeles's evolving population. The group has exhibited major installations at the Wexner Center for the Arts, Columbus, Ohio, and the Museum of Contemporary Art, Los Angeles. Theoretical projects such as *Huellas Fronterizas*, which examines the urban intercultural dialogue across the U.S.–Mexican border, are joined by real projects such as *La Posada*, a shelter for homeless Latino youth. This combination of theory and practice, avant-garde and social purpose, has established ADOBE LA as an important cultural force in the continuing evolution of the Southern Californian landscape. *Huellas Fronterizas* was funded by the Fideicomiso para la Cultura Mexico/U.S.A.–U.S.A./Mexico Fund for Culture (Bancomer Cultural Foundation, Rockefeller Foundation, and Mexico's National Fund for the Culture and the Arts).

Gösta Ågren lives in Ostrobothnia on the western coast of Finland, and writes in Swedish. Politically to the far left and quasi-separatist in stance, Ågren was one of the founders of the Ostrobothnian publishing company, Författarnas Andelslag (Writer's Cooperative), which has been active in publishing writing by Swedish-language regional authors. In 1989, he won the Finlandia Literature Prize for his collection *Jär*. A translation of his selected poems, *A Valley in the Midst of Violence* (Bloodaxe), was published in 1992.

Max Aub was born in Paris in 1903, and moved to Valencia, Spain with his German father and French mother in 1914. After the Spanish Civil War, he moved to Mexico. His work was banned in Spain during the Franco regime. A playwright, poet, and essayist, he was best known as a novelist and published such titles as *Jusep Torres Campalans* and *La gallina ciega*. Aub died in Mexico City in 1972. His conversation with Luis Buñuel in this issue of *Grand Street* was published in Spanish in *Conversaciones con Buñuel* (Aguilar).

Henry Bauchau was born in Belgium in 1913. He studied at a Catholic *collège* in Brussels and went on to obtain a law degree. In 1943, he joined the Belgian Resistance, and after the war, he moved to Paris where he knew Gide, Camus, and Jean Denoël. In 1958, his first book, *Géologie*, was published and received the Prix Max Jacob. During the 1960s, he befriended Lacan and Derrida, and in 1972, Henri Flammarion commissioned Bauchau to write a biography of Mao Tse-tung, which was published in 1982. In 1990, he was elected to the Académie Royale de Langue et de Littérature Françaises de Belgique. *Oedipus on the Road*, from which *The Wave* is excerpted, was published in the United Kingdom by Quartet Books, and has been translated into seven languages.

Janet Catherine Berlo is Professor of Art History at the University of Missouri in St. Louis. She received her Ph.D. from Yale University in 1980 and has since conducted research on the indigenous arts of North and Central America. She currently holds a Senior Scholar's Research Grant from the Getty Foundation, and her exhibition catalogue, *Plains Indian Drawings, 1865–1935: Pages of a Visual History*, will be published by Abrams in the fall of 1996.

Andrew Bromfield was born in Hull, England, and graduated in Russian Studies from the University of Sussex. His career has included teaching Russian for twelve years and teaching English in Yerevan, Soviet Armenia. From 1988 to 1993, he lived and worked in Moscow, where he was involved in founding *Glas*, an English-language journal of contemporary Russian writing, of which he was also coeditor. He has translated both poetry and prose from Russian.

Luis Buñuel was born in Calanda, Spain in 1900. From 1920 to 1923, he studied entomology at the University of Madrid, where he became close friends with Salvador Dalí. Together, they established Spain's first film club, and, in Paris in 1925, Buñuel collaborated with Dalí to write and direct his first film, the silent, twenty-five-minute *An Andalusian Dog*, a series of unconnected images intended to create a "poetic" effect similar to that achieved on canvas by the Surrealists. His second film, *The Golden Age* (1930), which was intensely critical of the bourgeoisie, was shown for two months before French censors yielded to public pressure and banned it. After a brief, fruitless stint in Hollywood, Buñuel returned to Spain in 1932. In 1940, he began work at the Museum of Modern Art, New York, re-editing footage from Leni Riefenstahl's pro-Nazi films to be used as American propaganda. He resigned from this position, however, after Dalí publicly revealed that Buñuel was both anti-Catholic and a member of the French Communist Party. Buñuel then returned to Hollywood, where he worked for Warner Brothers, and in 1947, he moved to Mexico. Several movies followed, including *Los olvidados, The Devil and the Flesh, The Daughter of Deceit, El, Illusion Travels by Streetcar, Nazarín,* and *The Exterminating Angel.* In 1966, Buñuel returned to France, where he directed *Belle de Jour, The Discreet Charm of the Bourgeoisie,* and *That Obscure Object of Desire,* among other films. He died in Mexico City in 1983. His conversation with Max Aub in this issue of *Grand Street* was first published in Spanish in *Conversaciones con Buñuel* (Aguilar).

Sam Cornish teaches at Emerson College in Boston, Massachusetts. His new collection of poetry, *Cross a Parted Sea,* will be published by Zoland Books in early 1997.

Ann Cvetkovich teaches English at the University of Texas at Austin. She is the author of *Mixed Feelings: Feminism, Mass Culture, and Victorian Sensationalism* (Rutgers University Press) and of articles in *Lesbian Erotics* and *GLQ: A Journal of Lesbian and Gay Studies.*

Lydia Davis is the author of *Break It Down* (Farrar, Straus & Giroux) and *The End of the Story* (Farrar, Straus & Giroux). She is also the translator of works from the French by Maurice Blanchot and Michel Leiris. She received a Whiting Foundation Award for Fiction in 1988 and the French-American Foundation's Annual Prize in 1993. Her short story, *St. Martin,* will appear in her new collection, *Almost No Memory,* to be published in the fall of 1996 by Farrar, Straus & Giroux.

Mike Davis is the author of *City of Quartz: Excavating the Future in Los Angeles* (Verso).

Alexander D. Fisher was born in Brooklyn, New York. He received his M.F.A. from Milton Avery Graduate School of the Arts and has most recently published poems in *Dew Magazine* and *Epiphanies in P Major.* He lives in Portland, Maine, where he is associate editor of *The Cafe Review.*

Cola Franzen's translations include *Mean Woman* (University of Nebraska Press), a novel by Alicia Borinsky, and *Si regresso/If I Go Back* (Cross Cultural Communications), a collection of poetry by Juan Cameron. She recently completed a translation of Saúl Yurkievich's *A imagen y semejanza/In the Image and Likeness*.

Forrest Gander's most recent books are *Deeds of Utmost Kindness* (Wesleyan University Press), *Lynchburg* (Pittsburgh University Press), and *Mouth to Mouth: Poems by Twelve Contemporary Mexican Women* (Milkweed Editions), a bilingual anthology.

Anne-Marie Glasheen was born in Liège, Belgium in 1945. She completed a degree in French and English at Lancaster University in 1966, and began translating in 1978, while researching post-war developments in Belgian theater. She has translated novels, poetry, art history, and several plays by contemporary Belgian playwrights. Her translation of Henry Bauchau's *Oedipus on the Road* was published in England by Quartet Books. Glasheen also teaches, writes, broadcasts, runs translation workshops, and organizes European cultural exchange programs for women.

Merril Greene is a writer and works in the film industry. She divides her time between the East and West Coasts.

Lee Harwood was born in 1939. He lives in Brighton, England, and worked until recently as a train conductor. Since the early 1960s, he has published eighteen books of poetry and two collections of translations of Tristan Tzara. His most recent books include *Crossing the Frozen River: Selected Poems* (Paladin), *Rope Boy to the Rescue* (North & South), and *In the Mists: Mountain Poems* (Slow Dancer Press).

Rachel Hecker was born in Providence, Rhode Island in 1958. She has been painting and teaching in Houston, Texas since 1982. She is producing a new body of work for a May 1996 exhibition at ArtPace in San Antonio.

George Herms was born in Woodland, California in 1935. His work was recently featured in the Whitney Museum of American Art exhibition, *Beat Culture and the Making of the New America, 1950–1965*.

Concurrently, Herms exhibited at the Tony Shafrazi Gallery, New York and at Jack Rutberg Fine Arts, Los Angeles in the show *Beat Epiphanies and Home Runs*. Herms has had a historic impact on the art of assemblage and is an enduring force in contemporary art.

Franz Kafka was born in Prague, Bohemia in 1883. A German-speaking Jew raised in Prague's Jewish ghetto, Kafka enrolled in Ferdinand-Karls University (against his father's wishes) in 1901. There he met and befriended fellow-student, Max Brod, and soon decided to pursue a law degree. In 1905, he began work on his first novel, which he abandoned unfinished (later published as *Description of a Struggle*). In 1908, he was hired as a clerk and technical writer at the Workmen's Accident Insurance Institute, and in 1911 he began working evenings also at his family's asbestos factory. In 1912, he wrote two of his most successful stories, *The Judgment* and *The Metamorphosis*, the former of which was published to acclaim in Brod's periodical *Arkadia*. In 1917, Kafka suffered his first tubercular hemorrhage and spent the next two years convalescing. By 1922, he had completed *A Hunger Artist* and most of *The Castle*. Despite brief respites, however, his health continued to deteriorate and, in 1924, he succumbed to tuberculosis at a sanatorium in Kierling, Austria. The prose fragments published in this issue of *Grand Street*, which were found by Max Brod after Kafka's death, appeared in German in Franz Kafka's *Träume*, published by S. Fischer Verlag in 1993.

Robert M. Laughlin is a curator of meso-American ethnology at the Smithsonian Institution in Washington, DC. He has spent much of the last thirty-five years in the highland Chiapas region of Mexico.

Bernadette Mayer's most recent book is *The Bernadette Mayer Reader* (New Directions).

David McDuff is a translator of Russian and Scandinavian literature, and has translated works by Dostoyevsky, Leskov, and Babel. In 1994, he won the George Bernard Shaw/*Times Literary Supplement* Prize for his translation of a selection of Gösta Ågren's poetry entitled *A Valley in the Midst of Violence* (Bloodaxe). Carcanet Press has published his translations of a novel and a selection of poetry by Bo Carpelan.

Ange Mlinko edits *Compound Eye* from Somerville, Massachusetts. Her collection of poems, *Immediate Orgy & Audit*, was recently published by Lift.

Margaret Sayers Peden lives in Columbia, Missouri. Among her recent translations are Isabel Allende's *Paula* and Fanny Buitrago's *Señora Honeycomb* (HarperCollins). Forthcoming is a *Selected Works of Sor Juana Inés*, to be published by Viking Penguin.

Victor Pelevin was born in Moscow in 1962. He has received degrees from the Moscow Institute of Power Engineering and from the Russian Institute of Literature. His work has appeared widely in Russian magazines and has been translated into French, German, Japanese, and English. His collection of short stories, *The Blue Lantern*, won the 1993 Russian Booker short story prize, and *Omon Ra*, from which the story printed in *Grand Street* is excerpted, was nominated for the 1993 Russian Booker Prize. It was published in the United Kingdom by Harbord Publishing, and will be published in the U.S. in April 1996 by Farrar, Straus and Giroux.

Danna Ruscha is an actress, photographer, and former animator who lives in Los Angeles. She is the publisher of Jim Shaw's *Thrift Store Paintings* (Heavy Industries Publications).

Edward Ruscha was born in Omaha, Nebraska in 1937. His first solo exhibition was held at the Ferus Gallery, Los Angeles in 1963. His recent solo museum exhibitions include those at the Musée National d'Art Moderne, Paris, the Whitney Museum of American Art, New York, the Museum of Contemporary Art, Los Angeles, and the Serpentine Gallery, London. He is currently exhibiting his *Chocolate Room*, a reconstruction of an installation from the 1970 Venice Biennale (in which the gallery walls are hung with 360 sheets of paper silkscreened with chocolate paste), in the show *1965–1975: Reconsidering the Object of Art*, at the Temporary Contemporary, Los Angeles. He lives and works in Los Angeles.

Jim Shaw was born in Midland, Michigan in 1952. He is an artist who lives and works in Los Angeles. Published collections of his work include *Thrift Store Paintings* (Heavy Industries Publications) and *Dreams* (Smart Art Press).

Daniel Slager is a writer, translator, and doctoral student in Comparative Literature at New York University. He is currently translating a collection of short prose works by Robert Walser.

Nile Southern is a writer, filmmaker, and creative director of Alternative-X, a literary site on the Internet (http://www.altx.com). He lives in Boulder, Colorado with his wife, Theodosia.

Terry Southern was born in Alvarado, Texas in 1924. He began writing satiric, outrageous fiction at the age of twelve, when he rewrote Edgar Allen Poe stories "because they didn't go far enough." After serving in the Army as a Lieutenant in World War II, he wrote short stories while studying at the Sorbonne University in Paris. There he befriended British novelist Henry Green, who convinced André Deutsch to publish Southern's first novel, *Flash and Filigree*, in 1958. *The Magic Christian* followed in 1959, and *Candy* (written with Mason Hoffenberg) was published by Maurice Girodias's Olympia Press in 1960. Southern published numerous short stories in England, France, and America (anthologized in *Red Dirt Marijuana and Other Tastes* in 1967), and coedited *Writers in Revolt* with Richard Seaver and Alexander Trocchi in 1962. In the 1960s, he wrote or cowrote screenplays for several movies, including *Dr. Strangelove*, *The Loved One*, *The Cincinnati Kid*, *Casino Royale*, *Barbarella*, and *Easy Rider*. In the 1980s, he began writing for Saturday Night Live and teaching screenwriting at New York University and at Columbia University. His last novel, *Texas Summer*, was published in 1992. Terry Southern died on October 29, 1995. Grove Press will republish *Flash and Filigree* and *Candy* in March 1996.

Karlheinz Stockhausen was born near Cologne, Germany in 1928. He studied musicology, philology, and philosophy at Cologne University and, in 1952, he moved to Paris to study with the composer Olivier Messiaen. In 1963, he founded the Cologne Courses for New Music. As a composer and theorist, he has pioneered electronic music, new uses of physical space in music, open forms, live electronic

performance, "intuitive music," and other important developments
in post-1950 music. In his writings as well as in his music, he has
evolved a uniquely coherent system of generalizations from the
premises of total serialism, paying attention to aesthetic and philo-
sophical consequences as well as to matters of technique and music
theory. He has also been widely active as a teacher and has taken
part—as either a conductor or a performer—in many performances
of his own music, forming his own performing group in 1964. He
lives in Kürten, Germany. The *Helicopter String Quartet* was performed
as part of the Holland Festival at the Westergasfabriek, a former gas-
works plant that has become a theater, in Amsterdam on June 26, 1995.

William T. Vollmann is a novelist and journalist, and also a contribut-
ing editor and writer for *Spin* magazine. He lives and works in Sacra-
mento, California. His new book, *The Atlas*, from which *The Rifles* was
excerpted, will be published by Viking in April 1996.

Susan Wicks has published two collections of poetry, *Singing Under-
water* and *Open Diagnosis*. Her book of autobiographical prose, *Driving
My Father*, was published by Faber and Faber in October 1995.

Saúl Yurkievich, Argentinian poet, critic, and professor of Latin
American literature at the Université de Paris VIII, has published
more than twenty volumes of creative and critical work. His most
recent books include *El trasver* (Fondo de Cultura Económica),
A imagen y semejanza (Anaya/Mario Muchnik), and *Julio Cortázar:
Mundos y modos* (Anaya/Mario Muchnik).

Current international poetry and prose

Trafika

PO Box 250413
New York NY
10025-1536
USA

Veverkova 20
170 00 Prague 7
Czech Republic

5

Subscriptions (four issues) USD 35 individual
USD 40 institutional
Sample copies USD 10

ILLUSTRATIONS

front cover ADOBE LA, *La Mona (The Doll)*, 1995. A five-story house built in the shape of a nude woman. Photograph by Julie Easton. Courtesy of ADOBE LA, Venice, California.

back cover Jim Shaw, *Dream* (detail), 1995. Pencil on paper, 12 x 9 in. Courtesy of the artist and Rosamund Felsen Gallery, Santa Monica, California.

title page Black Hawk (circa 1832–1889, Sans Arc Lakota), *Dream or Vision of Himself Changed to a Destroyer and Riding a Buffalo Eagle* (detail), 1880–1881. Pencil, colored pencil, and ink on paper, 10 x 16 in. Courtesy of the Mr. Eugene V. and Clare E. Thaw Collection of American Indian Art, Fenimore House Museum, Cooperstown, New York.

pp. 8–22, pp. 37–39, pp. 46–78, pp. 108–122, pp. 134–138, pp. 159–176, pp. 186–198, pp. 209–212, and pp. 226–260 Edward Ruscha, from *Hollywood Boulevard*, 1973/1995. Frames from six black-and-white contact proof sheets, from a complete set of twenty-seven. Courtesy of the artist and Leo Castelli Gallery, New York.

p. 9 and p. 11 Photographs courtesy of Photofest.

pp. 25–32 ADOBE LA, *Huellas Fronterizas: Retranslating the Urban Text in Los Angeles and Tijuana*. Titles and descriptions appear on **p. 24**. **p. 25 and p. 32** Photographs by Alessandra Moctezuma. **pp. 26–30** Photographs by Julie Easton. **p. 31** Photograph by Ulises Diaz. All courtesy of ADOBE LA, Venice, California.

pp. 40–45 *Flight of the Spruce Goose.* **p. 40** (inset), **p. 43, and pp. 44–45** (three insets) Photographs courtesy of AP/Wide World Photos. **pp. 40–41** (background), **p. 42 and pp. 44–45** Photographs courtesy of Bettmann.

pp. 81–88 George Herms, *The Bricoleur of Broken Hearts.* Titles and dates appear with illustrations. **p. 81** Assemblage, 24 x 24 x 6½ in. **p. 82** Assemblage, 28 x 24 x 5 in. **p. 83** Assemblage, 26 x 24 x 2 in. **p. 84** Sculpture, 7 x 3 x 4 in. **p. 85** Assemblage, 49½ x 49½ x 9 in. **p. 86** Assemblage, 24¼ x 36 x 6 in. **p. 87** Assemblage, 56 x 50 x 11 in. **p. 88** Assemblage, 42 x 14 x 23 in. Photographs by William Nettles. Courtesy of L.A. Louver Gallery, Venice, California, and Tony Shafrazi Gallery, New York.

p. 90, p. 95, p. 100, p. 102, and p. 106 Five black-and-white photographs, each 8 x 10 in., by John Swope. Courtesy of Robert Laughlin.

pp. 124–131 Jim Shaw, *Dreams.* Four pencil-on-paper drawings, each 12 x 9 in. Courtesy of the artist and Metro Pictures, New York.

p. 142 Black-and-white photograph, 8 x 10 in., photographer unknown. **p. 146** Black-and-white photograph, 11 x 14 in., by Steve Schapiro, 1964. Copyright © Steve Schapiro/LIFE Magazine. **pp. 150–151** Black-and-white photograph, 11 x 14 in., by Michael Cooper. **p. 157** Black-and-white photograph, 11 x 14 in., by William Claxton. Copyright © William Claxton. All rights reserved. All photographs courtesy of Carol Southern. **p. 143, pp. 147–149, pp. 152–156, and p. 158** Original manuscripts courtesy of Nile Southern. **pp. 144–145** Original letters courtesy of Richard Seaver.

pp. 178–184 Rachel Hecker, *Almost Heaven.* Seven paintings, acrylic on canvas, titles and dates appear with illustrations. **p. 178** 60 x 60 in. **p. 179** 60½ x 60½ in. **p. 180** 72¼ x 60¼ in. **p. 181** 72 x 72 in. **p. 182** 70 x 94 in. **p. 183** 72 x 94 in. **p. 184** 108 x 72 in. Courtesy of Texas Gallery, Houston, Texas.

ILLUSTRATIONS

pp. 201–208 *Spirit Horses and Thunder Beings: Plains Indian Dream Drawings.* Artists, titles, and dates appear with illustrations. **p. 201** *From Sioux Indian Painting,* by Hartley Burr Alexander, published in 1939 by C. Swzedzicki, Nice, France. Courtesy of the Cleveland Museum of Art, Cleveland, Ohio. **p. 202** Pencil, colored pencil, ink, and watercolor on paper, 11 x 5 in. Courtesy of Mr. and Mrs. Charles M. Diker Collection, New York. **pp. 203–205** Pencil, ink, and crayon on paper, 5⅝ x 8⅝ in. Courtesy of Buffalo Bill Historical Center, Cody, Wyoming. **pp. 206–207** Ink and pencil on paper. Mrs. E.M. Johnson Collection. Reference prints courtesy of State Historical Society of North Dakota, Bismarck, North Dakota. **p. 208** Pencil, colored pencil, and ink on paper, 10 x 16 in. Courtesy of the Mr. Eugene V. and Clare E. Thaw Collection of American Indian Art, Fenimore House Museum, Cooperstown, New York.

pp. 217–224 Karlheinz Stockhausen, *Helikopter-Streichquartett.* **p. 213, pp. 218–223, and p. 225** Score courtesy of Stockhausen Verlag, Kürten, Germany. **p. 217 and p. 224** Four color photographs, each 5 x 7 in., by Stefan Müller, Berlin.

p. 272 Posted in lower Manhattan, January 1996.

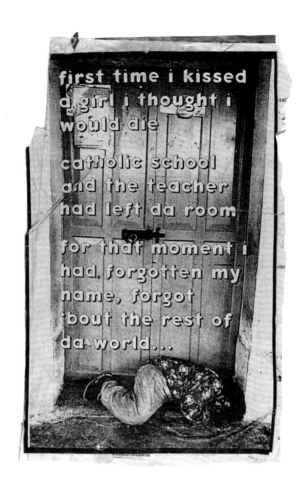

Grand Street would like to thank
the following for their generous support:

Edward Lee Cave
Cathy and Stephen Graham
Barbara Howard
Dominic Man-Kit Lam
The National Endowment for the Arts
The New York State Council on the Arts
Suzanne and Sanford J. Schlesinger
Betty and Stanley K. Sheinbaum

The New American Theater

Conjunctions: 25, guest edited by John Guare

INTRODUCTION BY JOYCE CAROL OATES

In its 25th issue, *Conjunctions* strikes out in a new direction and brings the stage to the page. Guest edited by John Guare, one of America's premier playwrights, *The New American Theater* is a celebration of the art of writing for the stage and will feature over two dozen new plays commissioned especially for the issue.

Jon Robin Baitz • Christopher Durang • David Ives • Arthur Kopit

Tony Kushner • Romulus Linney • David Mamet • Donald

Margulies • Ellen McLaughlin • Robert MacNamara • Joyce Carol

Oates • Mark O'Donnell • Han Ong • Eric Overmyer • Keith

Reddin • Jonathan Marc Sherman • Nicky Silver • Paula Vogel

Wendy Wasserstein • Mac Wellman • and others

Contact your local bookseller or send a check
($12 for this issue, $18 for a one-year subscription) to:

Conjunctions, Bard College, Annandale-on-Hudson, NY 12504

Back Issues of Grand Street

An Indispensable Collection

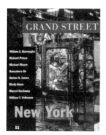

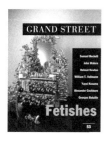

Some of the bookstores where

GRAND STREET

can be found :

Barnes & Noble, Hoover, AL
Bookman's, Tucson, AZ
Barnes & Noble, Berkeley, CA
Black Oak Books, Berkeley, CA
Cody's Books, Berkeley, CA
Bookstore Fiona, Carson, CA
University Bookstore, Irvine, CA
Bookstar, Los Angeles, CA
Museum of Contemporary Art, Los Angeles, CA
Occidental College Bookstore, Los Angeles, CA
Barnes & Noble, Marina del Ray, CA
Barnes & Noble, Montclair, CA
Barnes & Noble, Newport Beach, CA
Barnes & Noble, Oakland, CA
Diesel, A Bookstore, Oakland, CA
Barnes & Noble, Pasadena, CA
Barnes & Noble, San Diego, CA
Bookstar, San Diego, CA
The Booksmith, San Francisco, CA
City Lights, San Francisco, CA
Modern Times Bookstore, San Francisco, CA
Barnes & Noble, Santa Barbara, CA
Logos, Santa Cruz, CA
Arcana, Santa Monica, CA
Bookstar, Studio City, CA
Small World Books, Venice, CA
Bookstar, Woodland Hills, CA
Barnes & Noble, Boulder, CO
Barnes & Noble, Denver, CO
Newsstand Cafe, Denver, CO
Stone Lion Bookstore, Fort Collins, CO
Barnes & Noble, Littleton, CO
Barnes & Noble, Danbury, CT
Yale Co-operative, New Haven, CT
Barnes & Noble, Orange, CT
Barnes & Noble, Waterbury, CT

Barnes & Noble, Westport, CT
Bookworks — W.P.A., Washington, DC
Politics & Prose, Washington, DC
Barnes & Noble, Jacksonville, FL
Bookstop, Miami, FL
Barnes & Noble, Orlando, FL
Barnes & Noble, St. Petersburg, FL
Barnes & Noble, Tampa, FL
Barnes & Noble, Atlanta, GA
Oxford Bookstore, Atlanta, GA
Iowa Book & Supply, Iowa City, IA
Prairie Lights, Iowa City, IA
University Bookstore, Iowa City, IA
Rosetta News, Carbondale, IL
Pages for All Ages, Champaign, IL
Barnes & Noble, Chicago, IL
Mayuba Bookstore, Chicago, IL
Seminary Co-op Bookstore, Chicago, IL
Barnes & Noble, Deerfield, IL
Barnes & Noble, Evanston, IL
Barnes & Noble, Skokie, IL
Box of Rocks, Bowling Green, KY
Barnes & Noble, Florence, KY
Lenny's News, New Orleans, LA
Barnes & Noble, Boston, MA
Boston University Bookstore, Boston, MA
M.I.T. Press Bookstore, Cambridge, MA
Broadside Bookshop, Northampton, MA
Provincetown Bookshop, Provincetown, MA
Water Street Books, Williamstown, MA
Barnes & Noble, Annapolis, MD
Bookland of Brunswick, Brunswick, ME
University Bookstore, Orono, ME
Books Etc., Portland, ME
Raffles Cafe Bookstore, Portland, ME
Barnes & Noble, Ann Arbor, MI
Shaman Drum Bookshop, Ann Arbor, MI
Cranbrook Art Museum Bookstore,
  Bloomfield Hills, MI
Book Beat, Oak Park, MI

The bookstores where *Grand Street* can be found (continued):

Barnes & Noble, Okemose, MI
Baxter's Books, Minneapolis, MN
Minnesota Book Center, Minneapolis, MN
Walker Art Center Bookshop, Minneapolis, MN
Barnes & Noble, St. Paul, MN
Hungry Mind Bookstore, St. Paul, MN
Odegard Books, St. Paul, MN
Barnes & Noble, Des Peres, MO
Whistler's Books, Kansas City, MO
Left Bank Books, St. Louis, MO
Barnes & Noble, Springfield, MO
Bookstar, Cary, NC
Barnes & Noble, Pineville, NC
Barnes & Noble, Raleigh, NC
Barnes & Noble, Lincoln, NE
Nebraska Bookstore, Lincoln, NE
Dartmouth Bookstore, Hanover, NH
Barnes & Noble, Paramus, NJ
Encore Books, Princeton, NJ
Micawber Books, Princeton, NJ
Barnes & Noble, Springfield, NJ
Barnes & Noble, West Long Beach, NJ
Bookstar, Albuquerque, NM
Salt of the Earth, Albuquerque, NM
Cafe Allegro, Los Alamos, NM
Collected Works, Santa Fe, NM
Barnes & Noble, Amherst, NY
Community Bookstore, Brooklyn, NY
Talking Leaves, Buffalo, NY
Colgate University Bookstore, Hamilton, NY
Book Revue, Huntington, NY
The Bookery, Ithaca, NY
A Different Light, New York, NY
Art Market, New York, NY
B. Dalton, New York, NY
Barnes & Noble, New York, NY
Doubleday Bookshops, New York, NY
Gold Kiosk, New York, NY
Gotham Book Mart, New York, NY
St. Mark's Bookshop, New York, NY
Wendell's Books, New York, NY
Barnes & Noble, White Plains, NY
Barnes & Noble, Yonkers, NY
UC Bookstore, Cincinnati, OH
Bank News, Cleveland, OH
Student Book Exchange, Columbus, OH
Books & Co., Dayton, OH

Kenyon College Bookstore, Gambier, OH
Barnes & Noble, Toledo, OH
Barnes & Noble, Eugene, OR
Barnes & Noble, Portland, OR
Looking Glass Bookstore, Portland, OR
Reading Frenzy, Portland, OR
Barnes & Noble, Bryn Mawr, PA
Farley's Bookshop, New Hope, PA
Barnes & Noble, Philadelphia, PA
Faber Books, Philadelphia, PA
Encore Books, Mechanicsburg, PA
Encore Books, State College, PA
Brown University Bookstore, Providence, RI
College Hill Store, Providence, RI
Chapter Two Bookstore, Charleston, SC
Open Book, Greenville, SC
Bookstar, Germantown, TN
Bookstar, Memphis, TN
Xanadu Bookstore, Memphis, TN
Bookstar, Nashville, TN
Barnes & Noble, Austin, TX
Bookpeople, Austin, TX
Bookstop, Austin, TX
University Co-op, Austin, TX
Barnes & Noble, Dallas, TX
McKinney Avenue Contemporary, Dallas, TX
Barnes & Noble, Houston, TX
Bookstop, Houston, TX
Brazos Bookstore, Houston, TX
Diversebooks, Houston, TX
Bookstop, Plano, TX
Bookstar, Salt Lake City, UT
Sam Weller's Zion Book Store, Salt Lake City, UT
Barnes & Noble, Richmond, VA
Studio Art Shop, Charlottesville, VA
Williams Corner, Charlottesville, VA
Northshire Books, Manchester, VT
Barnes & Noble, S. Burlington, VT
Barnes & Noble, Bellevue, WA
Newsstand, Bellingham, WA
Bailey Coy Books, Seattle, WA
Barnes & Noble, Seattle, WA
Barnes & Noble, Milwaukee, WI
Barnes & Noble, Appleton, WI
Pages, Toronto, CANADA
Magpie Magazine Gallery, Vancouver, CANADA
... On Sundays, Tokyo, JAPAN